No matter what anyone said, it was because of her past actions that people were dying and all her fault...

Martha had to pick it up and see who'd called. It was Lizzie. She laughed in relief and held the phone out as she told Tom. "It's only Lizzie. No way is she going to tell me a horror story at this time of night." She played the message.

"Martha, someone just blew up our entire garage! I wasn't in my car, but my husband was! Martha—he's gone!" The message ended, and Martha crumpled into her chair, gasping and sobbing hopelessly. She felt Tom's arms go around her. He swept her up and carried her into the living room. He laid her on the couch and knelt beside her, his arms around her, uttering soothing words, trying to comfort her if he could.

Martha couldn't listen to his soothing words. Her guilt rose before her like a specter of evil. "Tom, I've brought this death to my best friend in the world! It's because of me that her husband's dead. How am I supposed to live with something like that?"

"You didn't do this, Martha—you know that. It's not your fault that some sick son-of-a-bitch is trying to kill off everyone you ever knew. You've never done anything that didn't need doing. It's not your fault!" He shook her shoulders gently, trying to make her believe him.

"I've got to call her. She'll know why this happened. It was caused by me—she knows the whole story, Tom." Martha rose off the couch and headed for her phone, nearly sobbing. "I'm about to lose the best friend I've ever had."

Martha Lavery Chance is a woman with a dark secret—a wild-hearted, amoral, alter personality, Serena, created to save her sanity as a child in danger. At present, living with a wonderful man, Martha refuses to marry him, believing it will cost him his life. A detective, he brings home the sad tale of another small child taken, sexually devastated, and murdered. His anguish sends her alter, Serena, into a rage against child predators, and she aches to get busy again, destroying the sexual capacity of these monsters. Can she disable a few more of those predators while staying free of prison herself?

KUDOS for *Predator*

In *Predator* by Ramona Forrest, Martha Lavery Chance and her alternate personality, Serena, are back targeting child predators. She has castrated several in the past, and while the cops in her old home town of Colorado Springs looked the other way, she now lives in Denver—and with a police detective, Harry Johns. He knows about her past, and he sympathizes with her because his own little daughter was sexually abused and killed and Martha's grandson was sexually abused. Even though her grandson is still alive, Martha fears he will never be the same again and will never be able to live a normal life. But Martha and Harry both know that Serena has no morals and her nighttime endeavors could easily land Martha in jail, along with making her a lot of nasty enemies who may target those close to her as well as Martha herself. Told in Forrest's unique voice, filled with wonderful characters, fast-paced action, and a solid plot, this is one you will want to keep on your shelf to read over again whenever you feel like the bad guys are getting the upper hand. ~ *Taylor Jones, The Review Team of Taylor Jones & Regan Murphy*

Predator by Ramona Forrest is the third book in her Martha Lavery/Serena series. In this book, Martha and her alter personality, Serena, still want to castrate child predators, hoping that will help protect young children from these monsters. The problem is that word has slipped out about Martha/Serena and her little hobby, and even though the cops often look the other way, someday Serena might do something that they can't ignore, and Martha could end up in prison. It's a thought that haunts Martha, but she is unwilling to stand back and do nothing while more and more children are abducted, sexually assaulted, and murdered. So she needs something that can castrate a man without letting him know he's been castrated. And she may have found a clue in the world of veterinary medicine. But will it work on humans, and if so, how would she do it? And, of course, the big question—can she do it without getting caught? *Predator* is intense, down-to-earth, fast-paced, and compelling. Combining mystery and suspense with a hint of romance, it's a worthy addition to the series. ~ *Regan Murphy, The Review Team of Taylor Jones & Regan Murphy*

Predator

Ramona Forrest

A Black Opal Books Publication

Black Opal Books

BECAUSE SOME STORIES JUST HAVE TO BE TOLD

GENRE: CRIME THRILLER/MYSTERY/WOMEN SLEUTHS

PREDATOR
Copyright © 2018 by Ramona Forrest
Cover Design by Jackson Cover Designs
All cover art copyright © 2018
All Rights Reserved
Print ISBN: 978-1-626949-41-6

First Publication: JUNE 2018

Published by Black Opal Books **http://www.blackopalbooks.com**

Predator

Chapter 1

Martha Chance, happy these days in her new life with Detective Harry Johns, nevertheless fought a frequent battle with that other person who lived within her mind. Her alter ego, Serena, was a recently discovered phenomenon. She was one who continued to wage a quiet, insidious war, quietly, but always there with her continual wanting. And Serena's ever present quest remained a constant, nagging thing—vengeance on every child predator in existence.

Martha lived happily from day to day, enveloped in the love and tenderness between her and Detective Harry Johns. Yet, in spite of the security and comfort of an idyllic life lived in that gentle environment, she had little respite from those insistent inner leanings. She'd been warned by her doctors, her lover, and her family that, in time, if she was unable to stop herself, she'd move toward some final, fatal step that would ensure her doom.

That previously unknown entity, Serena, had saved Martha's sanity against the horror of what had happened to her as a six-year-old. Serena had taken over for her that year, and Martha had no memory of her first grade year, though she'd been told her grades had been excellent. After the abuser had gone into the navy, Martha was herself again, but completely unaware of Serena until the rape and sodomy of her grandson, Will. At that time, her hitherto unknown alter ego had come forth to avenge the crime against her small grandson.

That deed and subsequent actions were done out of utter desperation and rage at the inefficiency of the law. Because of the strange occurrences happening to her at that time, she had sought medical help. A gentle, competent, psychiatrist in Colorado Springs had acquainted her with the wild-hearted Serena, her alter personality. From that time on, Serena had gained a strong presence in Martha's consciousness.

The avenging and illegal things Serena had done in recent years had placed Martha in severe jeopardy with the law. But she'd been lucky. She smiled, remembering that understanding detective in Colorado Springs, Ryan Mapus.

Martha moved about her home, enjoying the comforting routine of dusting, cleaning, and preparing meals. Even now, with a great meatloaf sizzling in her oven, along with two sizable baking potatoes, Martha enjoyed setting the table for two. That act alone comforted her with the fact she was no longer alone in the world. Her alliance with the detective, Harry Johns, made that lovely difference.

Living with Detective Johns brought continued relief from those hidden desires, yet they hung over her, clinging, as a thick dark cloud. And because the last man she'd fallen in love with and married had died, she feared Harry would die, too, and leave her alone again. She had refused to marry him.

Martha worked as a registered nurse at Hillsdale General, a local hospital outside the bustling city of Denver. She worked per diem, which allowed her to choose to work when she felt the need. Her shifts at the hospital enabled her to get out and join the community as a useful and competent member. Affecting the norm in every outward appearance, she lived a quiet, legal, and decent life. Yet, while carefully placing the plates and silverware, she frequently acknowledged the scores this inner creature had helped her settle, and she quietly rejoiced in them.

Shivering at how close she'd come to prison and death, she'd faced the reality of why she'd needed this inner person. Martha had then understood the cause. In her abhorrence of the things she'd done, if no one was around to hear her talking to thin air, she often verbally chastised her tormentor. Yet all the while, she rejoiced in having ruined the sexual capabilities of several destroying, inhuman, child predators.

Until Will's abduction, Martha had lived blissfully unaware that she even had an alter ego. And once she'd become cognizant of that other personality, she had also come face to face with the horrendous events that had caused the need for Serena to come into being. Once it'd been discussed and dealt with by her psychiatrists, Martha's real healing had begun.

From then on, Martha had found the strength to face—to learn to live with the evil things that had happened to her as a small child. She now lived a loving and peaceful life. While Martha's own sense of right and wrong fought a continuous battle with her alter ego, Serena had no real sense of right and wrong.

Often when alone, Martha went over her past—those deeds done by her alter-ego, Serena. First, the predator who molested her grandson—Fred Callahan. Then his good buddy, child rapist and murderer, Denny Garver. He now resided on death row near Canyon City. She went on to name them all in her mind, including how she had taken care of those computer dates. Those fiendish— older males who posed as young amorous boys. They used computer lingo to lure underage, lonely girls into illicit liaisons. They lured them to a sleazy motel, only to rape them and tear into their innocent young flesh, destroying their trusting innocence forever.

"Knock it off, Serena. I really don't relish spending the last years of my life in the slammer." She uttered the last words aloud, hoping to quell the rising urgency and desire to get busy once again. "Not when I have a great guy like Harry to keep me from giving in to the likes of you." She straightened a wayward fork alongside a plate and returned to the stove to check dinner preparations.

Outside the sun was lowering, and the new spring growth had greened up the deciduous trees. Apple trees bloomed, and the snow had melted, except for the patches she saw up in the higher reaches of the Rocky Mountains. How often she delighted to see them soaring to lofty heights above their home.

Her reveries of past adventures with Serena faded at hearing Harry's truck drive up the graveled driveway. Her heart beat faster, and she nearly dropped the butter dish. She knew intimately every squeak and rattle of his favorite old Ford pickup. He didn't use a company car these days. Undercover work went a lot better with a personal conveyance. A lot of his cohorts did the same, and at their own cost, success being a powerful motivator.

Their solid, slightly rustic ranch style house stood on the outskirts of Denver, amid groves of orchards and open fields, surrounded by scented, stately pines. Farther out, past the dense greenery of the forested areas, the high Rockies jutted majestically, reaching far into the clear blue sky. The high rocky crags and peaks with patches of snow crusted in the frigid shadows gave it a solid look of clean and wild magnificence. They enjoyed the high, bracing air, and in their happiness, often had the feeling of living in a magical Eden.

The truck scrunched to a halt, and the rasping sounds of the door opening made her heart rate quicken. He'd arrived home with his steadying love and big warm body to hold and comfort her. Harry had saved her sanity, and she thanked him silently for it every day.

Martha realized that her days of peace and serenity came with a price. It allowed Serena to quietly foment and seethe with vengeful ideas that grew incrementally stronger. But Harry was home now, and his presence always helped dispel the darkness of Serena. Martha's heart raced as she heard him coming into the house.

Without tripping over their two yelping, nearly grown pups, she ran out the kitchen door to greet him, leaving behind her worries. Uttering the words between clenched teeth, she snarled, "Serena, stay away from me with your mad ideas. I can't, and I won't, screw this thing up. You just leave me the hell alone!"

She met Harry full on as he moved toward the arms she held wide open without realizing it.

"Hey, hon, what's going on?" He always knew when she was troubled. His voice, though gentle, was also commanding, "Come on, spill, my darlin'."

Martha uttered a weak laugh. "You know, same ole same ole."

He opened his own arms. She nestled close against his broad chest and let her troubled soul sink into his warm masculinity. Together, laughing, they tried to walk into the house, warding off the happy welcoming of Max and Skunk. The half-grown pups had been welcome replacements of their earlier dogs lost to the jealous insanity of a mad man. They spent time petting and roughing the glistening fur of the two animals,

Max, a larger German Sheppard mix, eclipsed

Skunk, who was smaller with the softly blotched furring of an Australian Shepherd mixed with Blue Heeler. The pups, certainly equal in eagerness, made fending them off a happy, forgetting time for all concerned. Martha, wiping the moisture from Max's tongue off her arms, laughed, and looked Harry in the eyes.

"How was your day?" Seeing the sickness in his eyes, she knew it hadn't been a good one. They never were when he looked like that. Together, they made their way into the kitchen.

"No, you don't, my darling. You go first." He was no pushover. A strong man, she'd never been able to bulldoze him into going along with her ideas, and she respected him all the more for it. And at this moment, she hated to dampen the heated way she felt just seeing him again after only a day away. One of Denver's finest detectives, he was good at what he did.

"Just the same ol, same ol," she repeated. "You know what I mean." She looked into his eyes. "I'm sick of talking about it. Now tell me what's with you. I see it in your eyes, and it's not good—I'll listen if you'll tell me." Martha knew Harry was careful to say only what was fit for her ears, and the indecision in his eyes told her this was one of those times.

"Yeah, but I don't want to say it. We have a missing child, a five-year-old girl coming home from kindergarten, alone. This one strikes too damned close to home for me." She took him into her arms, and together they silently commiserated on the hideous possibilities. "Her mother was a bit late in picking her up…"

She felt him shudder and knew his helpless tears had started.

"Any leads?" She couldn't stop herself from asking. "How many sexual predators living in her near vicinity—this time?"

His arms tightened spasmodically around her as his body stiffened. Her throat went dry to the point she thought she might choke. She already knew the answer.

"We found about twenty, all within a mile's radius. How in the hell can that be? And why do we allow these rotten bastards to live peacefully among us? Where in the hell are they coming from? That's what drives me up a wall. No wonder you did those things you did. I've always understood it, considering my own past. It made a hell of a lot of sense to me." He tightened his grip on her trembling body. "Is it getting so bad we need the days of the old West back again when men like that were strung up by the balls and left for the buzzards?" She felt him getting worked up and angry and sought to deter it if she could.

"Hold on, honey." She held him close against her own body. "Of all people, I feel your anguish. You know my feelings about these things." His story was even more devastating than hers, and she hoped to deflect his pain. "Come on into the house, I've supper nearly ready." She pulled him along with her. The anguish in his deep gray eyes hurt her terribly and made her feel sick inside.

Maybe a cup of coffee and something to eat would help. "I don't know how to help you with this, and as you know, something like a lost child sends a part of me into a raging fire." She sat him in a chair, uttered a helpless laugh, knowing he understood her meaning.

"I'd give Serena a damned solid gold medal, and a great big one, if I could." He laughed, giving her a look. "And I know just where I'd pin it, too." He leaped up and grabbed for her, kissing her into near oblivion. "You know how to help me—and you damned well know it, girl."

"You're an animal if I don't watch out for you, Mr.—" Martha's eyes shone with joy while she chastised him. For a few stolen moments, they forgot all the heart-ache the outside world had to offer. She sat on his lap, nestled her body against his chest, reached up, wrapped her arms around his neck, and kissed him until he was ready to drag her bodily to the bed.

"Oh, no you don't! Supper's ready, and you need to eat." It wasn't fair, and she knew it, after she had him so very ready for the bedroom. She giggled as she struggled off his lap. Moving into the kitchen, Martha set about dishing up the food. Harry sat there watching her through narrowed eyes. A twitching of his lips matched that devil's shine in those gray eyes that always thrilled her to the depths. "Now move up here and get at it." She took her seat across from him and, in the joy of togetherness, they ate their dinner.

He tore into a soft roll and buttered it lavishly before he sopped the gravy from the meatloaf and shoved it into his mouth. How she loved watching him eat. The way his jaw worked and the movements of his face were very masculine and different. For some reason, a small thing like that had always fascinated her. She never tired of feeding this man or lying in bed with him, either.

"Say, now, this is good. You're a mighty fine cook, girl, you do that the same as you do everything else." His eyes burned with the passion he held for her. A wild surge of happiness swept through her, knowing she could do this much for him. His pain had dissipated since they'd been together. She knew how to keep his thoughts occupied, at least for the present, though some things never really left the mind. She knew that well enough, too.

She reluctantly brought up something that had continually plagued and taunted her. "Harry, I don't want to upset you but I've been looking on the internet for something, and I believe I've found it."

"Now, what?"

His caution was evident, and his tone reflected it. She hated to continue. But she kept on and watched as his fingers gripped the arm of his chair, matching the tightening of his long jaw.

"I think I know how I could put some of these monsters out of commission without bringing suspicion on myself." Waiting for his reply, her heart raced uncontrollably, while she swallowed her fear of his opinion.

"Yeah?" His face held an expectant look, but he held his council and waited for her to begin. It was important to her, and he indulged her.

"Well, if they didn't know what had been done to them, just a simple assault with robbery as the intent, no one would connect me with a thing like that, or look in my direction, now would they?"

"Maybe not. What are you thinking?" His narrowed eyes had darkened and his voice, tightly controlled, had lowered.

"There is a medication used on dogs, well actually on puppies. It's a new product, used for chemical sterilization—injectable, too, no cutting, no bleeding," she quipped, grinning. He said nothing and she went on, "Getting it and determining the proper dosage is the major concern." She waited. "You're not saying anything."

"I admit, you've got me thinking about it. I can't deny how I feel about that business, any more than you can. The things you've done have become an integral part of both of us." Distress came over his face. "But now that I've found you, I fear losing you during one of these escapades, Martha. That worries me the most."

"I feel that way, too, and certainly don't relish spending my last years in prison, but I can't stop thinking about those innocent kids. I'll never forget how it hurts a child.

My Will is better these days, growing older, but those shadows have never left his eyes. You've seen him enough times to know what I mean. Can he really become a normal man after what was done to him?" She shuddered. "What horrible memories—or feelings does he have or see in his mind, and hides them from us?"

"Martha, I totally understand. You *have* your grandson, damaged as he may be, but I'll never see my little girl grow up, go to a prom, fight off her boyfriends—none of that—not ever." He twisted in his seat, his face a pale mask of pain. "It's something to think about. Might have a way to take care of a few, but you know we'll never get them all." He shivered involuntarily. "My God in heaven, Martha, this is fast becoming a very sick world." He frowned and his brow wrinkled. "Tell me what you've learned. Maybe I can help with it."

He looked at her. All romance had fled the scene as he waited to hear what she had to tell him.

"I know we have to get our dogs fixed soon. That is, if we plan on that." They were his dogs, and the decision would be his as well. "Looking on the internet, there are several options these days. The one item that sparked my interest is called Neutersol. It's not totally perfected, but it is injected and shrinks those little trouble makers down to uselessness in most cases."

She watched his eyes for his hidden opinion, imagining this sort of thing must go against the grain for any male.

Seeing no opposition, she continued, "We would need to scope out a few of those many predators and be sure to target the right ones, but a simple mugging, disguised as a robbery and assault might work."

"I believe you're assuming he won't notice sore testicles?" He laughed. "Even a little bit?"

"Not if the assaulter did a little extra kicking

around." She tried not to giggle. "I could add some No-vocain."

The shine in her eyes told him Serena had quickly wormed her way into this project, if she hadn't instigated it in the first place. Serena was definitely the major player. Neither he or Martha had any illusions about that.

"I'll find a few good suspects for you—Serena." He smiled and nodded to her, his eyes narrowed. "I wouldn't mind knocking off a few of the bastards myself, you know that. There are always some under the radar, abusing their own kids, hammering their wives, and who knows what abuse goes on inside their neighbor's homes? Add to that, the legally registered ones so kindly let out on bail by our politically correct judicial system."

She watched the heat of his anger rising and felt the closeness of it, because it was a part of her, too. It made them both uncomfortable at the helplessness they so often felt. She agreed with his comment when he said with a grim smile, "We'd have to be careful, my darling." He had a look of deviltry across his face as he snorted. "They mollycoddle these devils and would certainly look your way if anything took place that closely resembled those things in your past."

Martha replied, "Why can't they just lock them all away? I don't get this new way of thinking. You and I know, and so do they. The recidivism rate among child predators is nearly one hundred percent. This whole country's crawling with men looking for some small child to savage for a few moments of gratification."

He saw her rising agitation. "Hey, want me to do up the dishes." He rose to grab the dirty plates and headed for the kitchen sink.

"You're trying to settle me down, and I appreciate it, Harry, but oh how good it'd feel to know a few more of them are out of commission." Her head came up, and she looked him in the eye. Knowing he wasn't totally against her idea made her pulse rate speed up with intent.

"You're something, you are, girl." He reached for her with hands wet from cleaning up. "Now where were we when you made me sit down to supper?"

He heard her shriek with joy and kept on until they headed for the bedroom.

Later, they sat in front of the television, looking for something to watch that wouldn't hurt. The last thing he needed was a news flash about that little girl, yet it was splashed on nearly every channel, forcing them to face it and work it out emotionally. He'd lost his own little girl a few years before in exactly this same way, and that horror haunted him in unguarded moments. They each had personal ghosts. Each knew and understood the pain of the other.

Chapter 2

Harry had left for work, and Martha stood at the kitchen window, thinking. Her mind was in a whirl from her daughter's frantic phone call, telling her Will had tried to strangle the little cocker spaniel puppy they'd gotten him. Feeling sick inside, Martha buried her hands deep in hot suds as she cleaned the kitchen. She felt the desperation all over again. She worried so often that her nine-year-old grandson would never be able to grow into a normal, loving man.

Deep in her own thoughts, Martha half listened to the dogs yelping outside. She initially thought they yelped in excitement, yet when the snarling tempest increased into sounds of fury, followed by a sharp yowling of pain, her heart raced with a newer worry. She forgot about the phone call.

She headed for the door. "Now, what?" Outside in the yard, she spied what remained of a good-sized rattlesnake. The slithery carcass lay torn, filled with gravel and dirt. Nudging it with a stick, she made sure it definitely lay unmoving before approaching.

She knelt down to Skunk, who was trembling. "Oh, no, poor puppy, somebody got bitten in this fracas." He lay on his stomach as she examined him, mucus draining from his mouth, and a few drops of blood dripped from his leg. Martha crooned to the dog, "Hold on, buddy boy, I'll get you down to the vet. I hope it's not too late." She pulled the soft belt off her robe and applied a tourniquet to his leg. "I knew I should have gotten dressed sooner," she muttered as she lifted him gently, laid him in her car, and ran into the house.

Inside, she hurriedly donned jeans and a black sweat-shirt, ran a brush through her hair, grabbed her purse, and took a quick peek in her mirror. "This'll have to do," she murmured to herself as she ran to the car and it revved up. "I'm nearly out of gas! Thank God, the vet's clinic is close by." She tore out of the drive and down the road.

Pulling into Doctor Gleason's Animal Clinic, she grabbed the nearly inert pup in her arms and ran inside. She told the receptionist what happened. The young woman blanched pale, turned, and ran to the back, calling for the doctor. The woman emerged shortly, and, sounding more settled and sure of herself, informed Martha, "He'll be right here, dear."

The doctor came out, wiping his hands, and took a look at the pup she held in her arms. "He's been bitten, you know that for sure?"

"I saw the snake and heard both dogs fighting it. I saw the blood on his leg and placed a tourniquet on it." She gestured at the right front leg.

"You may have saved his life with that maneuver. We have an effective anti-venom." He scooped Skunk from her arms into his and headed toward the back recesses of his office. Martha followed, taking a brief but careful look at the medical equipment used in the care of animals.

Murmuring soothing words as though his patient was a small child, the veterinarian laid Skunk on the examination table and bade Martha to hold him. He turned to his glassed-in cabinet and selected a vial. "This should do the trick, but he'll be a very sick boy for a while." He drew up an injection and, cleansing a small area on the muscular area of Skunk's hind leg, Dr. Gleason injected the lifesaving antivenin.

"Thanks, Doc. I'm glad you were so close, and that I was at home today." Martha heaved a sigh, hopeful Harry wouldn't lose another beloved pet. As she stood beside the dog, her mind swirled with questions she was afraid to ask. But luck was with her this day, because the doctor had a question of his own.

"I understand you're a nurse, is that right?" He bent a steady look at Martha with solid gray eyes, not unlike Harry's. The man, most likely, stood several inches over six feet, and his build was thin and bony.

"Why, yes, I am. Why do you ask?"

"There are times I could use a medically trained person in this office, if you wouldn't think working in a vet's office beneath the dignity of a medically trained professional—for humans, that is." He ended the sentence with a grin. "Good help is hard to find around here. I wouldn't need someone every day, maybe two days a week would suffice, to help out with some surgeries, and to order supplies and medicines for a start."

Martha's heart leaped. *There is a God after all, and he's looking down on me.* She replied with a tone as devoid of emotion as she could manage. "Well, I work at Hillsdale, a small, local hospital a few nights when I can. I worked in Denver, but not so much anymore since I've come to live way out here—too far to drive." She frowned, hoping to appear a bit nonchalant. "I might consider taking a couple of days. It'd be all new to me, but seeing how good you are with animals, I realize your work is very meaningful to you, the same as mine is to me." Martha smiled up at him. "It's important work, in

any case, and you obviously care about your animal patients. I think in any caring profession, empathy is almost
as important as the education and training."

"Good then. I'm okay today, but my receptionist out
there is getting married and leaving the area. I'll have to
train another one for the front desk, but back here I need
more talent. I'd like to be able to call on you if I need an
extra hand, especially during more difficult surgeries."
He had a questioning look in his eyes as he spoke.

"You know, I believe I just might like to do it." Martha knew if she worked here she could manage to order a
few extra supplies without his knowledge, and this would
fit into plans not yet completed. She petted the nearly inert form of Skunk as her mind raced with ideas as exciting, and as wrong, as anything her active mind could
manage.

Dr. Gleason broke into her heavy thoughts. "I'd like
to keep this poor fellow here…Skunk, is it?" He chuckled. "Just for a few days to be sure he's doing as well as
I'd like." His long, bony hands caressed the pup as he
spoke.

"Sure, good idea." Martha murmured, stroking the
dog, too—her mind filled with ideas. "How does he look
to you—now he's had that shot?" she remembered to ask,
but only after Skunk managed to give a weak, half-
hearted lick to her hand. It brought her swirling thoughts
back to earth.

"Can't tell a lot at first, but we've had good results
with this product. Try not to worry too much and feel free
to call me anytime at all." He ushered her to the door.
"I'll get back to you about when to start. I'll certainly be
glad to have your help, I know that."

Martha shook the man's hand. "Thanks so much,
Doctor."

She left for her car, her mind working overtime on

how to proceed. She knew she had to soft-peddle things until she had an agenda worked out, but knowing she might have a good avenue of access to the drug she needed had her thoughts racing.

She walked into the house and Max followed her. He wiggled, licked her hand, and, looking about, emitted a soft whine. Martha decided he was lost without Skunk. She patted his head and stroked his fur. "He'll be home in a day or two, sweetie, don't you worry about him." She made herself a fresh cup of coffee and sat down in the living room.

Turning on the TV, she heard the news. *Round-up of probable child predators nets four possible suspects in the sexual molestation and brutal death of little Mindy Lassen.* Her heart raced, and her temper flared. Her ears rang, and her mouth went dry. "Oh God!" she cried out into the emptiness of the room. "I hope they've caught the right one. Surely they must have gotten DNA from the poor child's remains." She listened carefully to catch the site of the arrests. There were many more sexual predators in the same area, according to Harry's information.

❧❧❧

She heard Harry's old truck pull in around six that evening. He was later than usual which had set her to worrying for the past hour. Her heart rate increased at the sound of his footsteps dragging as he came into the kitchen. Hearing that, she knew something had happened at work—he wouldn't be the same Harry tonight. He never was after some heinous event had occurred at work. She waited to hear what had made that awful difference in him from this morning until now.

She felt a jolt pass through her body at the sight of

his pale face and the look of utter defeat across his face. She gasped. "Harry, what is it? What has happened?"

"Oh, heavenly God, Martha, I saw what was left of that child!"

She went to Harry and held him close, unable to think of anything to say that would help this poor man through what he's suffered today. Without question, he had relived all over again the horror of the rape and murder of his own little girl. A good part of his agony had to be that.

"Please, God, may I never have to see a sight like that again." He sank into a chair and pulled her across his lap. "Martha, I'm not man enough to face a thing like that—not all over again. I can't do it!" He shoved his face into her bosom and sobbed.

She held him as he let out the harsh, choking sounds of sorrow. While he cried it out, Martha decided if anyone thought it unmanly, she didn't give a damn. She knew what he was feeling, and he needed her right now. Harry Johns was man enough for anything this sick world had to offer, and she was glad she could offer him what comfort she had to give.

"What happened to me is long past, Harry, but I sometimes see it enough to bring back the horror of it. I don't think a person can ever forget. How can anyone who has suffered at the hands of a sick fiend—like the one who did those things to this little girl?" She wanted more details about the suspects but held back. He'd tell her when he could—if he could.

Instead, she changed the subject. "Harry, I took Skunk to the vet today. He was bitten by a snake. The doc said he'd be real sick for a few days, but that he has a good chance to make it." She felt him stiffen in her arms, and his sobbing stopped.

He raised his head to look her in the eyes. "And?"

"And what?" She averted her eyes from that steady gaze that could see straight into her thoughts.

"You know what I mean and don't play your games with me, Miss Serena." He managed a laugh. "I know to whom I speak, and don't mistake it."

Martha ignored his reference to her alter ego. "Harry, the vet offered me a job—and I took it. It's most likely two days a week, but that'll be enough." She couldn't stop the slow grin that spread across her face.

He squeezed her tight. "You are really something, Martha. You sure as hell are!" But with a frown on his face, he added, "Are you sure you want to get yourself involved like that again? I'm not sure I'm man enough to stop you, not anymore." He gave her a look of determination. "I'm not sure I'd want to."

"I heard from Jeannie today, too." Martha slumped forward, crossing her arms over her chest and fighting the tears burning her eyes as she recounted what her daughter had said. "Will took that new puppy they—" She gasped for air. "He took it out behind the house and tried to strangle it! He tried to kill it with his bare hands, Harry!

"God in Heaven, Martha!" His face had gone pale at what she'd said. "I want to get in there and help you in every way that wayward part of you can begin to imagine."

She grasped his hands. "What are we to do?" Her face felt so tight with anger, she brushed across it, hoping it would soften. She crept into his arms looking for comfort and release. She added, her tone filled with hopelessness, "Will said he didn't know why he did it."

"Oh, Martha." Harry hugged her tighter.

"Jeannie says he is doing well in school, learning his lessons, and all, because he knows the nuns won't put up with any nonsense from him. We had such hopes that would be the answer for him, and it has been in some ways. But now we know even they can't really change what happened to him. It's been more than four years now, and look at what's happened." She gritted her teeth so hard she worried they might crack.

"Oh, Harry, he was such a sweet little guy before that happened to him!" Martha threw herself into his arms and sobbed.

"Martha, anything you want to do—God help me, I'll help you."

Chapter 3

In the new prison facility in Florence, a small city near Canon City, Colorado, Denny Garver sat in his dismal cell. Every day was the same—boring food, nothing fit to read, and no decent TV. And added to that, stations showing children's programming were not allowed on Death Row, not for child predators anyway. In the bargain, along with all his other miseries, he daily faced the depressing surroundings in which he found himself— bleak gray stone walls, iron bars for décor.

He occasionally overheard the surly guards talking softly, and sometimes snickering. He heard enough of their snide remarks to believe they were intended to add to his suffering, and the others, in their quiet way. The dirty bastards didn't mind it at all if he happened to overhear their comments about that last walk and about him being strapped to that table, clean and sterile, and covered in white.

They were required to treat him with dignity. He was a man destined to feel that small needle stick for the IV medication that would end his life. At that depressing thought, a tear escaped and rolled down his cheek. His wounds were long healed, but he was forever changed. Gone were the feelings of deep urgency and the familiar rise in excitement when he gave thought to the softness and innocence of a small female body. A soft, little, male body wasn't all that bad, either. Oh, how those images once made the blood roar through his veins with thoughts of what he would do with that helpless wriggling and struggling little body!

Daily, his mind worked on thoughts of finding a way to punish that evil soul who'd altered him forever on that fateful morning. He had merely stepped out to empty his garbage on the routine pick-up day. After all, he was a fastidious man, one not given to slovenly ways. He'd always taken pride in how his kitchen shone and sparkled with cleanliness. In no way did he deserve that hideous attack on his manhood by an unknown assailant.

Not once in the process of his court appearances and conviction did he ever learn who his attacker had been. That hidden fact had torn at him constantly and tortured him with thoughts of vengeance. His mind dwelt often on what he'd do to that evil bastard if he ever found the chance.

Hell no, he'd never discovered who'd done it to him—that sick fiend who'd brought his world crashing down around him. Why make such a damned secret of it anyway? Now, because of the police searching his home after that fateful day, here he sat—on death row, awaiting that damned white table and that tiny needle stick. "I guess keeping those ribbons wasn't such a smart idea, but they meant a lot to me, so pretty—brought back some hot memories, too." He heaved a sigh of disgust at himself. "All that DNA—shit!"

Denny had spent long hours thinking of a million ways to avenge himself on that person who'd made these changes to his masculinity. His frustration at the helplessness of his situation kept his blood pressure spiking to the top. The prison doc worried about his health. He'd ordered a medication to quell Denny's raging blood pressure. Denny grumbled aloud, "Why in the hell should he give a tinker's damn about my health? Why bother? Want to keep me healthy enough to face that damned white table?"

Sergeant Mort Lesser came to Denny's cell, clinking his keys on the bars. "Hey, dude, time to go outside for your daily airing."

Denny saw a friendlier gleam in Mort's eye compared to the other guards. In fact, he had already felt a certain kind of edginess in the man. Instinctively, he recognized some sort of a salacious need in him. No words had been spoken or hinted at so far, but he felt that he soon would. Something was there. So far, Denny hadn't figured out what Officer Mortie boy had on his mind. But something was sure as hell eating at the man.

"How's the weather out there?" he asked the officer.

"Good enough for the likes of you." His words were surly, but his tone was softer than usual. "I'm the guard out there today, so get along, will ya? You're not the only one I got to keep an eye on." Mort slid the bars back and indicated the hallway that led to an exit.

Denny appreciated the recent move to this newer facility as he had some access to the outdoors on a regular schedule in this prison. He came out of his cell and moved along beside the officer. He heard his cell door slam, closing with that hated metallic clang. The sound of it made his hatred come boiling up inside. He held his anger in, but clenched his fists tighter than usual. The longer he'd spent here, the more he'd come to hate that sound clear down into his bones.

Denny seethed inside frequently. Angry at finding himself in this situation, his jaw clenched so tight it made his head ache. But he was careful to keep his boiling thoughts under wraps. *These pigs got no damned feelings at all.* But still, this guy—Mort—he had a feeling...

The guard shuffled along behind him, staying closer than needed. It wasn't likely he had any place else to go, not in that stinking postage stamp exercise yard. Oh yeah, he could smell the newness of spring in the air and could see the sky, all right. If he was lucky, he might catch a breath of fresh, wet, laundry-laden air. If he looked straight up, was there a patch of blue? He caught the edge of a few branches sprouting out with its new leaves and saw a small flock of doves circling about. They taunted him with their care-free easy freedom. The hurt inside him grew tight enough to twist his gut.

"How about taking a seat right here? You ain't goin' any place out here, anyway."

Officer Mort Lesser was insistent this morning. He had something on his mind, and Denny had formed a damned good idea what the man wanted to know. Yes, Denny knew the man was right—he wasn't going any-where. Egging this sick-minded prison guard on afforded a little bit of entertainment. Keep him tense and nervous, waiting. Denny knew plenty of men who had the same feelings about small children, the same as he'd once had. Denny had recently gotten the idea, Mortie old boy, just might be one of them.

Mort sat down beside Denny. Fraternization between staff and prisoner of any sort was frowned upon, but the man sat there twisting his hands together. Mort occasion-ally wiped a bit of sweat from his brow until he finally found the guts to open his mouth. Denny merely sat there—waiting.

"You've got a hell of a history, man—what made you want to do stuff like that?" As he looked at Denny, his face had gone pale, his hands shook, and his lips tightened. "What—ah—what in hell did you do to those little girls, man?

Denny grinned—he knew what sort of information the officer wanted from him. "That's not for publication. You ought to know better'n to ask a thing like that."

"Hell, I know it, but it's kinda got me thinking, and...uh...you know, wondering." The guard, in his trembling, anxious voice, was asking for the sick, twisted, and foul details of the kind of things only Denny could tell him. Mort's sick appetite begged for what Denny knew, and he felt his pulse rate rise—he'd made a decision. His eyes grew narrow, and his heart soared with excitement. *At last, maybe I can make things right!*

"Anything I say comes at a price, and it ain't cheap." Denny rose to walk about, slowly, leaving the sweating, fidgeting, anxious guard on the bench. At last, he had a gleam of hope—a way to make that bastard pay for what he'd done. If this Mort was the person he'd been hoping for, Denny knew he'd found a way to make that hellish someone into a sniveling mass of pain?

He also knew the right man to make it happen. If he only knew who the dirty bastard was. Some upset Daddy? He didn't know—he'd never once caught the name of the one who'd taken a knife to his privates. But soon—he nodded his head in the affirmative—he knew he would.

He returned, ambling slowly, and sat down again. "Nice to get outside a bit." He offered the inane comment, curious to see if Mort would get up the guts to ask what he was in a devil of a sweat to know.

"Yeah, we're inside all the damned day ourselves." Mort twisted in his seat, his face looked pale as he asked, "Say. Denny, could you tell me a bit about some of those things?"

"What things? What are you askin' me?"

"You know goddamned well what the hell I want to know. You sure as hell do, don't you?" Mort exploded, furious, and embarrassed. But he kept his voice down. His face had gone red as hell, and his hands gripped the edge of the bench so tight his knuckles were white.

"I could go on for hours, man, and you know I could. But before I say one damned word, I need to know something first. If you can answer one question, I'll talk for days, and you won't be disappointed—no way in hell will you." Denny uttered a soft laugh. "You'll be sweating blood, mister."

Mort Lesser looked at Denny, his hands trembling, his face white, and asked, "What is it, then? What do you want from me?"

"I want the name of the person who clipped me. Just that, nothing more."

"Hell, they've kept that little bit of news so tightly under wraps, I doubt I can find that out." He shook his head and sent a look at Denny that almost aroused in him, a small bit of pity for the man. "But I'll sure as hell try to get that for you." He shook his head with a frown. "That's all you want?"

"That's all. Whoever he is, he's ruined every damned part of my life, and I'm stuck in here for what's left of it." Denny's jaw clenched tight as he sought his answer in Mort's hazel brown eyes.

"You're carrying a hell of a big hate around in there, aren't you?" Yet Mort saw more than hate in Denny's eyes and face, and in the silent nod of his head. He couldn't name the feeling, but what he saw sent an icy chill along his spine. In spite of his inner need for what this man would tell him, Mort had a feeling he'd come to regret giving even this small bit of information to a man like Denny Garver. But he'd been aroused to the point it was painful. He couldn't stop his own cravings to learn those sick, evil things no man should ever hear about or know.

"I heard it was done by a woman, Denny, but that's all I know right now. It was so hush-hush, I had to wonder if it was the truth. They didn't need anything more than what they found at your house that day."

"A few mementoes, yeah." Denny uttered a sick laugh. "Damned fool me, huh?" After a short moment of thought, he muttered, "A woman?"

"Well, let me nose around a bit—see what I can come up with." Mort rose from the bench. "Let's get you back inside." He beckoned the other few prisoners, and along with two other officers, ushered them back to their cells. Mort, excitement rising inside him, knew who to call in Colorado Springs.

Denny felt lighter in spirit and walked with a spring in his step. He had something in his corner at last. "A woman, huh?" he scoffed. "I wonder if it was the same sick bastard that did Callahan—never said who that was either that I ever heard." He had a feeling they were one and the same.

സൗന

Two weeks later, Mort came to take him out for his daily bit of fresh-air exercise. He seemed edgier than usual, and Denny's heart rate sped up as the officer unlocked his cell.

"Time for some out-door time. It's rainin' out there, but there's a cover over some of the exercise ground. Go on, git movin', the days goin' fast." Mort's voice had a lilt in it that told Denny plenty. He rose to his feet, walked out of the cell and down the passage to the outside yard. He heard the steel bars slamming shut once again behind him and felt his gut seize up just as he hit the fresh, damp air. He looked up to see the rain coming down straight. Even that looked good today, old Mort was going to tell him something he's waited weeks and months to learn, and he was more than ready to hear it.

"Say, Denny, this bench is under cover, have a seat." Mort nearly paced in the small space as he waited for Denny to take his place on the slatted bench.

Denny sat down, leaned back, and crossed his legs like a man without a care in the world. Officer Mort Lesser sat beside him. Only a few inches separated their bodies. Denny felt the heat of Mort's body sitting so near and found it intensely disgusting, almost nauseating.

"I found out who it was, but she's gone from around Colorado Springs anyway." He sounded as though he believed his information was no good because the woman had moved away. Denny felt his heart rate increase. He didn't give a damn if she'd moved to another state. He played it cool. All he needed was a name.

"I could get in a lot of trouble telling you a thing like this—you damned well know I could." His fear-tightened face had taken on a pallor.

Was it his need for the salacious material he craved, or guilt at what he was doing? Denny held back a grin. He wasn't what you'd call a good guy, but neither was this messed up, bloated officer of the law.

"You know it won't do me any good in here. I just wanted to know, that's all. Wouldn't you want to know who did a bastardly thing like that, if it was done to you?" Denny allowed a bit of pleading to enter his voice.

"I guess so—hell, yes—I know I sure as hell would." Mort straightened his rotund body on the bench and faced him. "I hear it was some older nurse. And you're right, it started because of what that Callahan did. I guess she got herself started and couldn't quit or something."

"So, does this bitch have a name?"

"Yes, I was told it was a woman named Martha Lavery. She moved away right about that time—you know, well, maybe a few months after it happened."

"Know anything more about her?"

"Hell, no, I was lucky to get this much. Of course, she was never prosecuted, so what does that tell you? She must have had an *in* with the cops, if you know what I mean, that's what," Mort scoffed. "It's sort of old news now, being nearly four years past like it is."

He edged closer, and by the rising excitement, and anticipation he saw in Mortie boy's face, Denny knew it was his turn to talk.

He didn't care what he said or how bad he made himself sound. He let it all out, embellished his evil deeds, filling the officer's mind with things no man ought to hear of or know about, let alone actually do. Denny spent the entire exercise time period promoting an evil knowledge that could one day impact the life of some small child. He embroidered heavily, adding to his own sadistic feelings that drove him to transmit his foul, sickening information.

Denny derived a kind of satisfaction from the telling of his evil deeds. He knew he fed the imagination of, until now, a man, innocent of such things. He let the words flow, the doing of it—the thrill of it—the fulfillment it gave—the feeling he owned the Earth if only for that short period of time.

What he didn't tell Officer Mort was the horrific aftermath—the sick way you felt inside, hating yourself, knowing what you'd done to a small, sobbing child, and the dark, depressing sadness of knowing you'd do it again. He left out how it felt to know it was evil. How your mind finally became tortured with the guilt of it. He also knew you could never blot out those things, you'd remember everything you'd ever done, how you felt, and the hellish feeling that you'd do it again when you found the opportunity.

Denny was hot to make a phone call, but he dared not after his little session with the officer. He'd wait, better yet, he'd write a letter. No need to put this officer on his trail. Later, who in the hell would care? But he'd read the papers and, at last, have the satisfaction of knowing he had repaid his stalker in full. He would have satisfaction and repayment for all he'd lost. He would gloat in the ruination of all that devil-woman ever loved. She would know the pain of all she'd lost and finally see her own life lost. If he could accomplish this, he'd gloat all the way to that dammed white table they had waiting.

Chapter 4

In the small community called a damned slog-pit by the inhabitants, a letter came to Rayburn McGill. He recognized the handwriting immediately, and his heart rate leaped when he saw where it had been posted, a city called Florence, right next to Canon City. He knew more than enough about that place, too. He slipped it into his pocket and walked back inside his low-slung two bed-room house, and took a seat in his ratty, overstuffed chair.

"Wonder what's on his mind writin' to me this way. He wants somethin'. I know that damned sick bastard well enough to know that." Murmuring to himself, he tore it open and felt an icy shock zip its way down his spine as he slowly read the contents:

Dear Ray,

I know you might be facing hard times right now with the economy on the skids as it is. I need some help. No, not with getting to hell out of the shit-hole. I don't hold out any hope for that. Remember what we spoke of that time in Indiana? I need to see you. It will be to your advantage. Could you say you are my brother and come

see me? You'll know how to find me when you see where
this is from.
   Yours, my brother,
   Denny

Ray stared into space for a long time. "Wants to see
me, huh?" He frowned and muttered, "Son of a bitch! I
got nobody huntin' me right now, life's been real quiet.
Got me a nice job at the grade school, too. Lots of young
stuff to look at around that place. Things goin' along
right nice for a change—real nice." He got up and paced
across the floor, his hands flung out. "Wonder what the
hell he's wantin' of me?" He paced again, knowing he
would visit his "brother" on death row. "Says it would be
worth somethin' to me. If it's not money, I ain't interested. I'll sure as hell tell him that."

                              ✌✍✌

"Hey, Denny, your brother's here to see you."
He'd waited an eternity to hear those few words. He
got up from his bunk and waited while the guard opened
his cell door.
He was taken to a small room which he'd not yet
seen. He had no real family that could come to visit, but
he knew who had come to see him. Denny was seated
behind a thick Plexiglass screen, with hand-held micro-
phones for communication. He looked up to see his long-
time friend and associate. Oh, yes, they knew each other
very well, and in some cases had even shared the wealth,
so to speak.
Denny picked up the speaker and murmured, "How's
it going, Ray?"
"How the hell you think?"

He didn't miss the look of apprehension across Ray's face and smiled.

Ray didn't want to be seen in this hole, not for love nor money. But that damned Denny had him by the balls any time he wanted to open his mouth, and old Ray knew it. He damned well did.

"Ray, I'm not ever getting out of here, but I need some work from you. I'll make it worth your while," Denny purred into the microphone.

"How worth my while—what to hell you talkin' about?" Ray's eyes squinted, and he unconsciously leaned closer, though it made no real difference.

"Somebody did me in, Ray. I'm not letting that go by the board. I'm mad as hell, and I'll die a happy man if that filthy bitch who did this to me gets hers." He lowered his voice. "I will leave you all I have if you can handle this for me."

"Filthy bitch, huh? A woman? What do you want from me, Denny, my boy?" He smirked. "What in the hell do you have to leave me? I never knew you to make any real money."

"You'd be damned surprised, now wouldn't you, asshole?"

"Prove it." Ray straightened up and stuck his jaw out a bit. He had all the power for once in dealing with the wily Denny, and he planned to sit back and enjoy using it to the max.

"There is a key to a lock box." Denny knew he'd caught Ray's attention with that statement. "It wasn't in the house at the time they searched the place. I was arrested from the hospital and never had the chance to get it. I can tell you where it is. But you have to swear to do this little job for me."

"So where in the hell is this so called key?"

"Not so fast—I need something first." Denny worried Ray might take the stash and never do the job. "You'll take care of this for me?"

"Hell, yes, I could use a few bucks right now." Ray seemed overly anxious. It was for more than his need of money—Denny had him over a barrel. One word to the cops, and Ray would be in an adjoining cell, and he damned well knew it. He had a lot to lose, his job, for one thing. Working around all those little bodies every day was like grazing in tall cotton. His mind went crazy listening to their giggles and silly talk. It happened over and over while he was at work. All he had to do was look at them to get himself swollen and painful, whether pushing a broom or cleaning the toilets.

"Well, go on, spit it out," Ray growled, as he quelled his wildly inflamed thoughts.

Denny had little to give him, but he said the name and added, "When I hear this bitch, and everyone close to her—people she cares about, has been fed to the worms, I'll tell you where the money is." He grinned in his dark way. "You won't find it on your own, but I got paid a ransom once and stashed it someplace real good. Didn't want to look suddenly prosperous, you know how it is—or was."

"Know anything more than a name?"

"I know she left town right after it happened," he snarled, "And that's all the hell I know." Denny shook his head in frustration. "Goddamn it, Ray, you're a free man. Get on that damned computer of yours. You know how to use it better than anyone I know. Hell, man, you could find the devil himself on that thing!" Denny snorted into the Plexiglass and gave Ray a narrow-eyed look and a sly nod that meant more than words. But, to Ray, it meant dear old Denny could and would, put him right into the cell next to him on this damned death row, if he didn't do as he was asked.

Then Denny lowered his voice into the microphone. "Remember—just you keep in mind—that devil-bitch has robbed me of everything in my life—everything! Get my meaning? I read the papers—and don't you forget it. If I don't see the results I'm looking for in the newspapers pretty soon, your ass'll be sitting right in here with me—"

"All right, all right, I got the damned picture." Ray slumped in his chair, and his blood had turned icy as hell. He couldn't help the shiver that passed through his body.

Satisfied he had a good man taking care of business on the outside, Denny turned and signaled the guard. He was ready to go back to his cell.

❧❧❧

Ray left the prison. His mind spun in a whirl, and he muttered as he drove slowly back to Denver. "Like I ain't got enough against me—now he wants—" Ray shuddered. He hadn't liked the feeling he'd gotten in that grim, gray-walled fortress that held Denny Garver. The forbidding place had left him chilled to the bone. "I swear that bastard wants to see me in there with him. Son of a bitch! I wish I could put *him* out of business instead of some damned woman I don't even know."

He entered the Longworth section of Denver and drove slowly down the street. The homes were modest to say the least. But now and then he noticed how nicely some people kept their snug little homes. Though for the most part these smaller homes were left unkempt—yards filled with weeds and broken toys; clotheslines filled with laundry; and curtains, torn and hanging crooked in the windows. It made a man depressed just to drive down the street.

Some yards had broken down old cars sitting there with young kids working on them. Did those poor, unfortunate, and impoverished teens hope to create a set of dream wheels from those broken parts scattered about? He snorted at the thoughts of how hard they'd work trying to build something other kids had easily gotten from their parent's open wallets.

How well he remembered back to his earlier years when having a set of cool wheels had occupied his own youthful mind. His boyish dreams had come to nothingness as time wore on, and it still rankled inside his guts. So when he saw the hopeless need for cool wheels that these young fools dreamed of, it was like looking into a broken, cracked mirror at his own failures. He was just like the rest of these poor fools who lived in this pathetic shit-hole part of town. Pushing a broom for a shit-eating wage. And the car he drove proved the point for him as nothing else could.

Ray pulled his own worn out, faded red Pinto into another of the small houses, shrugged at the uncut lawn and dried up flower beds. "A man's got to live like a damned hog in these filthy little flea-bag rent houses." He needed money all right—he sure as hell did. He walked in, sniffed the dank air and his full garbage can. He sat down in front of his computer, a lap top, but a good one. He'd made sure of that when he'd ripped it off from a nice home he'd just happened to rummage through.

He remembered that night. A little girl lived there, one he'd seen at school, but no one was home. He'd had made detailed plans for that soft little body. The fire inside his body had cried for release, and she wasn't there! How carefully he'd watched that home and knew their habits. He'd swallowed his disappointment as best he could. But when a couple of days later, he saw another small child wandering about alone, maybe on her way home from school, he knew his prayers had been answered.

He'd quickly swept the child off the street and taken her to his small home. She hadn't made a big fuss screaming and kicking like some of them. She had seemed to be frozen with fear, all stiff and big-eyed the way she'd been. His swelling response kept him in a glow as he remembered it all—everything in full detail. He knew her name now, too. The papers were full of the death of little Mindy Lassen.

Chapter 5

Martha had worked for the vet several times, assisting him in several surgeries, with neutering, spaying, broken bones, gashes, and the treatment of illnesses. Most of these things, she had never heard of. But of course in learning a new aspect of medicine, this was expected and no surprise to her. Any facility, including the care of human-kind, had new areas too and new skills to be learned. She had welcomed the challenge.

When she could, she quietly looked at the paperwork on the drug Neutersol. She felt defeated when she read the literature. It indicated it might not work on a full grown man. She nearly cursed under her breath. "Damnation! Looks like it's only for puppies."

When she found the right opportunity, she held up a vial of Neutersol and asked Dr. Gleason. "You ever use this on pups?"

His reply wasn't what she'd hoped to hear. "According to what is put out on this drug, it isn't all it's cracked up to be. Unless they make some changes in it, I don't think I'll be using it any time soon."

"Why ever not? It seems so humane, what do they say is wrong with it?"

"It fails to reduce the aggressiveness of the male for one thing. Partly, we neuter these young pets to reduce aggressiveness as adults, as well as preventing so much unwanted breeding."

"It doesn't prevent them from breeding then?"

"I didn't say that. It does prevent breeding. The problem is that it fails to prevent tom cats from spraying all over the house and running off as they mature. And dogs can still be aggressive with other animals and people. And in that case, they could be a bit more dangerous as pets for children." He went on. "It won't prevent a dog from biting a stranger the same way surgical neutering usually will."

He turned to leave the surgery, but Martha was still curious. "You could still use it, then, if it was right for a patient?"

"Some vets might, I suppose so, but if it isn't the whole package, I won't bother with it."

"Gee, that's too bad. It would have been nice not to have to do surgery on the poor little things." Martha made sure she presented the perfect picture of a worried pet owner.

"I suppose you're right about that. But if a drug doesn't do as well as the surgical procedure, it isn't all it's supposed to be, is it?" Dr. Gleason shrugged. He wore the face of a man who patiently did his job the best he knew how. He added, "This happens frequently with new things. I have learned to take all the wonderful new literature with a good sized grain of salt."

Martha understood he was disappointed with the drug, Neutersol. It wasn't as though this had never happened before with a new medicine or drug. Dr. Gleason had been in practice for many years and was used to it.

Martha asked, "Do you want me to toss this stuff, then?"

"Well, I suppose so. I won't use it. Just use the same procedures you would use in your own practice for drug disposal." He turned and left the medication room. As his tall frame exited the area, Martha's heart did a crazy flip-flop.

"I know just how I'll destroy this stuff! Oh, yes, I surely do!"

She quietly gathered up the numerous vials and placed them in her bag. She also tossed a couple of good-sized syringes in too. After a proper interval, she carried a few sample vials out and placed them into the sharps container. Those filled containers were routinely delivered later to an area for incineration.

Later in the day, Martha walked out the door of the Gleason Animal Clinic and stepped into her car. Driving home, her heart had begun beating rapidly, and her mind had gone wild with thoughts she never wanted to have again. Her once-quiet life had taken on a feeling so familiar, it made her fearful, yet terribly excited. Maybe Neutersol didn't do all it was supposed to do, but if it dampened the desires of even one child predator, she would be happy. Maybe she had found a way.

෫৯෫৯

Martha waited for Harry's return with more than her usual eagerness. She sought details on the location of this latest scene of travesty. She wanted to drive through that neighborhood. Was it another housing area where young families lived with small children and way too many sexual predators running free? She was haunted and sickened by thoughts of another little child dying to satisfy some inhuman monster's sadistic need. It had taken place yet again with little Mindy Lassen, and in that neighborhood.

Oh, yes, they had the usual suspects—the usual fruitless rounds of questioning—the look of surprise and innocence across the faces of those same suspects—and the sometimes rather thin proof of where they had been about the time the crime had been committed.

She wanted complete secrecy and would try for it, but Harry knew and, in many ways, approved of her feelings on this subject. He had applauded her actions many times over, but it was the underlying fear he would lose what they had together that kept him from letting her go on her hunt for these inhuman monsters. She saw the indecision across his handsome features whenever it was discussed, right along with his inner raging at what that child had suffered. And knowing, all the while, his own little daughter had suffered the same fate. And from the heartbreak of that terrible crime, he'd lost her and in time, his wife also.

Martha trembled inside with eagerness—could she hide it from Harry's probing eyes? Did she even want to? He would try to soothe her and calm her madness, and by now, she had the niggling inner feeling it was a sort of madness. It had, in fact, begun to worry her, way down deep. *Am I becoming some kind of monster myself?*

When she finally heard that noisy old truck crunching gravel in the driveway, her heart took a leap and began pounding. *Best play it cool, Serena, my eager other self. You have something to work with now.*

Harry came in, his shoulders slumped in that way she knew so well. Things hadn't gone well today. "Hi, Harry, not so good today, huh?"

"You know me so well, girl. Nothing good happened today. They took in a few possible suspects for questioning." He uttered a hopeless sounding, half-laugh. "I don't believe I have ever seen so many pristine, innocent looking faces in my whole damned life, Martha."

"Any that rang a bell with you out of those questioned today?"

"We sat behind the glass. Being undercover, we're not seen by any of them, but we get to have a look during the questioning. I saw a few nervous tics, side glances, and certain hand movements. I have a few ideas, but nothing to write home about. No, darling, not today—nothing concrete."

"What area are we talking about, anyway? I am familiar with most of Denver." Coy in her questioning, she busied herself in the kitchen, mixing a batch of biscuits. If anything might disarm a suspicious man's mind, it would be the smell of freshly baked biscuits in the oven. She looked into his eyes to see if he was on to her.

He was—he knew her so well. "What's on your mind, my darling?"

"Oh, nothing different than usual."

"I can't lie to you and I won't, but this latest child's murder has been on TV anyway. I'll lay it out to you as best I can." He spent enough time to inform her of the general whereabouts of Longworth, the area in question, as he watched her shove the biscuits into the heated oven.

"Longworth? I haven't been in that area. You say that sorry spot contains that many sexual predators—enough to easily pick out enough suspects to keep you behind that glass for several hours?" Martha felt her face grow cold, and her jaw tensed so tight it became painful.

"That's not the only area in this berg, either, and I hate to have to say it, but Longworth is just the closest to where the little girl was found." Harry held his face in his hands. He didn't want to look at Martha right now, knowing what he would see in her eyes if he did.

"Harry—please, I want to drive through that area." Seeing his face tighten, she added, "Now don't go thinking things. I'm curious, of course. But right now, I want to know how it feels to drive along those streets, imagining what monsters those houses contain. It can't be everyone, it couldn't be!"

"Of course not—it just feels that way, especially after a thing like this. It feels that way to me, at any rate. Sometimes I feel like the world is filled with rot, and we are drowning in it!"

Martha went to him and crawled into his arms. "What are we to do?"

He pulled her close and growled into her ear. "I know damned well what a part of you wants to do, and don't try to deny it."

"Of course I want to get busy. I ache with the need of it." But as the smell of freshly baked biscuits filled the kitchen, Martha got off his lap and went to the oven. "But right now, let's eat, my wonderful darling."

As they sat down, Martha looked into his eyes. "Harry, if anything happened to you, I don't know how I could go on living."

"What on earth ever made you say a thing like that, love?"

"I don't know, but I just felt a chill pass through me." She looked at him, her lips firm and tight. "I do worry about you every time you go to work. You will be careful out there, won't you?"

❧❧❧

Jeannie Moulton awaited the squeal of brakes. They were way down the block, but she always heard them at this time each day. With anticipation, she awaited Will's arrival home from his school. He attended the Catholic Primary Academy, and bus service was provided if the children lived more than a half mile from the school. The boy only had one short block to walk from his bus stop, and Jeannie sometimes worried about that. There were so many trees and bushes along the way as he walked to the house, it made her nervous.

Will came charging up the steps of their fairly new home in the suburbs of Denver. She thought his gait seemed a little slower than on some other days and as she was always quick to see signs of trouble in her son. She awaited him with increased tension. It was always something, and today would be no different.

He opened the door and came slowly inside. She saw the pallor across his cheeks and the slowness of his steps. She knelt down, hugged her son, and questioned, "Anything happen today, Will?"

"Aw, nothin'—nothin' happened, Mom."

"Oh, yes, something did happen today. I see it on your face, love."

He looked at her, and she saw a haunted look on his face.

"Mom—a man was looking at me today. He was across the street. There were about ten of us, but it was me he was looking at." He manfully fought his tears. "I know it was, Mom. I know it!"

"Oh, honey, tell me everything you can about this. After what happened four years ago, I can understand why you're fearful. Just tell me what you can remember about what happened today."

"He had an old junky car, all faded, sort of red-like. His eyes kept right on me as I waited for our bus. Mom, I knew he was looking at me." Will's face was tight and pale. He was afraid, and rightly so. A thing like this might bring back more of his old memories. Jeannie felt her rage grow and the familiar sickness deep in her stomach at the thought of it. "I stayed close to the other kids, Mom." He held his chin firm, but she saw the tremor of it as he worked to fight his fears.

"You did the right thing, son."

She led him into the kitchen where she had pulled some snacks out of the freezer for him. She let him take a look at the stuff but left the choices up to him. He chose a few pizza bits, and she popped them into the microwave.

"I will speak to the principle of the school about this, but I have something else in mind, too. I have thought about it a lot lately." She saw the light of interest come into his eyes.

"Like what, Mom?"

"Life can be full of dangers for anyone, but even more so for small children as we know all too well. I cannot keep my eye on you every moment." She took him by the shoulders. "Will, I think it's time you learned how to defend yourself. You are a small child yet, but you are strong and healthy for your age, and there are things you can learn to help protect yourself. Learning these things will give you some needed confidence too." The microwave rang, and Jeannie took the pizza rolls out. "Here you go, honey."

Will sat at the counter but took nothing. "Mom, I think about that, too. I watch these guys on TV. No one gets the best of them. They can kill with a flick of the wrist sometimes." The excitement in his eyes sent a chill clear through her body. From long experience, after his rape and molestation, and his recent attempt to strangle his puppy, she knew he could easily go too far if they weren't careful with him. She feared he had the capacity to become enraged and violent with little provocation.

"Will, if we do this, it is with the strict understanding that you must only use what you learn to save your own life, or maybe to help someone else. You cannot become a bully with the skills and knowledge you will learn."

"Yeah, I know that, Mom. But just think, if one of those bad guys came up to me, I could deck him real easy, couldn't I?"

"Yes, you just might be able to do that, and if it was a man with bad ideas like that, he'd have it coming." She shoved the plate of pizza rolls at him. "Here, Will, have something to eat. Aren't you hungry after school?"

"Yes, I'm hungry, but I want to learn how to fight off a bad man, too. I want to learn how, Mom." He took a pizza roll and bit into it.

"Okay, I'll discuss it with your father, of course, but as soon as possible, I want you to get started. I'm not sure why I feel this way, Will, but one day it might mean your own personal safety, and that's what I'm thinking about."

Will quietly munched his pizza roll as his mind busily dispatched molesters, lechers, bullies, and maybe a few snotty girls he had in mind. He would learn all he could because somehow Will knew he would need this knowledge one day. Thoughts of what might happen sent an icy chill across his body. He wasn't sure why, but he felt his chest expand with the idea he would be full of tricks and surprises if the wrong person ever grabbed him again.

¢∕≥¢∕≥

The phone jangled, and Martha quickly grabbed it up. "Yes?"

It was her daughter, Jeannie, and Martha's heart rate leaped. It was never good news when she called.

"Mom, Will came home with his face white as a sheet," Jeannie said. "He told me some man was watching him from an old, ratty, faded reddish-colored car. Will was so filled with fear that it made me furious and sick at the same time!"

"Are you sure the man had singled Will out?"

"Who knows for sure? But Will says the man looked at him and not the other kids. I only know that my son was devastated. He seemed to have a deep sort of terror all over again." She sniffed back a sob. "Mom, he will never be able to forget what that man did to him."

Martha could hear her daughter breathing rapidly, and her anger against what had been done to Will soared all over again.

Then Jeannie said. "I am going to enroll Will in a course on self-defense. I'll speak to Martin about it, but my mind is made up. I can't have him living in fear like this. He needs to know he can defend himself."

Martha instantly approved. "That's a great idea. I agree with you about that, Jeannie. He may learn to be more aggressive, but hopefully, they can help him understand how far he dares to go. I believe they teach restraint right along with his new skills." She paused a second. "I think every child should know the basics of self-defense. Even the small ones. We no longer live in a safe world, my dear."

"Humph! Did we ever, Mom?"

Martha hated the defeat and sarcasm in her daughter's voice.

"But I'm glad to have your input, and especially, your okay. I know he is still a small boy, but he has been through so much—too much. He is no longer an innocent little soul like most other kids."

"He will learn some lethal skills, Jeannie. Are you prepared to face that?"

"Yes, I spoke to him about it. I think he got a buzz from hearing about those things. I hope we won't be making him into a Rambo-type killing machine."

"Jeannie!" Martha almost choked on the words, thinking of that little boy as a lethal machine. "We won't let it go that far. We can't."

"No, we can't, but we have to do something to give him confidence and to help him protect himself, too."

"Well, a good course in self-defense ought to do that for him."

After Martha hung up, she got busy making dinner for Harry. She always got the warm fuzzies just thinking about that man. When she heard the crunch of his truck tires on the graveled driveway, she felt a wide grin break out. He always did that for her.

But the way his shoulders slumped as he came through the door, made her want to cry for him. "Again, Harry?" It was all she could think to say. His job was a tough one, and he saw too much.

"Yeah—again, dear." He went to her and held her tight for long moments before he could even speak.

"So what happened today?"

"Another small girl went missing. We haven't found her or any sign of her. The parents are so distraught, they want to go out and shoot someone. Thank God, they haven't got a target, not yet anyway."

The phone on Harry's hip went musical. His face was white when he answered it. "Yeah, Harry here." He listened for a moment, and Martha saw an expression of relief come over his face. He clicked off and turned to her. "She's home—was at a friend's house." He slumped into a chair at the table, put his head in his hands. She brought him a cup of coffee.

"Harry, sometimes I think your job is going to be the end of you. Maybe it would be best if you didn't care so much."

"How can I do that, Martha—could you?"

"I guess you can't any more than I can." She stood before him. "Harry, will you drive me through that Longworth section? Isn't that the area you mentioned?"

"Still on that kick, huh?" His eyes took on a wary look, but Martha was not deterred.

She nodded. "You know I am, and will always be as long as I have the strength to stand and walk. I want to drive through the streets of that section, just to get the feel of the place."

"I'm off tomorrow, how about we take a drive then?"

"Why, Harry, darling, I'd love it."

"But for now, forget the dishes, forget everything. I need you like I've never needed anyone before. I'm burning up with need, you lovely woman. I don't care how much you rake me over the coals, or hard you are on me tonight. I don't give a damn." He got out of his chair and headed for her.

The heated look in his eyes set her fully ablaze, her body on fire. She was glad to meet him way more than half way. They nearly ran down the hallway to their bedroom, clothes flying off as they moved.

Chapter 6

Ray had the feeling his car had been recognized and was a dead giveaway. He'd scoped out the Moulton home, and followed the mother about as discreetly as he knew how. That Moulton boy was someone Martha cared about. He could be the boy who'd set this crazy woman on her path of destruction—for Denny and some others. If so, he'd be one of those that Ray had orders to destroy, eliminate, or whatever other kind of hell he could devise. He needed to know more about the kid, aside from the fact he was too old and the wrong sex for Ray's fancy. But whatever. Ray figured he might as well have some enjoyment along the way.

The boy didn't attend the school where Ray worked, but he had the kid spotted. Following a bus was no big deal. But the look that came across that child's face told him that this child was always on the look-out—for what? But if he was Martha's grandson, Ray knew what the child feared. That decided him. By damn, this boy *was* the one. "He'd had some nasty things done to him, but what's he all worried about? He's alive, isn't he?"

Denny would be watching for results, and Ray had better get something done. He had to act, but he needed a change of cars. It was time to be the brother again. Becoming frantic to avoid having Denny shoot off his mouth about him, Ray never noticed how the trees were leafing out, or how nice the weather had gotten. He needed money and answers. Uttering a sigh of disgust, he got into his pathetic excuse for a car and headed to Canon City.

℮℠℠

"Denny, you've got a visitor."

Again, he was escorted to the secluded room reserved for death-row inmates to meet a visitor. He sat down and looked through the thick Plexiglass. Ray. But then, who in the hell else would it be?

"What the devil you want now?" Denny snarled the words into the microphone.

"First, I need some money. You can't ever spend it, and I need a change of vehicles. My old junker has been spotted, and maybe more than once." Ray shifted on the hard seat. "Tell me about the Moulton kid. He is someone of interest to the old bitch—why?"

"Keep it down, will ya?"

"Who gives a shit, Denny? Not you, that's for damned sure."

"He's most likely the kid that old Freddie boy did." Denny laughed. "He got off on that one." But his face sobered. "It all went to hell after that. Something got the bitch in an uproar after that happened. She went after Freddie way before she went after me."

"Related to her—that it?"

"Looks that way."

"The old gal's shackin' up with one of the top detectives. Looks real cozy in that department, too." Ray chuckled quietly to himself while Denny sat and watched. "I'll really enjoy fixin' that for her. Oh, God, how I will!

But the kid is getting a bit old for my taste. Like 'em younger, and the other kind, if you know what I mean."

"Forget that, you sick bastard! I don't give a flying fart what you want. You'd better come across if you know what's good for you."

"Sick bastard, eh? Look who in the damned hell is talkin'." Ray sneered at Denny, his unease driving his rage. "Well, if I want to get anything done, I need a different car already. That kid has spotted me in my old piece of shit. I saw his scared-lookin' face clear enough to know. I need that money, Denny, if I'm to do these things you want. I need it now—have to have some things, a newer car, or for sure a different set of wheels, for one thing. What the hell do you care when I get it. You've already got me where you want me—you know that, don't ya, you sick bastard?"

Denny hastily wrote something on a slip of paper and shoved it through the slot at the bottom of the glass. "Here you go. Get yourself whatever you need. Some decent clothes might be a good start. You look like a god-damned street bum." He lowered his voice and growled, "I'll be watching the papers and don't you forget it."

"See ya, bro." Furious with Denny for putting him in this hellish spot, Ray couldn't help adding the last quip. "Keep 'em hangin' loose if you know what I mean." He almost didn't give a damn any more.

"I'll see you hangin' loose, you bastard. See if I don't—if you let me down, you'll be hearing from me. You'd better come through, Ray."

Ray left, and Denny signaled he was ready to return to his dismal cell. His step felt lighter, and he hardly felt his feet hit the drab gray-shaded concrete. In spite of being in this living hell, his heart beat stronger. Old Ray had a few things in the works, and he'd damned sure earn his money. Denny knew that and smiled as he walked.

Ray scanned the bit of paper and knew where to look for this key. "Clever bastard, that Denny. Who'd ever think to look in a place like that?"

He drove rapidly toward his goal, Colorado Springs, and Denny's old home. If it was occupied, he'd need to be damned careful—he knew that, too. He'd have to wait and see. His car was in such rotten damned condition, it was close to limping. If there was enough money hidden in that damned lock box, he'd find himself something a hell of a lot better than this piece of shit.

Ray drove along the street where Denny had lived before his arrest. "Looks abandoned. If it is, it's my lucky day." He parked and decided to knock on the door. He felt his tension rise as he approached the door. He had no real reason to feel that way and straightened his shoulders. He knocked on the door.

Hearing no response, he stood still for a while, then looked into a handy window. It looked empty. Then he began to scan the rock-work around the front door. Some of it was cemented, and some were squares set into the ground, but loose. Looking carefully around, Ray knelt down and pried one of the loose squares up. After two of them, and finding nothing, he began to curse the day Denny had been born.

After another quick glance at the street, in case he might be seen, he tried another one. Beneath it he saw a scrap of heavy plastic and grabbed at it. It came free and inside he saw a key inside a small plastic bag. "Shit-damn! Here it is!"

Now he had to find the locked box. This wasn't a large city and he knew he would. He hastily replaced the stone squares, hoping he'd made it look untouched. He scattered a few leaves over the area and left the yard.

Ray was in a big hurry to get shut of that area for some reason. Just being near that house cast a spell of gloom over his entire soul. He figured it was Denny and the evil things he'd done. Even though Ray had a pretty rotten history himself, he believed he wasn't anything near the devil that Denny was. "Why do I feel this way, anyway, dammit it all to hell?"

He shrugged his feelings away and got into his faded little car. "Now, where to? I need a phone book." He drove to a small diner and went in. He borrowed their commercial yellow pages, took it to his booth, and started searching.

He ordered a small lunch and kept looking while he ate. Finding enough info, he almost tore out the pages, but decided to take the book with him. He shoved it under his coat, and after laying a few bucks on the table, walked out.

After three tries, Ray found the right place, a bus station with private, small boxes. Inside he found a canvas bag containing several bundles of hundred dollar bills. "Wow, somebody sure as hell paid a real nice ransom, the bastard wasn't lying." He also knew that some poor little child never saw home again, not with Denny pulling the strings. "Must be thousands here." He felt his excitement rise, knowing he had the power of money in his pocket. But he had a job to do—a price to pay, and knew he'd better get at it. "The bitch and all she holds dear, eh?" He shook his head. "Bastard don't want much, does he?"

Ray knew he had to be careful not to draw undue attention to himself throwing bundles of money about. "A car will be the first thing. Something different, but not worth a lot." He headed back to Denver. He had a lot of work ahead. "That kid is one of 'em, and that woman who did Denny lives with a goddamned detective." It wouldn't be easy, but he had to show some results or face the slammer right along with Denny. He felt sick just now.

He tried to set his mind to thinking about something that would make him feel on top of the world again. At least for a little while.

Lost in thought, Ray drove back to Denver. He had a big job ahead of him, and all of it illegal. These nasty little jobs could end his life in the doing. "Just when I had a nice little set up. Lots of nice stuff right in front of me every damned day, and here I am, stuck between a rock and a hard place." He puffed out his breath. "There's no way out for me."

Yet, hopeless as he felt, he had a pot full of money, and that was something he'd never had in his life. He drove into his small driveway and went into his shabby little home. "If I suddenly move, it might cause suspicion. I could be under the gun so damned easy, just because of something that happened a long time ago. Those bastards never forget."

He made himself a cheese sandwich and took a beer out of the fridge. "Need to pack in a few groceries one of these days." After he finished his meal, he got the title to his shabby little car and headed down to the used car lot. "Maybe things will look better after I get some newer wheels."

Later, Ray drove away from the car lot with a nice used pick-up. It had a small camper on the back. "I might get some use out of a thing like that one of these days."

His mind settled on seeing himself in there with a small child wriggling and fighting in his grasp. He hadn't seen the right one, not yet. Maybe even that boy he had spotted. *A little too old for my taste, but two birds with one stone as they say*." He smiled as he drove into his yard with a new set of wheels.

Chapter 7

Will had been to his self-defense class several times, and already he felt a sense of empowerment. *There is something I can do. There really is!* He felt his chest expand. *Wait till I tell my daddy what I learned today. Won't he be surprised?* Knowing he would soon be able to take care of himself, keep himself safe, gave Will a feeling of elation he had not felt for several years. He could never forget what that man had done to his body, but now if someone ever tried that sort of moves against him, he knew he could do something.

He was a small boy, but good sized for his age and strong. Now he was no longer without some means of defense. His new training made Will feel more than equal to anyone.

Later that evening the family sat together for the evening meal. Will sat quietly eating, and Jeannie, ever on the alert for signs of trouble in her son, saw the shine in Will's eyes. She waited to see what would come next, and something always did with Will.

Finally, she had to ask, "And how was your lesson with the Self-Reliance Team today?

"Mom, we are learning a lot. What I am learning

makes me feel safe, like I can protect myself." He softly added, "Even against a bigger person."

Jeannie felt satisfaction at his words and, for once, she did not see that strange gleam of thoughts in his eyes that no boy should ever have. His eyes reflected confidence and pride in himself. She wanted to cry with hope for her son but kept her cool. She thought about the puppy. That pet was gone, and she didn't have the courage to get another one. Not yet.

Will looked across the dining table at his father. "Dad, could we talk after dinner?"

"Why yes, son, we surely can." He looked to Jeannie, surprise in his eyes at the unusually mature request from his son.

After leaving the dinner table, father and son walked into the library where Will quickly took the initiative. "Dad, I am learning things that I never knew before. Did you know you can kill a man with some of the things they teach?" At the look of alarm on his father's face, Will quickly put out a hand, perhaps to prevent his father from worrying his son was learning something lethal. "Hold on, Dad. I know how this sounds coming from a young boy, especially one who just tried to strangle a puppy. I just wanted you to know what I'm learning. Keep in mind, Dad, they also teach us the responsibility that comes with learning these things."

"Thank God for small favors, Will. You have frightened me with what you've had to say. But I'm also glad you've told me and that you trust me to know these things as well." He reached out to pat his son on the shoulders.

"I didn't want to scare Mom with it, but I figured you could handle knowing what I'm learning."

Martin Moulton couldn't miss the look of confidence he saw on his young son's face. It was a look he feared he'd never see after the attack on him as a five-year-old. But what did it really mean?

They had gone through all the counseling they knew how to find for him. The Catholic School System, which was staffed by tougher-than-usual nuns, had done a lot for Will, too. But this self-defense program had seemingly turned a corner in the young boy's life. *Oh, God, if this could only be true!* He cried the words to himself, while he cautiously carried his worry inside.

They returned to the great room where Jeannie sat with her mending on her lap. Of course, she was burning with questions, but she kept her needle flying and said only, "Will, do you have some studying to do?"

"I'll get right on it, Mom."

He left the room without the usual hassle over doing his homework, which left both parents close to shock. Jeannie questioned her husband, her brow wrinkled. "What's going on, Martin?"

"Later dear, later." He smiled at her with mystery in his eyes, and her pulse rate shot up to double time.

"You men! No woman can figure you out!"

In answer, Martin merely raised his eyebrows.

※※※

Two days later, Will waited for the bus that would take him close to his home. More conscious of his surroundings since seeing the man in the faded red car, his eyes darted about as he laughed and chatted with his friends.

"What you lookin' for?" a short, freckle-faced boy asked.

"Nothin'. I just like to know who's around, is all." Will wasn't about to enlarge on anything personal or let his friend know he had anything to fear. Instead, he stuck his chest out. "I'm takin' some classes in self-defense, and they teach us to be aware of everything and everybody around you."

"Wow! Just like Rambo?"

"Naw, just everyday stuff. My mom thought I oughta learn how to take care of myself, you know." He wanted to change the subject. The freckle-face kid, Jimmy, was getting too close and personal. Anything like that still made Will feel uncomfortable. He would always carry hidden things around inside himself, things he couldn't tell anyone.

He saw the bus coming and heaved a sigh of relief. He also saw a pick-up with a camper on the back drive slowly past as the bus pulled up. Seeing the truck drive slowly like that gave him a chill. But maybe it was the look on the man's face that gave him a creepy feeling. His face pits and scars, and Will saw them from where he stood.

He reached home that day and said nothing about the vehicle to anyone. But this other man in the reddish colored car had had the same pits and scars on his face, too. Will got a part of the license number until the truck drove too far away. DXL His chest puffed out a bit as he wrote those letters in his school book. Though learning to take care of himself, he wondered if he'd ever get the chance to use the skills with which he was becoming adept.

❧❧❧

Martha worked at the small community hospital and had enjoyed her shift. It was med-surg, her favorite area with its clean surgeries, illnesses, and a few broken bones—the usual stuff. This hospital, being small, put their orthopedic patients on med-surg, as they had too few to open an orthopedic floor.

Martha left the hospital and drove home in her small Buick Century. Stopped at a light, she noticed to her right, a pick-up with a camper on the back. It sat close beside her, and when the driver looked her way, something in the man's eyes made her take notice. The driver had taken more than just a casual glance, and it had bothered her for some reason. Was she being too suspicious?

Later, as she neared Harry's rustic, cedar-sided ranch home, it cruised on past her and shortly turned off onto a lonely country side-road. "Was the man in that truck following me?" It didn't make sense or even seem possible, yet she had the feeling he'd done just that. It set her to thinking—wondering.

She met Harry at the door. She usually worked the evening shift, and he always waited for her return. Reaching him, she melted into his arms. When he held her out to look in her face, he questioned her, "What is it, dear? Your face is white, and you're stiff as a board. What's going on?"

"Harry, I think I was followed on the way home tonight. A truck came even with me at that last stoplight, and the driver gave me a look. It felt off, somehow. I can't explain why I feel this way, but I do. I also think that man followed me out here." She gave off a shiver. "Could that be possible?"

"Anything is possible. Given your history, you might have an enemy in the works. Can you think of anyone in particular?"

"God, no!" She felt ice filling her veins as she told Harry, "A few men might wish me dead ten times over if they knew who I was. Harry, is this a dream or a nightmare I'm having?" She gasped. "Maybe I just imagined it."

"And maybe not." Harry had that firm, determined look across his face, and Martha became quietly thoughtful. Was there someone out there who might want to seek revenge on the person who had ruined their sexual capability? She knew that was a possibility, but only if they knew her identity. She couldn't think of any time her name or identity had been brought out. But, certainly, there were those who knew all about her and what she'd done.

She went over the list in her mind. *Freddie boy? Never, not that wimp! Then who? Denny's on death row, so it couldn't be him.* She mentally went over the list of sexual predators she had disabled—if only in the gonad department. She understood that some predators were out to hurt and maim young children, whether sexually or just physically. The vision of those little victims made her shudder physically.

Harry grabbed her and held her tight. "What's the hell's going through that mind of yours, dear?"

"Just thinking of anyone who might have me in their sights and want a bit of revenge." She grinned at him and shrugged. "It's a rather long list, Harry."

He pulled her into his arms and gave her a long, hard kiss. "Yes, it is, you devil woman." He held her out and looked into her eyes. "Your name has never been mentioned in public as a vigilante, Martha. Not that I have ever heard—not even once, as far I know."

"I know that, but people do know about me, actually quite a few. It wouldn't take much for an interested person to find out who had done the deed on them. Not if they had an agenda." She looked him in the eye. "Harry, I could be on someone's hate list. I sure could be."

"I'll keep a look-out for a truck with a camper. Since no actual crime has been committed, we cannot issue an all points. Colorado has a lot of them so if you see it again, try to get the license number. That's all we'd need to put him away if he threatens you."

"If—it's often way too late by then. You know that, yourself."

"Oh, God, Martha, I couldn't handle that!"

"Relax, Harry, we don't even know if this is more than a figment of my over-active imagination." She kissed him and headed for the bedroom, and Harry was right behind her.

⁂

Ray continued on down the country road. "I know where you live now, my lady. But before I take you—I will take everyone you care about, first. No one has a greater right to suffer losses than a filthy destroying bitch like you." He felt himself grow hot with anger and hate. "Maybe your losses won't be the same as you've caused for some other poor bastards, but they'll be losses enough to break your bitch's heart."

He smiled to himself, thinking of all she had to lose—her grandson, her daughter, her son-in-law, and best of all, that goddamned detective she was shacked up with. Ray drove on into the night, his grip tightening on the steering wheel. What was he up against? He didn't know, but he had some plans to make, and he had to be careful about it. "Now that she's seen me, I think I'd better find another damned piece of junk to drive. Shit-damn, I liked this camper, but now that I think about it, that damned kid has seen me in this, too. Damn, I had plans for how I'd use it, too."

Chapter 8

Harry was home from work, and Martha again requested that they drive through Longworth. She had a strong desire to see that area, maybe she would get some kind of feeling about it. After a light dinner, they set out.

Harry nodded to Martha as they entered the Longworth sector of Denver, "I don't know what good it will do either one of us, but I understand your reasons for wanting to drive through here."

"Neither do I, but I've wanted to see this place ever since you came home with the news about the Lassen child." Martha laid a hand on Harry's leg as she saw the crowded little homes along the main street of the area. She noted the poorly kept yards and the broken, disabled cars parked in weeds and uncut grass.

"Sort of a poor little place," Harry commented. "I don't know if being low-income promotes slothful living, or are they just too tired trying to keep their heads above water to care about a nice lawn or a few weeds."

"Do any of your interviewees live in this area? I believe you said they did. The ones you saw being interrogated I mean."

"I have some of the addresses with me." He handed them to Martha.

She scanned them quickly. "There is one on this street, somewhere along here." She peered intently at house numbers and found half of them missing. "How do they get their mail, if you can't read an address?"

Passing one home, she held the paper to the light. "Oh, oh, I think it must be this one. Weeds in the yard here, too." She looked out the windows to see a feeble light coming through a smudged and dirty window. "Must be too busy out molesting kids to do a bit of cleaning." Martha regretted the quip the moment she'd uttered it.

"Hon, I know how you feel. Sometimes a joke about things eases the pain. I think it's an American thing." Harry grinned at her and turned a corner.

"Here's Delgado Lane. Anyone on that list living here?"

"No, not that I see here. Nothing on this street." Seeing a truck with a camper on the back, she turned to Harry. "That truck with the camper has a familiar feel about it. Sort of like the one that followed me home a couple of nights ago." Martha shivered involuntarily.

"Write the license number down for me." He winked at her. "Maybe driving through this little cesspit of predators will be worth the gas."

Martha hastily scrawled the number as best she could. "Part of it's too muddy to read, Harry, all I got were the first three letters." She felt a small chill pass through her body as she took another look at that truck. "Will said he saw a truck with a camper drive past him the other day, too—while he waited for the bus." She looked at Harry, her face tight. "Do you think it's possible we're being stalked?" She frowned. "But why us especially?"

"Don't be so paranoid, dear. It can't be anything like that. No one knows about you around Denver."

"We've already discussed this. Some people know a lot about me—in your department here in Denver, and in Colorado Springs, too." She shivered again and wrapped her arms around her body.

"Let's go visit your daughter, Martha. I want to ask Will about seeing that pick-up. It might head us in the right direction." He turned his old truck about and headed out of Longworth housing area.

"Are you sure that's wise?"

He looked at her and nodded. "I'll be careful how I conduct this little interview with him, and I'll speak to Martin about it first."

cœo

Ray just happened to be looking out of his darkened bedroom window and saw the old truck drive slowly past his home. "Whoa, now." He gritted his teeth. "Someone checking *me* out?"

He wasn't sure if anyone in that truck had their eye on him. But he remembered the intense questioning downtown for some of those who lived in this area regarding the Mindy Lassen case. He was on edge. There were several men of his persuasion living in Longworth. But with a sly smile, he wondered if they'd found a suspect yet.

The truck continued on its way, and Ray sat down in his grubby little living room, unable to enjoy his favorite TV show. He'd begun his own campaign to meet Denny Garver's demands on him, but now he worried that someone might be checking *him* out. Was someone driving by to give more than a passing glance at his residence—at him, in particular? NCIS held no interest for

him, now—not with his guts twisted into a knot that left
him breathless.

∽∾∽∾

Harry and Martha entered the Moulton's driveway.
Everything was kept up and neat about the place. It went
unspoken about the difference in the two areas, but aware
of it, Harry squeezed her elbow as the headed up the
sidewalk. He had a feeling, and it sent chills through his
tall, spare body. He worried now that some outside presence had taken undue notice of Martha and her family. It
was a subtle feeling, but it was there.

Ushered into that home's warm presence, Harry felt
completely welcome. He'd always enjoyed Martin's
company as well as Jeannie's. As the men entered the den
together, Harry asked Martin, "Would it be all right with
you if I mention that truck that drove past Will? I want to
hear what he has to say about it. These drive-bys have
happened more than once so I understand."

"Yes, it was twice, but different vehicles," Martin
replied. "Will said he was sure the man took notice of
himself, in particular. It must have been a rather close
observation—enough to set him on alert. Of all people,
he has more than the usual awareness of things like that."

"No doubt he does, Martin, no doubt at all. But,
lately, I've gotten the feeling that it's more than Will who
is under some sort of watch or observation. I have no real
reason for the feeling, other than that Martha felt she was
followed home from her hospital shift the other night. Of
course, that is aside from this business with Will."

"My God! Harry, is that possible?"

"With Martha's past, anything is possible." Harry
grimaced. "She could have quite a few pissed off men in

the bushes, if what she tells me is the case. Of course, none of them knew who did the deed on them."

"Are you sure about that?" Martin queried.

"As far as I know." Harry shrugged, frowned, and then admitted. "There are a few who know about her. I imagine that kind of information could be gold in some departments. I'm seriously considering talking to that detective in Colorado Springs about this. I don't like feeling this way—not at all."

Martin frowned. "Jeannie has enrolled Will in a self-defense course. He tells me it is likely more intense than she imagined. But the boy is happy with it, feeling sort of empowered, if you will." He edged closer to Harry. "He tells me he is learning some serious stuff. He says with what he is learning, he could kill."

"Good God, Martin! Could he handle a thing like that?"

"If some sick bastard ever gets his hands on Will again, I hope he has the strength and guts to use what he's learning." Martin lowered his voice. "I know with his state of mind, a thing like this could possibly be dangerous." Then he smiled. "On the other hand, he's showing so much added confidence and self-assurance, so far, I have to applaud everything he's learning. And, Harry, he assures me he's learning how to handle the responsibility of it—right along with all the moves."

"I think you may have hit on the best rehab for a kid like him, outside of the good sisters' no-nonsense approach to learning. Martha tells me that's been a real big help."

"I believe it has, Harry. I always say, if you are going to live in this world, you must follow the rules of living. He has to learn that, and no excuses."

They were interrupted by the sound of feminine laughter and rose to join the ladies.

Martin led the way. "Better go see what's going on."

Will sat quietly in the corner, studying. His father went to him and bent down. "Son, Detective Johns would like to hear more about this vehicle that went cruising slowly past while you waited for your bus."

Harry saw the boy's face tighten and grow pale. He regretted that he had to bring the subject up but felt the need. He rose to approach the boy. "Son, I just wanted to know what you saw and what made you feel wary of the man in the truck." He put his hand on Will's shoulder. "We're pretty good friends by now. I hope it won't upset you to speak about it."

Will rose to his feet. "No, sir, it won't bother me...well, maybe a little, but I will tell you what I can. I only saw the man for a short time." He walked toward the den. "We'd best go in here," he indicated, and Harry, delighted at the boy's choosing a more private setting for this conversation, followed Will into the other room.

They took seats, and Will faced the detective. "I don't exactly know why it bothered me, but the first time, he was in an old pinkish car. It looked like a real pile of junk." He grinned with that statement. "Then, the second time—I knew it was him—I knew it. He has a sort of scarred up face, with pits and stuff where he must have had pimples or something."

Harry was pleased to see the boy had no fear of him as an officer of the law. He nodded, encouraging the boy to remember all he could.

"There were about eight or ten of us standing there waiting for the bus, but his eyes were on me. That's what made me feel he was watching me, or something. I was sure he was sort of looking for me, sir."

"Don't blame you one bit, son, for feeling like you did. You have more reason than most to be watchful.

Your dad tells me you are in training for self-defense. How's that going?"

"Oh, it's goin' real good, sir. I like it a lot, and I'm learning things that will help me if I ever need it." Will didn't elaborate from then on, and Harry didn't push him on it. But he saw the tightened jaw and squared shoulders of a determined young man.

"Well, I guess we'd better join the others. I sure thank you son, for what you had to say. Every little detail is helpful to us."

"What's going on, sir? Is somebody after us?"

"Not that I know of, but it pays to keep an eye out." Harry almost felt like a liar, but in no way could he add to the child's worries. But he had to add. "Son, if you see this man again, will you get his license number if you can?"

"I already did that. You wanna see it?"

"You bet I do. Good work son—very good work!" Harry followed Will to where he was doing his homework and took a copy of what he had written down. "It's not all here, but it's a heck of a start. Thanks, son, you're quite a detective, yourself."

As they entered the great room where the rest of them were relaxing and watching TV, Martha rose to her feet. "I think we should be going, Harry." She offered no reason for her statement, but he heard the tone of urgency in her voice.

"Okay, darling, I guess it's getting a bit late." He reached for his jacket, and Martha found her purse. They said their goodbyes, but when Martha tried to hug Will, he allowed the embrace, but was careful to avoid her kiss. She looked at Jeannie in surprise.

"He's growing up, Mom." Jeannie nearly giggled as she hugged the boy herself. He avoided her kiss as well as she asked him, "Aren't you, my darling?"

"Aw, Mom." His face reddened, and he skulked off to his room.

Jeannie and Martin stood close together as they said goodbye, and Martha was pleased to see the look of contentment on their faces.

Harry commented, "It's so good to see them that way, isn't it, Martha?"

"Yes, it is, but Harry we need to hurry home. I don't know why, but we need to." Martha clenched her hands together and sat stiffly upright beside Harry as he drove. Something was wrong, she was sure of it, but couldn't think of any reason for feeling that way.

As they reached the gravel driveway, they saw the light of low burning embers glowing behind the house, she cried, "Harry! What is that?"

"Looks like the old barn must have caught fire. I never use it now with the horses gone, but I liked having it there—always liked the looks of it." He saw the lights of a fire truck screaming down the road, "Someone must have called it in." He got out and waved them into the yard and on toward the glowing remnants of Harry's barn.

Martha felt a deep sickness in her gut. "It's happening, I know it!" But she cried it quietly to herself.

Harry was talking to the fire crew outside.

The men went toward the glowing ember pile, and Martha followed close enough to see the total destruction then went into the house.

After about an hour, Harry came inside. Seeing his whitened face, she asked. "So what have you learned?"

"Well, they said it was man caused, because they found the accelerant that was used. Whoever did it, seemed to have left the can to make sure we knew it was done deliberately."

"Like I said before, Harry, someone is out to cause us trouble, Will, me, who'll be next?" Martha laid her face on the table. "It's because of me, Harry, I know it is. It's all because of me."

Chapter 9

Ray decided on his next victim. "Don't see why that bastard gets to have all the comforts of home whenever he wants it." He nodded to himself as he tried to watch another episode of NCIS. Too restless, he got up and paced about as he remembered seeing that ratty old truck driving slowly past. "I wonder about that truck. I've seen it around here a time or two before this."

His thoughts left him worried and unsettled. "Maybe someone else is sniffing around this area." Something didn't set just right. Ray had learned long ago a man like him had to keep an eye out. He never felt safe from those bastard cops. "If they've spotted my truck and camper, I'll have to shuck it and get something else, now. Shit-damn, I wanted to get some use out of it, at least once." He still imagined himself in there with a small warm body and enjoyed the response those thoughts gave him. He reached for a bottle of pills and downed a couple.

❧❧❧

It was two weeks later, and Ray had set his mind on one target. He had scoped him out and followed as quietly as he knew how. He had changed cars. He had a small, dark tan colored sedan now. This car hadn't been seen by that jumpy kid, or that nut-clipping bitch, either. It looked like dozens of others, and he felt anonymous while driving it. No one would take notice of him, and he felt safe with his choice.

"That bitch's nosey detective appears to be on some kind of stakeout by the looks of it. Been hanging around the warehouses down on Jefferson. Plenty of nice secluded spots for me, too." His plans were finalized. It was growing late in the day, but Ray had enough light to see. He was an excellent marksman, so all he needed was a chance—a small window of opportunity, like when that other big dude who worked with Martha's shack-up left for a while. He'd been keeping any eye on these two for a couple of days and decided the big dude and the detective took turns going for food or drinks. He didn't know nor care which, but saw it as helpful to his plan.

In time, as the light began to fade, he saw the big dude drive off down the street and disappear around the corner. Ray hauled his 700 millimeter Remington Magnum out of its case and double checked to see if it was fully loaded. He always kept it that way, but his hand trembled as he rechecked to be sure. He didn't think he'd need more than one shot.

He was jumpy about taking out a cop. He hadn't blown away an officer before, and it made him a bit sick in his gut with a case of nerves.

Watching the detective, he waited patiently. For a short time the detective had disappeared, but soon he saw him walk out of the side entrance of a warehouse and lean against a tree. "Stupid clod! Are you making a nice target for me, or what?" He raised his rifle, took aim, and squeezed off a shot right into the man's gut. He'd made sure he used hollow—point ammo because almost anywhere a man was hit, one bullet was enough. His guts would be scrambled big time with that one hit.

He saw the man crumple and sag to the grass beside the tree. He smiled coldly. "Got the bastard. Good shot, Ray ol' boy!" He congratulated himself as he withdrew from the area, placed his rifle in its case, wrapped his overcoat around it to disguise it, and sauntered off several blocks to his small dark-tan-colored car. No one had paid him any mind as he walked along, listening to the scream of ambulances as they hurried to the scene. He smiled to himself, saying, "I believe that went well," and kept on walking.

♥⌀♥⌀

Martha stood at the kitchen window, watching down the graveled drive. Harry should have arrived home by now. She felt nervous inside in any case, because, lately, she'd felt the subtle signs of being watched or singled out. The arson of the old barn was a good part of it. She saw that as a deliberate message to herself, in particular, since the accelerant was deliberately left for them to find. She believed it was a declaration, a promise of things to come—but what?

Martha never could tolerate waiting. Already on edge from recent events, she found it too easy to imagine all sorts of things happening—none of them good. She hadn't worked at the small local hospital this week at all, but had done several surgeries with Dr. Gleason, the veterinarian. She admired the man for his skills, but most of all she appreciated the care and concern he had for his furry patients. It told her what kind of man he was. Max and Skunk were back together with the recovery of Skunk from his snake-bite episode. She fed them their dinner as she awaited Harry's arrival.

She had her hands deep in flour as she made his favorite—biscuits. When her cell went musical, she wiped her hands on her apron and took it up, her heart pounding with anxiety.

"Hello."

"Martha Chance?"

She heard the officious sounding voice and instantly felt sick. Her body filled with ice as her heart began to pound. Something was wrong, and she knew it.

"This is Martha Chance," she nearly whispered—a dreadful fear had closed her throat until her voice was barely audible.

"Mrs. Chance, this is Marcus Ebert. I work with Harry Johns."

"Yes, I remember you. What is this about?" She heard her voice rise a bit higher as her throat tightened further. Oh, yes, she remembered the head of the detectives very well. She had dealt with him in the past.

"Mrs. Chance, I regret to inform you that Harry has been shot."

"Is he all right?"

"We believe he will be. He's undergoing surgery at the moment."

"What happened, Detective Ebert?" She felt the ice racing through her veins, freezing her very soul. Something big was going down—she knew it.

"It was an apparent sniper-type assault. His partner got to Harry right away and called the paramedics."

"Where is he?"

"At Riverside, ma'am. I'll send an officer to bring you to the hospital. You'll not be in any frame of mind to be driving, not tonight."

"Oh, no you won't! I'm already on my way. I've worked there—I know where it is." She took a deep breath and said to herself, "I can handle this."

"But, ma'am—"

She hung up, grabbed her coat and purse, and headed to the car. She had the presence of mind to remember she had a full tank of gas, but couldn't remember filling it. And it didn't matter.

చ్రచ్ర

Martha pulled into the hospital parking lot, parked crookedly, and flung herself out. She slammed the door and hurried to the entrance and up to the receiving desk.

"I would like to see Detective Harry Johns, please."

The receptionist, an older woman with rounded rosy cheeks, took up and scanned the admittance sheet. "I don't see anyone by that name, ma'am."

"They told me he was in emergency surgery."

"Oh, of course." She pulled his name up on the computer. "Are you related?" she questioned. "He is listed as a no information patient."

"I am his significant other, and please, I must be at his side when he wakes up." Martha didn't plan to allow this old biddy to prevent her seeing Harry, but she tried to be nice.

"Let me make a call." The receptionist pressed the numbers and spoke softly into her phone. Her eyebrows lifted, and her expression changed as she nodded and said to Martha, "You may go on up. It's on the fifth floor. There is the ICU Unit and a surgical waiting room there."

With a curt thank you to the bemused lady, Martha hurried to the elevators, muttering under her breath, "Like I wouldn't know where to go." She had worked several years in this hospital and knew it well.

She walked on trembling legs toward the ICU and waiting room. Marcus Ebert saw her coming. He rose from his chair and held out his hand.

"Mrs. Chance, we haven't heard anything so far. It's been over two hours since he was taken in." She didn't miss his frown, and it gave her a sick feeling. Now she must wait along with Detective Ebert and another officer.

Ebert indicated the other man. "Mrs. Chance, this is Detective Tom Wells, another member of our staff. He and Harry were working together on a case when this happened."

She looked at the man but ignored his outstretched hand as she gasped, "You were there—you saw him get hit? Did you see anything—anything at all?"

"No, I heard the shot, but I didn't see anything—it came out of a treed area. No car drove away that we heard—so far nothing." His head sank lower as he replied, and Martha could see the man felt he'd failed his partner.

She sank a bit deeper into her own private hell as she realized she could lose this fine man, Harry Johns. He'd come along at a critical time in her life and had saved her in so many ways. She imagined Harry's strong arms holding her. She heard his soft words that had the power to turn her into a flaming mass of wanting. A wave of heat passed through her as she remembered how well he knew how to take care of that, too.

Seeing a chapel, Martha left the men to enter it. She sat there, barely knowing what to say to a higher power. Yet unashamedly, she begged, pleaded, and beseeched, with all the love she had in her heart for the life of this man she loved and leaned on. Harry Johns was a man who kept her straight and out of trouble, and she needed him so much.

She used her cell to call Jeannie and explain what happened. Then, feeling light-headed from the fear and intensity that held her in its close embrace, Martha left the chapel and returned to the men.

"Any news?" she asked, her voice high, tight, and almost squeaky to her own ears.

"Nothing yet," said Marcus Ebert. His look of sympathy did nothing to make her feel better.

Detective Wells sat there quietly, shoving his big hands through his gray-tinged black mane, saying nothing. His nearly black eyes took in every detail, and she wondered what was going through his mind. What were he and Harry working on? Did it apply to the threat she believed she currently faced? Martha couldn't bring herself to ask—not now.

On almost silent feet, a doctor appeared in the doorway. "Detective Ebert?" he asked.

Martha looked up, her heart pounding as she rose to hear the doctor's words. She stood beside detective Ebert.

"The surgery is over. Officer Johns is alive, but extremely critical and will remain that way for some time. He lost a lot of blood, which we are replacing. We removed his spleen, several sections of small bowel, and made the repairs as well as we could. Of course, emergency surgery in that area is, by its very nature, more hazardous without a complete bowel prep. Infection is always our greatest concern in a case like that. We have done extensive intra-abdominal lavage and irrigation as much as possible under the circumstances." He wiped the sweat from his brow, and waited, looking at them.

Martha moved to the front. "I am his significant other, Doctor. What may we expect—will he survive this—can he?" Her hands trembled to the point she clasped them together to quell some of the shaking. She felt the arm of Marcus Ebert go around her shoulders in support.

"It's touch and go from here on out. He's a very strong man, and that's a great help in a trauma case of this nature." He looked her in the eye with his declaration. Martha thought he looked familiar. She'd worked here, and had no doubt met him, but in her state of mind, she couldn't be sure of anything.

"May I see him?"

"It will be a while. He's in recovery now. Possibly in another hour." The doctor nodded, sympathy in his eyes as he turned and left them to return to his duties.

Martha sat down, stunned, and feeling faint. "I can't believe this has happened. I know certain things were aimed at me—but at Harry?" She was sure she hadn't said it loud enough for anyone to hear, but the detective, Tom Wells, directed his voice quietly to her.

"Ma'am, Harry and I were working on an idea. He felt it might be very possible you have someone out there—someone who is coming after you with retribution on his mind."

"What do you mean, sir?"

"Ma'am, I know of your history." At her look of shock, he quickly added, "Harry and I have gone over it as well as possible, in the past week. He felt it was necessary because he was of the opinion that someone could be seeking revenge against you—a payback if you will. Perhaps someone you did a bit of work on in times past." He tilted his dark head a bit as he looked at her, and held back the start of a grin.

Martha saw the crease of his cheek and knew what he was thinking. Not many men could look at her in the same way once they knew her predatory history against child predators. "So he filled you in, then." She couldn't stop the beginning of a smile herself.

"It's under wraps, but he felt I needed to know."

"If Harry had an idea, will you share it with me?"

"Certainly, but this isn't the place. I believe Marcus thinks you may be in a good bit of danger, yourself." He lowered his voice. "He has asked me to keep you under surveillance for your own personal safety."

Martha drew in a sharp breath before she could utter a word. "He what? That is entirely ridiculous! I refuse to allow it!"

"I'm afraid he doesn't think so, ma'am, and I'll do my best. Commander Ebert believes you have someone out there bent on your destruction, and by the way, so does Harry."

"First of all, I will not have some officer hanging around me or my place. I don't care one whit what officer Ebert thinks!" She couldn't stop there. "If they're after me, why shoot someone else—someone I care about?" But the moment she said it, she knew the reason. Her face grew cold. "They aren't just after me, are they? They are after my family! Everyone I care about, too—oh, my God!"

"Hold on, ma'am, what are you thinking?"

"A man has driven past my grandson, Will, not once but twice." She shuddered and went on, "He is very alert to anything like that, of course. If you know my history, you must know about him, too." She stifled a sob. "He came home all tied in knots after that first time the man drove past, looking at him. His mother has enrolled him in a self-defense class because of it."

"Harry had considered that whoever it is might be after your family, too. I thought it sounded a bit far-fetched, but you certainly have a point." Tom sat back and blew out his breath. "This could get mighty interesting before it's through."

Martha snorted at that. "For you, maybe!" What he had suggested angered her, though she realized she was being unfair. "I hope you don't think any of this is being done for your entertainment, sir." Her cheeks flushed hotly, but she held her temper the best she could.

"Hey, now, hold on. This is a rough time for you with Harry down like he is. I hope I haven't said anything out of line, but you've got to admit, this whole thing is a bit on the unusual side."

Martha backed down. "I'm sorry to be so touchy, but for a long time now, nothing has been easy for me. You say you know my history, but do you really?" This Tom was a tough, hard-shelled sort of man. One who might have been a navy SEAL, or army ranger at one time. She recognized the kind of quiet strength he displayed, without being overt about it. He reminded her of Duke, a navy SEAL friend of her dead husband, Bob Chance. A man who had been a big help to her in the past.

"I know what Harry has told me, but little else. I'd be interested to know more if you'd tell me sometime."

They were interrupted by the entrance of a nurse. "Officer Johns may have a visitor—for a small visit— five minutes, no more."

Martha stood up immediately, as did Ebert, but he motioned for her to go first. "You first, my dear."

The nurse led Martha to Harry's bedside. She felt faint, and her pulse hammered at seeing him this way, the tubes, the dripping blood transfusion, numerous IV's, and his face the color of the bed sheet. She was not a nurse now, only a mourning, frantic family member fearing for his life. She leaned over him to whisper. "Harry darling, can you hear me?"

She watched his eyelids flutter open. He looked up at her. "Hi, darlin', sorry to be such a..." His hand moved toward her but failed to reach her.

"Hi, Harry, how do you feel—have you much pain?" She grasped on to his hand, knowing her words were inane at best. She was dumbstruck to see him this way. "Darling, you've got to be all right!" She felt herself giving way to near hysteria, as his recovery nurse, ever watchful, slid an arm around her for support.

Harry murmured low, and she bent down to hear his words. "Darlin', please be careful. He's out to get you, hurt you—lay you low—take it all from you. I know it—please be—" His head rolled back. He was breathing, but she had a terrible feeling. As she wondered, *Who is it Harry speaks of who's out to get me—to take it all from me?* she turned to stone inside. *I'm losing this wonderful man, I know it!*

Chapter 10

Ray drove into his driveway feeling deflated, afraid, and sick inside. He'd done what he'd had to, to please Denny Garver and believed he'd gotten away with it. Successful, yes, but it had left a bitter taste inside of him. "Doing this kind of shit ain't my thing. That bastard, Denny's, got me by the balls. He knows I'll do what he wants—I have to. But he don't give a good goddamn about what happens to me. He's putting me through this to even his own score. Right now, I'm needing something for myself, too—oh God—I need it so bad I can't stand it!" Unwanted thoughts and visions entered his mind, and he felt himself responding. "I'd like to get my hands on that damned Moulton kid, or any kid, any sex. I'm gittin' itchy as hell, again. Oh, God, I know it ain't right, but I'm needin' it somethin' bad!"

He paced around the kitchen then sat down again. "Shootin' some bastard cop was all right, but it don't give a man what he needs—no way does it." He kept seeing the boy in his mind, imagining the things he'd do once he got him quieted down.

He twisted in his chair. "I ought ta go see that damned bastard, Denny, again. See if he's happy with my work so far." He gave it some thought, but he was reluctant to see that big gray monstrosity of a prison again. "If I go there too often, someone might wonder about it. I don't need no fingers pointed my way. Denny can write a damned letter as good as I can or anybody else."

The indecision of it drove him to down a few pills. "I'd better get a few winks. I'll be needin' my strength." He headed for the rumpled bed in the next room. The sight of it set him thinking about the kind of things that set him off, until finally, the pills did their job.

જ૭જ૭

Martha refused to leave the surgical waiting room while Harry was so critical. Jeannie and Martin sat with her. They alternately held her, hugged her, and went to the chapel and prayed with her. But Martha never left the immediate area for more than that. Jeannie brought her something to eat from time to time.

When Martha realized the dogs needed tending, she called the neighbor boy. He'd brought them the puppies all those happy months ago. "Harry will think me derelict in my duties if I let Max and Skunk go hungry." She managed a smile for Jeannie and Martin right then.

It was time to see Harry again, and she approached his cubicle. She fought against the feeling he would die and leave her to face life alone again. But the strong realization came over her, that no more would his strong arms hold her, protect her, and keep that wild person who dwelled inside her in check. As she neared the cubical, the nurse bid her enter.

Coming to his bedside, she instantly saw the increase in his pallor. Most frightening of all, she saw the encroaching pale, waxy shade she feared the most. She stood beside him, watching helplessly as that fearsome shadow of death slowly crept over the man she loved. His fingernails were even more bluish, nearly purple, in spite of the oxygen he received directly into his lungs. After the first several hours post-op, he'd began to have respiratory failure. They'd quickly placed Harry on a ventilator. He remained on that steady pumping machine that included the occasional sigh.

"How is he?" She directed her question to the small dark-haired nurse, Sherry, who had the care of Harry for this shift.

"About the same. He seems to have lost more strength, Martha. I can't gloss over how things are going. He doesn't look any better. He is fighting the infection with all he's got, but it's rather overwhelming with the abdominal wounds he's suffered. He was extremely traumatized inside, according to the post-op report." Sherry looked at the small bags of medication dripping slowly into his veins. "We're doing all we can, but he's very ill."

She had the beginning of tears in her eyes, and Martha saw them. She put her hand on the young woman's shoulder. "I know you're doing your best. I've been on staff here, myself. I know how it is, but that doesn't make it any easier when it's one of your own, laying there, fighting for his life."

She kissed his pale cool lips softly, left the cubical, and returned to the waiting room. Martin had gone, but Jeannie remained, her face turned expectantly toward her mother. Hoping to change their train of thought about Harry, Martha asked her, "How are things with Will, now?"

"He is very watchful, in case that man might drive by again. He got part of the license plate, but not all of it." Jeannie twisted her hands as she spoke.

Martha's temper soared, thinking of what Harry had whispered the night he came from surgery. "Jeannie, that night we were visiting at your home, we had driven past a certain house in The Longworth section. I saw an old pickup with a camper on the back, and I took a part of that license down, myself. I only got the letters, the rest of it was muddied and unreadable."

"And you never compared the two?"

"We didn't. Remember, our barn burned down, and we forgot about it. But I wonder if Harry did and didn't tell me. He had spoken to Will about it."

She hadn't heard any result from Harry and wondered if he had been trying to protect her from worrying about that truck.

"He never said if he did the comparison with Will's number?" Jeannie asked.

"I wish I knew. Harry's too sick to ask now." Martha lowered her voice. "We may be in for some big trouble, Jeannie. Harry woke up enough to speak to me when he first came out of recovery. He warned me that he believes someone is out to get me. His words were, 'to take it all from me.' If so, Harry is his first attempt. That's what it sounded like to me—his words were a bit slurred." She added, "That partner of his, sitting over there like a bump on a log, told me Harry said pretty much the same thing to him."

"That's impossible! Who would do something like that? Who could hate you that much, mom?"

Martha tried to hide her smile. "I can think of several, Jeannie—you know enough about that business." Remembering Harry's last spoken words, Martha felt a chill pass through her body. If what Harry had told her was the case, maybe someone was out to get her or her family. How could she trust anyone who came near her, after knowing that?

Martha had nearly dozed off during a quiet moment when a loud overhead voice proclaimed, "code arrest." It rang out over the intercom. She responded by leaping to her feet, her heart hammering. She followed the sound of running feet. A sick feeling overwhelmed her—those feet belonged to numerous medical people, and they ran rapidly, straight to the cubicle of Harry Johns! They pushed equipment and the code cart along with them.

Martha ran to the outside of the cubicle, but other than a peek through the curtains, she was not allowed entrance. She knew all about code arrests, but this particular one tore her heart out. It meant the loss of a wonderful man, if they couldn't bring him through it, and by his waxy pallor, she feared they wouldn't. If someone was out to deliberately destroy her life and happiness, he had hit the mark. Her anger flared, her fists clenched, and tears flooded her eyes.

The charge nurse came to her for a quick moment. "Sorry, Martha, it looks pretty bad, but we're doing all we can." She left to return to the fray of saving a man's life. Martha had no choice but to await the end of their desperate struggle to save Harry. She had to stand there, wringing her hands, facing the fact that she could lose the man she loved and the wonderful happiness she shared with him. She noticed the man, Tom, standing near her, his face pale and tense.

After what seemed like forever, the doctor came to her, his brow sweaty, and his shoulders slumped. "Martha, I'm very sorry to tell you—we lost him. We did all we could, but it wasn't enough. We just couldn't save him. I don't know what else to say—we lost him." He put his hand on her shoulder. "I'm so sorry."

"I know you did all you could—I know that." Martha murmured the words as she brushed past the doctor and headed into the cubical to see Harry. He lay there silently, his breath forever stilled. All the life-saving tubes had been removed, and a clean sheet covered him up to his shoulders. A few remaining, stunned personal, stood there, saying nothing, looking totally defeated.

She brushed his hair back from his fine, male features and kissed his cool lips. Her tears fell onto his stilled form as she whispered to him, "Oh, Harry, my dearest darling, I'm so sorry I've brought this onto you. I know that much about what has happened today! I am paying now for all the things I have done—but, my darling, why you?"

He could never answer her again, and that hurt the most. How would she ever make it without his strength? He'd kept her sane, and he'd kept her normal. Now, he was gone. She sank into a nearby chair, hardly noticing Jeannie's arms around her, and let go all her pent up tears.

She knew that crying released many painful emotions, and it helped Martha too. While she fought to get her head on straight, already Serena was busily fomenting a multitude of ideas and plans for vengeance on this unknown killer. Martha had an enemy, she knew it for sure, and so did Serena.

After she had settled a bit, Martha said to Ebert. "Harry said something about someone out to get me and all my family, or words to that effect, when he first came out of surgery. It's what he believed. Could he be right about it?" She tightened her grip on the chair and looked at Jeannie. "If this person is leaving me until last, he might come after you, or Martin, or—God forbid—Will!" She looked at Ebert. "Will is nine years old now, almost ten, but he has never gotten over what that rotten pedophile, Fred Callahan, did to him. And now a man has driven past him—twice. He looked at Will in a way a boy who has been through what he has could never forget. All this happened while he waited for the bus—do you hear me? While a small boy waits for the school bus that brings him home!"

"My God—have you called the police about that?" Ebert looked at Jeannie with his question.

"No, sir, we never thought about calling the police." Her tone let the officer know what she thought about the police. "But I did enroll him in a very good self-defense course. He's a small boy for his age but strong. Maybe he'll be able to defend himself if he meets one of those devils again."

"That was a good idea, ma'am—that is, if he doesn't learn things a young boy hadn't ought to know."

"Like what?" Jeannie retorted. "Being able to take care of himself?"

She refrained from further comment. She and Martin had never felt the police in Colorado Springs had done much in Will's case. But she knew who had and winked at Martha—a sly wink that referred to Serena's activities.

"Well, I know some of the things they teach in these courses. You can learn how to kill in some of them." Ebert shook his head and let the warning in his voice convey the rest but wisely said nothing more. He understood how she felt. Many others felt the same way, to his regret. Being an officer of the law these politically correct days was not an easy job.

After a time, Martha had to face the fact that it was all over for her, and she faced life on her own again. When she finally discovered that Ebert had ordered Tom to keep an eye on her, she struck back with heated words. "I refuse to have some big lout hanging about my house. I've been through all that before, and gunshots came through my windows anyway!" She referred to an earlier time, and Detective Commander, Marcus Ebert, knew what she meant.

She lowered her voice. "If what Detective Tom Wells told me is true, I am not in danger for now, but my family, no doubt, is. Why put a guard on me when some deranged killer will most likely go after them first?"

"Ma'am, we don't know that for sure. But it *was* Harry's idea. He believed it, and that's what we're going on."

⁌ʒ⁍

Tom stayed in the background. He was another person who had never left the facility during Harry's confinement. He'd had his orders. Martha Chance was in plenty of danger from someone with a personal vendetta. She had an enemy. She didn't know who or why for sure, but she stood to lose a lot more than the man she'd lived with. Harry believed whoever it was, was out to get all her family, her lover, and then, her. Tom believed Harry had the right idea about what was going on and so did Ebert.

What he wasn't sure of was keeping an eye on Martha Chance. She was cold to him, ignored him, and in general didn't want him around. If he wasn't careful, he might end up like some of the cases Harry had told him about. It gave him the cold shivers just thinking about it.

Tom knew he'd have his hands full. He chuckled. "Keeping watch on that woman won't be easy. She can't stand the sight of me already."

Chapter 11

Martha knew Harry's arrangements were up to her. He had no other family that she knew of—his life had been a lonely one until they had come together. She excused herself and told Jeannie to go on home.

Commander Ebert put out his hand. "Pardon me, Mrs. Chance. The department requires an autopsy in a case like this. Just let us know where you would like him sent after…"

He couldn't finish the sentence, and it didn't matter. It was just one more thing to tear her apart. She got hold of herself, nodded, and told him what he needed to know.

She left then to go home to Harry's house on the outskirts of Denver. She reached the darkened house and, along with the frantically wriggling and yipping pups, walked slowly in. She petted them and ruffled their soft fur as she cried out, "Left alone like those old Eskimo widows put out on the ice flows to die—it's the story of my life!"

She looked about the empty rooms of Harry's snug little ranch house. It continued to be a place of comfort for her, a place where she'd been very happy. And because of those memories, she decided she might as well continue living at Harry's place, unless some hitherto un-known relatives came to claim it.

Some time later, she heard the dogs set up a frantic yelping and barking. Fear rose within her mind, "Already?" she worried.

Had the killer came to get her so soon? On the positive side, that disturbing sound had startled her from her feelings of abandonment and worry.

Her heart rate had risen in a flash as soon as she'd heard the dogs yelping out there, but she decided no killer would bother to knock. Nevertheless, she looked through the tiny bit of glass set in the door to make sure.

She saw a big, solid body standing there, and Tom's black eyes calmly looking back at her. She flung open the door, and with anger in her voice, cried, "What on earth are you doing here? I told Ebert I didn't want some bodyguard type person lurking around under my feet!"

"Just following orders and likely I'll not be here for long. I'd appreciate coming in if you please." His voice was calm and firm.

Martha grabbed the door to slam it shut but knew she couldn't. Both men had worked closely with Harry, and Tom had his orders, despite her objection. She knew she could have flatly ordered him out of the house, but instead, opened the door to let him enter—only for Harry's sake.

"How are you planning to take your meals, then?" She sighed. "Are you hungry?" He didn't answer her but merely stood in the kitchen, taking in that area and gazing into the next room.

"What are you looking for around here? That killer won't be after me yet, not until he's wiped out everyone I've ever known."

"That's what Ebert isn't totally sure of."

"Then why aren't you outside prowling around. He isn't in here!"

"You sure of that?"

Martha felt her face grow cold and tight. Admittedly, she didn't know anything for sure. She shrugged. "Right now, I don't know a blessed thing, Mr. Wells, if that's your name."

"I doubt he is, ma'am, and yes, that's my name. I'd like to look about if you don't mind. And, by the way, I could eat a bite if you have something handy." He turned away to enter another room, while Martha sputtered beneath her breath.

"The colossal nerve of that man!" She was upset, yet deep down, realized she was glad not to be alone right now. Without Harry, the place seemed almost ghost-like, and she hated the lonesome feeling of it.

Nothing was the same anymore with Harry gone, but with an officer in the house, she believed she might sleep a bit better.

She looked about her kitchen. A hardened, dried pile of biscuit makings lay where she'd left them a couple days ago. A feeling of desolation swept over her as it felt like she'd been gone forever. Even the dogs had seemed subdued when she'd driven into the driveway. They had whined about, and she was sure it was Harry they'd waited for.

She busied herself cleaning up the mess that she'd left and noticed, if Tom was checking things, she never heard a sound from him. "Kinda sneaky, making no noise like that, isn't he?" she murmured to herself as she got out the makings for grilled cheese and tomato soup.

When she had things ready, she called his name. He appeared almost instantly and without a sound, and she looked at him with suspicion.

As they ate, she asked him, "Before this happened, we had driven through that Longworth section where that little Mindy Lassen was..." She couldn't even say the words. "We saw a pick-up with a camper on the back. I took what I could of his license plate, but half of it was muddied over. Then at my daughter's, we found out my grandson had seen what may have been the same vehicle driving past, giving him the once over. He also wrote that much of the license plate down in one of his books." She leaned toward him. "Can you find out who owns that truck?"

"That's great, ma'am. Let me have what you have. Not all those letters will be for pick-ups. It's something to take a look at."

Martha got her purse and handed him the slip with the letters, DXL. "That's what Will had written down, too. Sorry, that's all I could get."

"Every bit is a help, and this will be, too. Have you a computer I could use?" He finished his soup and sandwich and rose from his chair.

Martha led him into the great room where she had her computer on a small desk. "Here you are. I don't have an access code, so go right ahead. I hope it sheds a bit of light on this man—or on something."

Suddenly, Martha felt an overwhelming fatigue. Things had caught up with her to the point she could barely hold her head up. She was out on her feet and wanted to go to sleep if only to blot out, for a few blissful moments, all the heartache. And again, looking at the big man sitting at her computer, ticking away at the keys, she had to admit she was glad he was in the house.

"Officer Wells, I'd like to catch a few winks. I haven't really slept in several days, now."

"I'll be right here, ma'am, and wide awake." He turned back to the computer.

Martha told him to take the last bedroom down the hall before she ran for the bedroom, took a blistering hot shower, and fell into bed.

∽∾∽

When Martha came awake, she felt around for Harry's big form. Her hands searched for him, but there was nothing there, no warm body to touch and caress. With that, she remembered everything all over again. Near to tears again, she staggered out of bed and into the shower to face another day. Another day to face the disaster her life had become.

Dressed in jeans and a short-sleeved green sweater, she made it to the kitchen. Fresh coffee sat on the counter, but she saw no one around. She poured herself a cup, found it strong and hot, and murmured, "Wonder if that big dude made this." She knew he had.

The door opened to admit Tom and the dogs. They poured in, wiggling, whining, licking her hands, and shoving against her leg. As she patted them and ruffled their fur, Tom said, "I see you found the coffee."

He looked at the woman sitting there and easily understood why Harry Johns had found her so captivating. Older, maybe so, but there was something deep and mysterious about Martha Chance, and Tom saw it. In those snug-fitting jeans and a sweater that enhanced the greenish shade in her eyes, her figure was as good as any younger woman's, and her short, glossy hair had rusty overtones that defied description. "Sleep well?" he asked.

"Yes, thanks." She didn't look at him, but went on petting and roughing up the dogs' furry necks. She leaned down and kissed the tops of their heads.

"Feed the dogs?" She looked up at him with hazel-green tinged eyes that made him think of a lioness on the hunt.

"I don't know what you give them, how much, or where it is." He laughed and roughed Skunk's fur. "But I'd say they're ready to eat."

It was all so homey and friendly between them at the moment, she nearly forgot what was taking place. But this man in her kitchen wasn't Harry, and it hit her hard all over again. "Tomorrow is the services," she reminded him, and herself, too. Nearly bursting into endless tears again, she clamped her jaw tight and decided she'd cried enough.

Inside, she burned with hatred for whoever had done this to a man so fine and decent. Her face changed, taking on a firm set as she asked, "Find out anything about those license plates?"

"Not enough. There are several trucks with those letters, but only three with a camper on the back. If it was the one in the area of Longworth, it was very recently bought by a man named Rayburn McGill, located on Delgado Lane. And if it is him, he never completed his part of the registration. However, it will be followed closely. You never know, these letters may be all we need.

"If it's that man's house, it gave me a creepy feeling. I remember that about it, even though we didn't know who lived there at the time."

Tom shook his head. "We'll check him out." He looked around the kitchen. "Got any breakfast in mind?"

Seeing a trace of wistfulness on the big man's face that reminded her of a hungry little boy. Martha's attempt at anger disappeared. "Like some bacon and eggs? I think I have some yet—haven't been shopping for a while."

She saw him swallow, much like Max and Skunk when they saw a handy scrap of anything edible.

"Why sure, ma'am, that'd be fine." He sat in a kitchen chair, leaned his elbows on the table, and watched her every move.

Martha got busy and, against her will, found herself happy to be doing for this man. It was like having Harry back, only it wasn't—one look at that rangy dude was enough to see that.

She made a full breakfast—potatoes, biscuits—all of it, and managed to eat a decent breakfast, herself, for the first time in days. "Sorry, we're out of orange juice." She bit back the words, knowing she had just referred to Harry and herself as a couple. Tom stiffened a bit when she'd said it, and the reminder of her loss hurt like hell inside, but she held her sorrows in. She knew she had a long way to go if she was to regain her sense of life again.

She shrugged, stopped her meal, and rose, taking her plate to the sink. She'd had enough of feeling this terrible pain, and of this huge lanky man, too.

Tom rose from his seat. "Nice chow, ma'am, thanks." He headed outside and called the dogs. Martha wondered when he planned to leave her home. She was stopped in her tracks for any activity but grieving, and she didn't need him around for that.

Martha watched Tom out the window while wondering what he was about. Did he look for signs of an intruder—what? At a loss for what to do, she laid out her clothes for Harry's service tomorrow. She chose a slim dark skirt, with a matching jacket. Her blouse was a lacy confection Harry had loved, and it choked her up to see it again.

At the sound of crunching gravel in her driveway, Martha went to the kitchen window and looked out to see Lizzie's Caddy coming into the yard. The sight of that jazzy dame made her heart leap with joy, even at a time like this. It was the first tiny bit of happiness she'd felt in days. She ran out the door and met the car as it came to a halt.

"Liz, my dearest friend in the world, what a life saver you are!" She nearly pulled her friend out of the car. "Come on in, you wretch. What are you doing out here?"

"Couldn't let you go through this alone, dear—you know that." Lizzie gave Martha a healthy squeeze and looked into her eyes. "It looks like you need me a whole lot, girl. Aside from losing one of the best men in this world, how are you making out?" Her hazel eyes held the concern she felt as they entered the house. Lizzie tossed her purse into a corner. "Got any coffee?"

"In a minute, we've just finished breakfast."

"We?"

Tom stepped into the kitchen, his questioning eyes on Lizzie Marin. "Now, who do we have here?"

Martha's temper rose up, threatening to choke off her voice, but controlling herself, she introduced Tom and explained things to Lizzie. "He has orders to watch me like a five year-old kindergartener, Liz." She nearly sneered the words.

Lizzie looked Tom in the eyes. "And why is that?"

"Boss's orders, ma'am."

"He and his boss, actually Harry's boss, believe someone is out to get me, Liz." Martha knew this sentence opened up at least an hour of explanations, and she slumped into a handy chair.

Lizzie faced Martha. "What on earth is going on here?"

Martha told her friend enough about what had happened to answer her immediate questions. Feeling cold all over, she grasped Lizzie's hands. "I hate to say this, Liz, but your being here will identify you as someone I care about. In that case, you could become a target your-self.

"Are you kidding me?" She looked at Tom. "Are you also protecting her family, Jeannie, Will, Martin?"

"Not at present, but I think my boss is planning on it."

"Planning on it?" Lizzie's voice rose a few decibels with her comment. "Good God! No wonder people are being murdered in their beds!"

"Ma'am, if you'd just listen for a minute, you'd know how things are going down." Tom uttered those words filled with a smoldering anger of his own, and Martha saw Lizzie sit up and take notice, her eyebrows raised.

Martha stepped in. "Hold on, Liz. The whole thing is a supposition in the first place. But it's also what Harry thought. It's what he murmured to me when he first came out of surgery." She saw Tom heave a sigh of relief and flash a tight smile in her direction. Shaking her head, she added, "Those were also the last words he ever spoke to me, Liz."

Tom stood before both women. "You wonder why I'm here. I'll say what I can about it. Our commander of detectives is most concerned at this time for Martha's immediate safety. We have several areas we're working on, including contact with your old friend, Ryan Mapus, in Colorado Springs." He nodded to Martha. "He's been very helpful in this case, I might add."

Martha flushed, remembering that detective very well, and their last conversation regarding her vigilante activities. "How could he help with this?"

"He had some ideas, and is doing a bit of investiga-tive work on your behalf in his area." Tom smiled, re-membering some of the details discussed.

"Has he any information then?" Martha asked.

"I'll let you know if I hear of any, ma'am." He left them and went outside.

"So that's it—they don't know a blessed thing!" Martha snorted, and Lizzie laughed.

Ⴠ

They spent the rest of the day catching up, walking in the newly leafed out trees, and looking at the few remaining patches of snow up in the Rocky Mountains soaring high above them. It relaxed Martha to have this woman around. It always had. Tomorrow would be hell for her, and she was glad to have Liz with her. But Tom, with those black, searching eyes, she could do without.

Chapter 12

Everything was over now. Funeral arrangements had been made, and executed, marking the end of her life with Detective Harry Johns. Martha had sobbed to the point her eyes wouldn't focus anymore. Aside from her family, Lizzie had been there for her in a closer, more personal way, just when she'd needed that special person the most.

On the day she left, Lizzie wondered if she had really helped at all. Martha was a very complex person, especially with Serena added in. Lizzie wasn't sure of anything about her friend. Before she headed for her car, she hugged Martha warmly and said, "You'll make it through, dear girl. You have more strength than anyone I know."

Martha felt the loss of her friend instantly the moment she backed down the driveway. She stood there, waving slowly, as the truth sank in all over again about her situation. Another lonely widow left alone. She smiled to herself. In her thoughts about it, she realized she'd left out the part about the Eskimo woman left alone to die out on the ice flows.

Through it all, the specter of Harry's last words of warning had never left her mind—he'd been so sure she had a terrible enemy, a person who was still out there, planning to commit another horrible crime, designed, in particular, to hurt her further—another loss for her to suffer. Naturally, she understood the reason for it—it had to be revenge for clipping some filthy child predator, but which one? Was there one out there who had power and moxie enough to bring this about?

Another thing that aggravated her was the quiet presence of Detective Tom Wells. She knew by now that he was not a man to be put off. He hadn't managed to make friends with her, nor did he spend a lot of time trying. He got along well enough with Max and Skunk. He'd spent time talking and playing with the dogs, but he was always on watch. She believed his sharp, black eyes missed nothing.

In spite of herself, she was comforted by his presence, though it hampered her in too many ways. She had her mind on that grubby little house in Longworth. Something about it nagged at her. No doubt it was his truck that Will had seen, but they'd never been clear about that. She wanted to drive through the area again. If her car would be recognized, she could always rent a different one. God knows she had enough money these days.

Her first husband had left her well situated, and Bob Chance had added to that. Now Harry had left her more money and this nice home in the country. It was a comfort to know she had plenty to get by on, but not one red cent of it was worth losing three of the best men she'd ever known. Right now, nothing meant much to her without Harry Johns in her life.

Martha was strong, she'd always been, and somehow she'd live on the best she could. She realized all over again that her Serena self did not mourn the loss of Harry like she did. Certainly not. She quietly and continually pressured her to get busy. Her Serena half had always been her protector. She was created to be that so long ago.

If some evil soul was out to do her and her family in, Serena urged her to make the first strike. Take that devil out, whoever he was. Unfortunately, there were problems with this simple solution. First of all, she didn't know who it was. And with Tom hanging about, she felt hamstrung, hampered, and cornered.

What had slowly become uppermost in Martha's mind was the presence of those unused vials of Neutersol stockpiled in her bedroom, stashed beneath her lingerie. She figured Tom couldn't help looking into every nook and cranny of her home—he'd no doubt been trained that way. She hoped maybe he wouldn't go so far as to look through her underwear. And then again, she figured he wouldn't know what Neutersol was used for anyway.

She only spoke to Tom when she had to and had put him in the smallest, far away bedroom she had available. It was the one Lizzie had usually occupied when she came to visit. But for this last stay, Lizzie had occupied the second bedroom, the pretty one where Martha had stayed when she'd first come out here with Harry.

Now, Martha found herself eager for Tom to be gone. "I'm a rotten soul to feel the way I do, but the time has come—for Serena *and* me." She was glad Tom wasn't a mind reader. If he was, she'd be in real trouble.

She often wondered if he had a family. It didn't seem like he could have when he spent nearly every waking hour under foot at her place. She didn't plan to pay him enough notice to ask him about it either. The only time she'd be free of his scrutiny was if she worked with Dr. Gleason at his veterinary clinic, and out of respect for her loss, he hadn't called her since Harry's death.

So far, there hadn't been any sign of further action by that so-called predator. Someone was out to ruin her life, band Martha never stopped keeping an eye out. Jeannie had stopped calling so often, believing that the worst of losing Harry had passed.

Martha was glad she'd stopped worrying and calling.

But Jeannie couldn't possibly know how Martha still felt, how she ached with loneliness when she slipped into their big, wide bed at night. It was then her loss seemed the most overwhelming—her arms, as well as her bed, were so totally empty. The loss of Harry Johns made her feel cold all over in that bed.

e∽e∽

Ray sat in his worn out chair, thinking about his next move. "I see the bitch has some kind of fancy friend from out of town. Might add her to the list, after I take care of that daughter of hers or better yet, that husband. He looks like a city dude, dressed the way he always does. Should be easy enough to wire up his car. I can do it while he's at work. I didn't see any surveillance around the parking garage—piece of cake." He smiled to himself, thinking about a little blonde-haired first grader he'd noticed. He took a couple more pills and headed for his rumpled bed. He needed his rest.

But as his head hit the pillow, his mind swirled with a deep, fomenting resentment. "That filthy, rotten, god-damned Denny Garver has forced me into doing things he would never do on his own. He's makin' me into a killer, and I'd never been into things like that. I'll be caught and hung one of these days, and it'll be his fault, not mine!" He punched the pillow hard enough that feathers flew about the room.

e∽e∽

Martin kissed Jeannie goodbye and drove away in his new Buick Enclave. The roomy SUV was his latest purchase, and he drove it with pride and confidence. It was a great ride, looked smart and sleek, and held a lot of equipment should he need it for the day.

He left as he did every week-day morning, his mind on the more recent developments at work. This was a very busy time in the aeronautics business with new discoveries almost every day it seemed. Right now, they were working on a component of the USAF Flybot, a flying spy device far advanced in the works. Once fully developed, it would greatly increase the surveillance powers for the military. Martin found this work very rewarding and felt it was important to his country in the bargain. Right now, life was very exciting and rewarding too. And on top of that, his son was coming along, gaining confidence and important skills.

A small, mundane item like car care was a niggling problem to him. His SUV needed its first servicing, and he found scant time to take care of it. He hadn't the time to sit around and wait for an oil change and whatever else they usually did. Knowing the dealer had a service whereby they would pick-up the vehicle and return it before the day's end, Martin decided he would take advantage of it—a nice perk.

After he got to his desk, he gave them a call. He left a partial set of extra keys at his secretary's desk and, with a nod, told her to expect the service man when he came to pick up his vehicle.

こうこう

About eleven-thirty a.m., Martin entered the meeting room with several other engineers. This meeting was called to go over the latest specs for one small aspect of the Spybot. Martin's company, and those who worked there, were excited to have a hand in the creation of such a device.

Their meeting was suddenly interrupted when they felt the reverberation and heard a loud, muffled explosion. It rattled the entire building, and the floor shook beneath their feet. The windows rattled, and the whole meeting room seemed to be in motion.

"What in hell was that?" someone yelled in panic. "Are we being bombed?"

They had jumped to their feet at the explosion. It was quiet out there now, but they stood about in shocked silence after what had sounded like a massive explosion. They were still too agitated to take their seats around the conference table. Jim Ellison, a coworker, ran to a window and hurriedly pulled the shades up. He cracked the window and looked out. "Hell of a lot of smoke and dust coming out of the garage." He turned back to the others. "Sounded like a bomb went off down there." He brushed his hair back from his forehead. "Hell's bells, I've got a new car parked down there."

"So do I, Jim," Martin replied, and neither man was alone.

Almost everyone else in the room had a car parked in that garage.

Their boss stepped in to pass on what he knew. "I hear some vehicle just blew up down below. We'd best postpone this meeting. How about tomorrow at nine?"

Every man in the room wanted to head for the parking garage, but they knew they had to await an "all clear" before going down there to check on their individual cars. They also knew it could be a long wait. An all clear wouldn't be issued until after the police got through with their investigation and whatever else they did in a case like this. Martin paced about in his frustration, but there was nothing he could do about anything at the moment.

Martin immediately called Jeannie. "Hon, there was an explosion down in our parking garage. I just wanted you to know everyone here is just fine." He listened a moment. "Now Jeannie, don't go thinking things like that. We don't know what happened, not yet. Just hold on. I'll call you when I know something more." He knew exactly what Jeannie worried about. It had crossed his mind the moment it happened.

He heard her voice, near to tears, begging him to come home.

"I know what you're thinking, Hon, But how could that be? Try not to borrow trouble, dear." Martin spoke a bit longer and closed his phone. "My wife's worried. We've had a rather severe threat against our family that we've had to pay attention to. I'm sure it had nothing to do with this—no way." But it hung in his mind that it very well could have been an attempt against another of Martha's family—one of her loved ones. He wouldn't say it to Jeannie over the phone, but he knew it might well have been him at the end of the day, getting in his car to drive home. Martin felt the guilt of knowing some other poor soul may have taken the hit that was meant for him.

Instead of taking action, his coworkers stood around in stunned groups saying little, each one of them wondering if their own car had escaped damage. Most of them had pulled out their cells and called home, also needing to reassure their families of their safety.

He'd have to wait, and waiting was the hardest thing of all for Martin. Anxious and worried, he wanted action. Unable to sit and relax, he paced about his office muttering through clenched teeth, "I'd like to get my hands on that slimy bastard!"

The others of his group slowly filed back to their

desks, cubicles, or offices, wherever they spent their day. However, not a one could concentrate on their work. Some grouped together to discuss the situation further. Talking about it—speculating over it—seemed to help, somehow.

Jim Ellison approached Martin's office. "I heard that comment you made out there, Martin, about a slimy bastard." His eyes searched Martin's face for answers. "What's going on—if you'll let me in on it? It sounded pretty intense."

"It's just something in my family. And, yes, it's intense, all right. In fact, the whole thing is a hell-in-gone situation. It's beyond belief. If you don't mind, it's very private and not something I could discuss with anyone. Sorry, Jim." Martin had to turn his colleague away and regretted it.

The two men walked out of Martin's office and wandered about, hoping for some news. In time, a police officer entered the area and was met by John McClellan, vice president of the company. They spoke for a few moments, then together they headed toward Martin. He had a sick feeling, seeing they were headed for him. He guessed what they were coming to say.

They entered his office, and Jim Ellison was left outside. "Mr. Moulton, I'm Sergeant Bill Morrison. I've come to inform you that your vehicle was apparently at the center of the explosion. We identified it as yours by the parking location. There was little of it left otherwise—a Buick Enclave, was it?"

"Mine?" Martin felt his face grow cold as his pulse rate soared. "What happened? It was supposed to be at the Buick Garage being serviced." With a very sick feeling, he remembered the Buick man had come to pick up the keys from his secretary only a few moments before the explosion. Horrified at this turn of events, he cried aloud, "God almighty! What exactly happened, Officer?"

"It appears the vehicle was wired with some sort of explosive device. When the man started it, it blew sky high and took out several other vehicles along with it. We have the forensics team on what's left of your vehicle now. They'll remove it to our yard when it cools down enough to complete their investigation. And if you don't mind, I'd like to ask a few questions."

But Martin, horrified at the probable fate of the poor service man, didn't heed the officer's request. "The service man who came to pick up my van—what about him?" he asked, but he already knew the answer. He felt sick inside, knowing that the bomb had been meant for him, not some innocent worker. "Oh, God—Jeannie! I have to let Martha know about this, too." He let those words escape before he stopped himself.

"Yes, I'm afraid whoever had started your vehicle has been killed, Mr. Moulton." The officer took out his book. "Do you know anything about this that might help us with this investigation, sir?"

Martin looked about to see the vice president standing there, and Jim Ellison lurking about outside his office. "Is it possible to have a bit of privacy here?" He shrugged and said to his vice president, "Sorry, sir, this is an on-going and extremely personal matter."

Sergeant Morrison cleared the room, closed the doors, and took out his book. "Now tell me what you can."

"Sir, it's a long story and a tough one. I can also put you in touch with a detective who knows as much, and probably a lot more than I do." Martin sat down and leaned forward toward the officer, his elbows on his knees, to tell what he knew. It went on for a long while.

He told Martha's story, including the most recent loss of the detective, Harry Johns.

The officer shook Martin's hand. "Wow, I've never heard of anything to top this. I'll get in touch with Detective Tom Wells, ASAP." He turned to leave and said, his hand out, "Thanks for your testimony, Mr. Moulton, and if you need a ride home, we'll provide you with one, just say the word."

"I'll gladly take you up on that, sir, and thank you for it. I'm feeling a bit shaky—that bomb was meant for me."

"I'd have to say you've had a close shave, and you have a wife and son to think about."

Martin nodded in agreement with the officer.

The officer shook his head. "Considering the things you've told me, we may need to provide you with protective surveillance until we get this person locked up."

"If you think we'll need it, of course. My wife will be a nervous wreck after this. But what I don't get is this: Your department has a detective out at my mother-in-law's place full time, twenty-four/seven, keeping an eye on her, when we've been led to believe this person is out to get the rest of us, before he goes for her. What's going on with that?"

"I have no idea—must be departmental business, but I'll check into it."

Martin was ready to leave the area right now. "I'll tell my boss I'm going home to my family, if you'll take me now."

Sergeant Morrison nodded. "Sure thing."

After a short chat with John McClellan, his superior, Martin and the officer headed for the elevators. As they descended, Martin asked, "Any chance I could get a look at the scene—see what's left of my Enclave?"

"I think we can do that, now. The smoke and dust may have dissipated some, and area quieted down enough. You won't be able to touch anything for now, however."

They exited the elevator at the third floor of the parking garage into a fuggy mix of smoke and burning materials. Martin surveyed the site from where they stood. "God almighty, that poor man had no chance at all." He shivered, thinking what might have happened to himself and not the unfortunate service worker. "Has his family been notified?"

"I imagine so, but that wasn't up to me," Morrison replied as he nudged Martin toward the elevator. "Better get you on home, son."

His gentle words reflected the edges of gray that appeared below his police cap. The man had seen a lot in his years on the force, and what he'd seen today bode poorly for this fine young man and his family.

As they drove through the streets, Martin felt the icy effects of shock settling into his body. He'd had a very narrow escape. His tremors worsened as they drove along until he clasped his shaking hands together to hold them still. He worried how this would hit his family. And Martha, what would this do to her?

As they drove into the driveway of his home, Martin saw Martha's car parked a bit crookedly in the street out front. Right behind it sat the detective's older model Range Rover. Martin told the officer, "Detective Tom Wells is here, too if you need to speak to him. The man hangs close to Martha. He says it's to keep a guard on her." He snorted. "It really pisses her off."

Chapter 13

"Thanks for the heads up. I'll see what the situation is with him while I'm here," Sergeant Morrison replied.

The men got out and walked up the few steps to enter the house.

Martin was met by Jeannie as she threw herself into his arms, sobbing and crying. "Oh, darling, are you all right? This thing is far more real than we thought, isn't it? Oh, Martin, what's going to happen?" She clung to him with a near death grip and looked up into his face.

He held her out and looked into her eyes, trying to reassure her. "I'm fine, honey—everything okay here?" Without waiting for her answer, he introduced Sergeant Morrison. "He's working on the case and kindly brought me home. The SUV is—uh—" Then he shrugged. "The Enclave is toast, sorry to say, dear."

"Thanks for calling me about it—if you hadn't when it flashed on the news, I'd have been worried out of my mind. How'd this happen, Martin?" Her face was the color of paste, and her hands shook like aspen leaves in the wind.

"I'll tell you what I know, which is next to nothing. They haven't completed their investigation yet, but from what we know already, I'm sure that bomb was meant for me." He sat down heavily in the nearest chair and wiped his forehead.

Martin noticed Martha standing back, waiting beside Detective Tom Wells. He spoke to her. "Martha, whoever is doing this hasn't finished with us yet." He rose from his chair and went to her. "He's still out there, and we're just a part of it—if what Harry believed is true."

Martha trembled, but not in fear. She fought the sudden anger that had risen in her at whoever had planned and executed this devastating murder. "Yes, I believe it's true, Martin. You were a lucky man today, but I wonder what he'll do next? If he failed to get you this time, what's next? I can't imagine your sending young Will outside this house to school or anywhere else. It's just not safe!" She turned to Tom, her fists clenched and her face flushed. "And you! Why are you hanging around, hounding me day and night? He's not after me—look around you. You should be right here watching *this* family!"

Tom tightened his lips. "I wouldn't exactly call it hounding, ma'am. And I do have my orders."

Martin thought he saw a hint of a smile cross Tom's lips at Martha's remarks, but it was quickly hidden. In spite of everything, Martin couldn't blame the man for his thoughts. Of course, Martha was outraged. She believed Tom guarded the wrong people. Martin also wondered what the deal was but wisely stayed quiet to see how things went.

Tom faced Martha. "You might call that friend of yours from Colorado Springs and give her a heads-up, too. She was at your home for several days. To an onlooker, that would suggest someone close to you."

Martha understood Tom's meaning, and Martin saw her face go pale. She quickly pulled out her phone and pressed Lizzie's stored number. With a frown at Tom, she went into another room to speak with her long-time friend.

Martin asked Jeannie. "What time is it? Isn't Will due home by now?"

She took a hasty look at the clock on the kitchen wall. "Any minute now." Then she ran to the window and looked out at the street to see if he was in sight. "I don't see him, Martin."

He heard the rising hysteria in her voice and went to her. "Hold on, darling, he's not late, is he?"

But Martin felt a rising anxiety of his own. From now on, no one in his little family would feel safe. They didn't have that luxury anymore. Someone had them in their sights, and they had no idea who it was that was threatened them—or for certain, why.

"Oh thank God! Here he comes, Martin!" Jeannie jumped away from the window and appeared ready to run to meet her son.

Martin grasped her arm. "Easy, dear, we must not alarm him. It'll be bad enough when he sees a police cruiser sitting out front. There are Martha's and Detective Wells's vehicles, too. That'll certainly set him to wondering."

Will entered the house, questions written across his young face. "What's goin' on Mom?" He nodded at Martha, Tom, a policeman in full uniform, and his dad. He knew his dad wasn't usually home this early in the day. "What's wrong?" He waited for an answer.

Martin went to his son. "Will, we had a bit of trouble today. Everyone is all right, but something has happened." He sat in a chair and brought his son close to his knees as he gently explained all the events of the day, and what they had planned to do about it. He saw the boy's face grow pale.

Will's eyes grew large and rounded. "Sounds like he was after you, Dad, doesn't it?"

Martin saw the boy square his shoulders as if readying himself for a fight. Martin applauded the move. It led him to believe it was because of the self-defense training the boy was receiving.

"He'd better not try to get his hands on me, Dad. I'll know what to do now if he does." Will had a shine in his eyes.

At any other time, Martin would not have liked to see a light like that in the boy's eyes, but right now, with the increased danger to the family, it looked good. Internally, he applauded those self-defense lessons.

Martha came up to the boy. "Hi, Will, how's school?" She really wanted to know all about his self-defense training.

"Oh, Grammy, it's okay, like always. Those nuns are really tough, but my other class is the best one of all. I'm learning all kinds of things."

His young chest swelled a bit with his words, and Martha readily saw the increase in his sense of self and confidence in his own abilities.

"That's good, Will, a person never knows when they might need to know those things."

"Like real soon, maybe." He gave her a knowing nod of his small head. "Don't worry, that bad man won't bother me."

"I hope not, Will. But you'll be very careful walking home from that bus stop, won't you?"

Will nodded. Then, casting a glance at the big man, he asked Martha, his voice lowered. "Who is that big guy you have with you? Who is he?"

She answered his query. "That man is Detective Tom Wells. He worked with Detective Johns—they were good friends." That seemed to satisfy the boy, though it had never satisfied her.

☙☙☙

Ray sat in his worn-out chair, mulling over his failure to kill or badly maim a member of Martha's family. "From what the TV says, it wasn't the Moulton dude that got it. Hell no, it was some damned garage flunky. Shit-damn, now I've got to do it all over again." Restless, he got up and peered out the window. "It won't be so easy after this. He'll be on the look-out for anything like that again." He knew this news wouldn't please Denny Garver, and hoped he had enough time to make another hit. He kept the TV tuned to the local news, hoping somehow they'd got it wrong.

Deep inside, Ray hated what he'd been forced to do. He couldn't keep on with this kind of thing for long. The killing of innocent people hurt him inside in ways he'd never believed possible. He imagined their lives, their families, their kids. He faced the fact that he actually did have a few moral values left, in spite of his fancy for small girls. That was wrong as hell, too, he knew that, but he hadn't been able to suppress it.

Ray had found a small way to rationalize his evil deeds. He'd made it easier on himself by deciding that, after all, they were created as females—made for the use of men, weren't they? But this hitting and blowing up these regular folks didn't sit right with him. They'd never done him any wrong.

Thinking of the dismal gray walls that held Denny Garver worked on his mind. He faced a dilemma no man should have to face. And Ray knew he wasn't done, not just yet. "Maybe I'll take a hit at that fancy dame in the Caddy. That oughta be easy enough—she's lived a fancy life. Snuffin' that snooty bitch out won't hurt me a bit—might be fun. If I figger out where she lives—someplace outside of Denver."

But though Ray knew he'd do it, he couldn't stop the creeping sense of futility that crept into his consciousness. Things weren't going right. "That bitch who caused all this trouble in the first place ought to be the first one to put down. It's all her fault!" He shook his head in frustration. "Now if she ain't got another big bastard of a cop living with her. Must be some kind of woman. One stud after another in her sack every damned night, that way."

He got up and headed for his bed, taking a couple of pills with him. He was glad he'd got the fancy dame's license plate, a thing like that made all the difference. "Tomorrow, I'll look up that Caddy's license plate. Easy enough to find that babe, no matter where the hell she lives."

He lay awake, his body burning—his mind on another thing entirely. She was a tiny thing—soft, piping little girl's voice and big wide blue eyes. He'd watch her every chance he got, playing on the slide or running with her friends. She lived about three blocks from him—played hopscotch on her sidewalk alone sometimes, too. So near, yet so far…

Why couldn't he just happen along one evening? He knew her name, now, too. Liza Hanley. He wouldn't sound like some stranger if he talked to her a bit at school. She wouldn't fear someone she knew, he was sure of it. He got so heated, he got up and walked about his house, drank a beer, snapped on the TV. Nothing helped. He burned—engorging painfully, imagining what that little one could give him.

In desperation, he downed two more pills and lay again in his rumpled sheets, thinking thoughts he knew were so very wrong.

ogeo

Jeannie fretted about the house. Will was safely at school. She was out of groceries and sundries and had to go shopping. Fearful of leaving the house, she had put it off for days, eking by on what she had on hand. But now, out of everything, she had to leave the safety of her home and get what was needed.

These days, every act seemed fraught with peril. It angered her that no one had figured out who it was that sought their death and destruction. The authorities had no doubt of the cloud their family lived under, but nothing had been done to stop this ugly threat. Despite the fact that nothing had happened lately, she didn't trust the feeling that the danger had passed.

Their needs must be taken care of. Jeannie shrugged away her worries and, with the long list in hand, grabbed her purse and headed to the garage. Her car, safely locked in the double garage, was safe. "I will keep watch, be careful, and do what needs doing. We can't run and hide forever." Nothing had happened for a couple of weeks or more, and some of the fear had worn off. But she had a moment's tension when starting the car—could it be wired? Jeannie relaxed when she felt the engine take hold. No sputtering and grinding sounds like in a movie she had seen.

She opened the garage door, backed her car into the empty street, and headed to the shopping complex. It was rather a large area, but it held all the shops she needed to visit. She reached the store and parked her car. After she took a cart and began her shopping, she slowly relaxed and enjoyed the feeling of normality it gave her. For a couple of hours, she forgot her worries.

After visiting several aisles, with her cart piled high, she checked out, made her way to her car, and loaded her supplies in the trunk. She got into the car, turned the key—noting happily how easily it started—and drove away. What she hadn't noticed was the small puddle of pale, oily fluid that had drifted out between the front tires. She had never thought to look for things like that before and had no habit of it.

With a CD playing her favorite musical group, she drove out of the crowded parking lot, headed down the street, and, after a mile of rather heavy street traffic, she merged onto the freeway that led to her housing area. It lay just outside of Denver. Humming along with the latest soft rock and tapping the beat on the steering wheel, she murmured, "At least the traffic is better here. It's clear driving."

They lived in the Wintercrest Subdivision, an above average housing area of individually crafted homes. Their home befitted an engineer of Martin's ability and was a thing of pride for them both. The school that Will attended was within a mile, and one of the reasons they had chosen that subdivision.

Jeannie sped along, tapping her fingers on the steering wheel as she thought about what to have for dinner. No make-do whatever tonight—they would feast royally for a change. She had bought the steaks to make it happen. And then there was the company dinner slated for next weekend. She went over her wardrobe, deciding on what to wear. She wanted to look her best for Martin's coworkers and bosses.

Lost in a slightly daydreaming mode, she was shocked to full alert as a small dark tan car came so close it nearly sideswiped her. Trying to avoid him, she turned her wheel rather sharply. Shocked, and suddenly frightened, she found herself careening off the roadway, across the bar ditch, and heading for what appeared to be a solid rock wall.

She didn't want to hit up against a thing like that and slammed on the brakes. She felt nothing—there was no response—no slowing of her car at all.

Instinctively, she put her hands and arms across her face to protect herself as her car careened toward the solid wall just beyond. The bar ditch had slowed her some, but not enough to prevent her car slamming hard into the wall.

Jeannie heard the crashing of metal on stone and felt the heavy shock of the impact. The instant slamming of the ballooning airbag heavily into her face was the last thing she knew. Everything went black.

Arousing, she heard voices and felt hands tugging at her shoulders. Someone asked, "Are you with us?" Warm hands pressed here and there, examining her. "Can you move your arms, ma'am?" and, "Can you move your legs—wiggle your toes?" She heard and felt her seat belt being unbuckled.

She finally opened her eyes. "What happened?" Overcome with nausea, she felt sick. "Where am I?"

"You went off the freeway, ma'am. You've had an accident." She heard a masculine voice explaining things to her. "Your car ran off the road into a rock wall." He took her pulse. "We are paramedics, ma'am. We want to help you out of this car as soon as it is safe to do so." He pressed about on her abdomen, had her move her legs, and head. "It does appear you have no spinal injuries, and you are able to move all extremities." He asked her again to move all her extremities until he seemed satisfied she could be moved safely. He took her blood pressure and checked her pulses, all around.

He sniffed her breath, and when Jeannie realized what he was doing, she declared, "I'm not drunk, I've had nothing that way."

"We can see that, ma'am. Just had to be sure."

He helped her move to the edge of the seat then lifted her under the arms to stand long enough to get the stretcher close. Two of them lifted her, placed her on her back, and covered her with thick blankets. "Need to keep you warm, ma'am, prevents shock. I don't see any bleeding, but you could have internal injuries. The ER doc will decide that."

Jeannie felt herself lifted and carried upward until they slid her into their vehicle. From then on, she let go and lay there, listening to the scream of the siren and feeling the movement of the ambulance.

She remembered and tried to sit up. "Did you bring my purse? I have everything in it, my insurance, and all."

"It's right here, ma'am," he said as he pressed her back onto the gurney. He held it up for her to see. "A lady has to have her purse." He smoothed her hair back from her forehead, as she awakened further.

"I remember when I put the brakes on, nothing happened." She felt the fear creeping in. "It was him, I know it!"

"It was who, ma'am?"

"Can you call my husband? His number is in my phone. It's in my purse." She wanted Martin. She needed him—he would know what to do.

She heard them put in the call. "Please, if you can reach him, I must speak to him." She reached out to take her phone.

The medic handed it to her. "Martin? Oh, Martin, I've had an accident. My brakes didn't work!" She started sobbing, and the medic took the phone.

He explained things to Martin and where they were taking her. "Yes, sir, she's going to Riverside." He chatted another moment, reassuring her husband that she was alert and talking. Then he patted Jeannie's hand. "He'll be there waiting for you. He's closer than we are."

Chapter 14

In time, Jeannie felt the ambulance come to a halt, back up, and soon she was removed from the vehicle. She felt the rumbling wheels as they took her through the doors. When she saw Martin's face above her, the tears started coming as she tried to reach out to him.

They placed her in a small room set up for the triage of incoming patients. Martin was asked to step outside after having a few minutes with her.

While he waited outside Jeannie's cubicle, he decided to call Martha. She needed to know what had happened. They both knew the reason for this accident. Martin again felt the helplessness of being a victim with no answers in sight. His fists clenched in anger and frustration, and his heart rate soared. Now he waited to find out how seriously his wife had been injured. She was alive and, for that, he thanked God.

❧❧❧

Martha received the call and shook with anger as she told Tom of her daughter's accident. He ushered her into his Bronco, and they headed for Riverside.

"He's after every one of us!" She fought her tears as Tom drove. She knew the killer who threatened them had hoped for a messy collision off a high-speed freeway, with the death of Jeannie as a result. Martha felt a small bit of satisfaction that he hadn't succeeded. Martin had said she was alert and talking and she took comfort from that bit of positive news.

After Tom parked the Bronco, they nearly ran to the emergency department. Martha and Tom were ushered into Jeannie's cubicle. Martha saw with relief that her daughter was awake and talking.

She looked at her mother and tears filled her eyes. "He tried again, Mom." Jeannie choked up but managed to add, "I hope they get that man soon. He seems to fail more than he succeeds, but he's bound to get one of us, soon."

Her daughter's face was so pale. Looking at her laying there under that sheet with an IV flowing into her arm, oxygen cannula in her nose, and the bruising across her face from the impact of the airbags, Martha felt a heavy burden of guilt. She'd brought this on her family. "I'm so sorry for this, Jeannie!"

"Mom, don't." Jeannie managed to give her mother a stern look. Looking at her mother, and remembering all the events of the past few years, she knew her mother was not really at fault. "You only did what you had to do. It was all for Will in the beginning. We can't forget that." She managed a smile, though her face looked increasingly discolored from the airbags, and Martha was sure her daughter hurt all over. Jeannie went on, trying to comfort her mother. "I have no regrets for anything that you have ever done in the past, and you can't either."

An orderly came in. "She'll be going for a CT scan now," he said and wheeled her away.

Martha turned to Tom and Martin. "What are we going to do about this? It cannot continue. He won't stop until he gets every one of us." She looked at Tom. "You too, mister. Can't you do something?" She was angry and wanted some action.

Right then, a police officer entered the cubicle. He introduced himself. "I'm Sergeant Allen Lines. I will be investigating this accident." He spotted Tom. "Excuse me, mind if I have a word with Tom, here?"

The men left the area, and Martha heard them speaking softly with each other. Of course they knew each other. She was curious about what Tom would tell the officer.

Shortly they returned and, since the patient was absent, Officer Lines asked Martin. "What can you tell me?

"She told me her brakes didn't work," Martin said. "She applied them as her car left the highway. You might want to check that. We believe there may have been sabotage to her car. I'm sure Tom has filled you in on that business."

Officer Lines nodded. He already had the gist of what was happening in their lives, though, perhaps, not why. Martha watched the proceedings with a jaundiced eye, all the while wondering if the police would do anything to find out who was behind these deadly attempts on their lives.

The devil behind it had succeeded in taking the best man she'd ever known away from her. By the way the assassin's failures were mounting up, she worried he might become increasingly rash or reckless in his attempts.

Her mind kept going back to that sorry little house on Delgado lane. Why, she wasn't sure, except for the truck with the camper on back and that she and Will had both taken the same three letters down. It made sense to her. He had driven past Will twice, and to her, that meant something.

The man had quickly gotten rid of that same vehicle, and that meant something, too. Why else would he have done that? Full of questions with very few answers, Martha wasn't sure what he drove now, but she believed it wouldn't be long until they found that out, too.

༄

Jeannie was returned from the CT scan. The officer waited to begin his questioning until he could ask the doctor if he was sure she was up to it. But she had no memory of the vehicle that had sent her careening off the road, other than that she thought it was a small, tan-colored sedan.

She told him that she had no brakes, and, otherwise, had seen nothing. He took down what he could and after another word with Tom, he left the hospital.

After another long wait, the doctor appeared to say, "I'm Doctor Miles Logan. Mrs. Moulton is in no danger. Her CT scan did not reveal any internal injuries, her blood work is normal, and her senses are intact. She's been very shaken up and has a lot of bruising about the face and chest from the air bag, but even there, nothing was broken. We can thank those things for saving another life, and I believe they did just that." He added, "We'd like to keep her overnight for observation if that's agreeable to you."

Martin looked at Jeannie. "How about it, dear? Would you want to stay overnight? You'll be okay, the doc said. You have an all clear as far as any serious injuries go."

Jeannie said, almost pleading, "Please, Martin, let's go home. I want my family around me, but most of all, I need your arms around me, to hold me."

Then she remembered, "Martin, my car was full of groceries. Could you go get them after I'm home? There are steaks, too. I had planned a really nice dinner for us." She shed a few more tears, and her eyes clouded over as she remembered it all over again.

They'd decided to leave, and the nurse busied herself getting the final papers ready. In time, these were handed to Martin along with a prescription for pain medication. Jeannie was helped into a wheel chair and taken to Martin's new Enclave. Both Tom and Martin checked the car over for explosives before they drove away. Martha and Tom followed them home.

It was after three in the afternoon and Will sat on the front steps waiting for them. He had a key, but hadn't used it. Martha felt a surge of alarm that her grandson had placed himself in a position of danger. But she softened her comment on it. By the confident expression on his face, he hadn't worried about it one whit. She knew it was a result of his self-defense training.

She asked him. "Will, why were you sitting out here like this? What if that man came by? Aren't you afraid of what might have happened?"

"No, Grammy, I'm not. I can handle him or anyone else that tries anything on me."

He had a look of confidence that she was glad to see, but Will was a small boy, only nine years of age. Martha felt a tightening in her gut, and a rise in her fear for him. His increasing confidence in his new self-defense abilities might well become a fatal trap for the boy, and Martha was fit to be tied.

❧❧❧

Martha's mind was in a turmoil, but she did not mention it to Tom. She had things to do, and he wasn't a part of any of it. Her daughter had made a full recovery, but with each passing day, Martha worried something else would happen. Will had gotten bolder each day, and that worried everyone. Martha feared he was deliberately putting himself at risk.

But for her, Tom remained under foot. That fact held her back from what she burned to do. Her goal was devious. Serena's urging was a part of it, too, but Martha believed that little house on Delgado Lane held answers to things she needed to know. What was it about that house that drew her there? What secrets did it hold? Martha burned daily with her need to go there in disguise and find out about it. She carefully kept her desires hidden from Tom. She had to be clever. He was no fool.

Tom said little and stayed out of her way most of the time, yet he was always there. When Martha was alone, she often complained on the phone to Lizzie about Tom's continuing presence. She had already warned her friend about the person who was out to ruin her life by destroying her family. She had detailed both Jeannie's and Martin's narrow escapes. But this sorry business could well include Lizzie, and Martha had explained the need to be cautious in every way imaginable.

She had also made a secret arrangement with Lizzie. Between them, they had devised a way for Martha to get free from Tom's observation, hopefully, for a few hours. Having decided she needed that arrangement today, Martha couldn't wait any longer. Tired of champing at the bit to investigate that place, she felt that now was the time, and she was ready.

Martha had started back with Dr. Gleeson at his animal clinic. After assisting with three surgeries today, she was about to leave. In the bathroom, she called Lizzie.

"Hey, girl, I need one of the favors we spoke about." She listened a moment. "Yes, today, as soon as I get home—give me about ten minutes. I want to do a bit of reconnoitering of a certain house. I don't need that Tom lurking about, watching my every move."

She listened a bit more as Lizzie declared, "Yes, I'm being very careful, and no, I haven't had any bombs stuck under my steering wheel—not so far."

Martha heard a carefree laugh with that last statement. "It's not funny, Liz. You know what that rotten devil, whoever it is, has already done—miserable failure that he is. Tom is worried he might target you as well."

Martha grimaced at something Liz said and then rang off. "That fool woman can't get serious about anything, I swear." She donned her outer coat. The day was far spent and the coolness of night had settled over the darkening landscape outside. She said goodnight to the doctor and headed for her car.

In her trunk, she kept a few items that would aid her in a disguising herself if she needed to, and tonight she planned to make use of the stuff. Just as Martha walked into her kitchen, her phone went musical. She reached into her purse for it, listened, and then answered, "Yes, Doctor. Why, of course, I will. I'll be right there."

She saw Tom leaning against the doorway to the living room. "Tom, Dr. Gleason just had a car accident victim come in. Broken bones, open abdomen, really a bad case. I'll be back when it's taken care of."

Martha left him without another word, jumped into her car, and roared out of the driveway toward the vet's' office. She drove right past his practice and headed the other way on the county road. She'd need to circle around some to hit the road that led into Denver, but she knew the way.

Down the road a mile or so, she pulled into a service

station, took her kit from the trunk, and suitable clothes. In the bathroom, she quickly reapplied rather gross-appearing make-up and donned the grubby clothing. Hopefully, it was adequate for her purpose. In any case, with that baseball cap pulled down over a good part of her face, she didn't look like herself anymore. She smiled at the view in the mirror. "It feels good to actually do something again." She knew her Serena side agreed with her, and Serena's excitement added to her own.

Later, she entered the Longworth section of Denver and drove to a quiet area away from her true goal. She wanted to walk—stumble—or whatever, down that street called Delgado Lane and pass that house that had given her those weird sensations. It was *that* house that had had the pick-up with a camper on the back of it. That had added a sense of urgency about the house, and she wanted to know what made her feel the way she had—why a chill?

After shuffling along for three blocks, she entered Delgado Lane. "I don't see a truck with a camper, in fact, I don't see any vehicle at all. If no one is home, maybe I can take a closer look—see what I can find." She talked softly to herself as she walked slowly. She passed the house, went on to the end of the street, and turned the corner. Seeing an alley behind these homes, her pulse quickened.

"Maybe it has a gate that won't be locked, if I'm lucky. I need to learn how to pick a lock one of these days." She entered the alley and, by the distant light given off by a street light and a newly risen moon, she moved carefully along. She passed several large garbage containers, broken bricks, old rotting boards, and tree cuttings. Martha counted off the fifth house from the south end. She came to a rickety gate of weathered slats that appeared gray in the softness of the moonlight. She pressed the latch and felt the gate move—it wasn't locked. She murmured, "Hallelujah—no lock at all! How careless."

She'd almost spoken too loud and quickly squelched her chatter as she moved into the yard. She made her way slowly as she encountered and nearly tripped over empty cans and rotting cardboard boxes. Martha shook her head in disgust. She stepped around half-full bags of garbage, partially submerged in uncut grass as she moved toward the house.

Reaching the side of the weathered clapboard house, she peered into a window. "No lights on anywhere inside, no vehicle—he isn't home—thank you, God." She moved slowly about in the encroaching gloom of heavy twilight until she found the back door. Turning the handle, she found it wasn't locked either.

Martha entered and moved carefully and slowly through the back hallway entrance. It was narrowed further with stacks of boxes piled there against a wall. After bumping into several items, she took out a small pencil sized flashlight and aimed it at the floor. She exclaimed in a muffled voice, "Ye Gods! This place is filthy—and the smell—disgusting!" She moved about, wondering what kind of miserable soul lived in a shack like this.

She saw drying food on a plate beside a large, worn-looking upholstered large chair. A half can of beer sat beside the plate. She hefted the can, found it half empty and no longer cold, if it ever had been. The hum of the refrigerator in the kitchen sounded. Hearing that, she knew the man had some method of food preservation.

She entered a bedroom, and her knees came up against a full size rumpled mattress with half the bedding tossed on the floor. She shone the flashlight about the room, carefully avoiding the windows. His clothing lay scattered about, shorts, T-shirts, socks inside out, and a uniform shirt that dangled from the back of a chair. Wrinkled pants lay crumpled on the floor. She noted the name of a school on the shirt. "Longworth Elementary— my God, he works at that school?" Her eyes narrowed, considering the kind of man that could be living in this house. "Around all those little kids." Her heart rate increased at the unwanted thoughts that came to her.

She moved farther into the room and shone her light on the furniture. She saw a picture of a small, dainty little girl on the wall. A man's hair brush, nail clippers, and a few coins lay on the dresser. She stepped closer to the bed, nearly tripping over an object.

When her light shone on a small patent-leather Mary-Jane style shoe, Martha felt the blood run cold in her veins and stifled her shocked cry, "My God in Heaven, this is a little girl's shoe! What is a child's shoe doing here in this house?"

She wondered if the man who lived here had children. Somehow, in spite of seeing a child's picture on the wall, something told her he did not.

Suddenly, she felt the urge to vomit and put her hand over her mouth. She had to get out of this place! Something wasn't right in this house—a terrible, sick feeling came over her. Thoughts about that shoe consumed her as she noted where she'd found it. It shouldn't have been there. What to do—who to tell? She could scarcely get her breath. She felt her lungs tighten, and she began to choke up. Martha knew she had to get some air. Gasping for her breath, she raced through the congested mess of that house to reach the back door.

As she closed that door and headed back to the gate, she heard a car drive into the front yard. She saw the headlights flashing against the trees. "Oh, wow! Just in time!" She hurried through the back gate, carefully closed it, and walked back through the alley. Once she reached the street, she breathed easier. Trembling with the excitement of her discovery, Martha quelled her nausea and moved rapidly toward her car.

She believed she'd left everything as she'd found it. But with the place so messy, how would he know if anyone had touched or moved an item or not? She had picked up the little shoe, however, and that bothered her. Had she moved it to another location when she had dropped it? Did the man even know that little shoe was there? If it had belonged to the murdered child, Mindy Lassen, it was crucial evidence, but the police had no reason to search this man's home.

If he was indeed a child predator and had savaged that little child, it had to be brought to the attention of the Denver Police Department. She had just committed the illegal action of breaking and entering, so a friendly phone call was definitely out.

Martha had to find a legal way to finger that person. She had some planning to do. She had plenty of ideas, good ones, and, thanks to Serena, violence was a good part of it. Martha's mind was filled with ideas and plans as she walked the several blocks to find her car.

Chapter 15

Martha pulled into the same service station long enough to change into her regular clothes and clean the excess make up off her face. The scrubbing left her skin reddened and with an urgent need for her regular make-up. She didn't have it with her. She would have to face Tom looking as she did right now—in desperate need of a long, hot shower.

Facing him made her a touch nervous, but it was late. Martha needed to get home and take something to settle her nerves. She couldn't get the sight of that little shoe off her mind, or that work shirt, either. What horrors had taken place in that sorry little house?

The lights were full on as Martha pulled into the driveway, and gritting her teeth, she knew Tom would be right there waiting for her. She entered her house, feeling like an errant teenager, and fought against the guilt of it. After all, who was Tom Wells, anyway? She'd never heard of him until that dreadful day at the hospital. She remembered how he sat with the rest of them just like he belonged there. As Harry's partner, she guessed he did. He had been a part of the group that waited for the wounded man to come out of surgery.

Tom sat at the kitchen table, reading the paper. He

hadn't had dinner by the looks of it. There were no dishes or signs of food preparation. It made her angry to think she had to feed him when she was upset and exhausted.

He looked up. "A bit late, aren't you?"

"As if it's any of your business." She couldn't stop the tremor in her voice and hands, as hard as she tried. And she knew he was fully aware of it.

"Something has happened to you, Martha. I know it has. I can see it plain as day."

"Well, that's a lot more than I see," she replied through tightened lips, her tone clipped and short.

"I called the animal hospital." He kept reading with his nose in the paper. She heard those damned papers rattling.

Martha put on a pot of coffee and got out some bacon and eggs. "Have you eaten?" By the negative nod of his head, he hadn't. Angry about that, she realized, by the ache deep in her gut, she was hungry, too. She slapped several slices of bacon in the pan to start sizzling.

"I can take care of myself, Martha. The question is: can you?"

Thinking of the little shoe, Martha faced away from him and felt the tears begin. She mopped her eyes and, when she caught the odor of him standing close behind her, she whipped around. "Don't think you're getting next to me, mister." She tried to move away, but he caught her.

"I'm not trying to get close to anyone, but you've got a lot of trouble brewing against you, ma'am. I'm here to help you with it." He put his hand beneath her chin and raised her eyes to see them brimming with tears. "All right, ma'am, tell me what happened. Something did and it's a hell of a lot more than you're ready to deal with. You damned well know it, too—don't you?" Holding her arms, he shook her gently as he searched her eyes. "You can't carry this load alone, Martha. You already know that Harry told me a whole lot about you, what you've got going on inside—he told me all of it."

Martha couldn't stop the tears and sank into a chair. She said, between sobs, "I guess I'd better level with you. You won't believe what I have seen tonight." Feeling a load of relief that she had someone to share the horror of what she'd seen, she straightened and faced him. Martha realized that, right now, she was glad to tell him where she'd been and what she'd done.

She told him all of it and knew it was safe to do so. "I just got out of there in time. I saw his headlights flashing on the trees. He was pulling into the driveway as I ran out the back door."

Tom went to the stove, turned the fire down beneath the bacon, and flipped it over before he replied, "We need to see what's going on in that house."

She finally asked him what she really wanted to know. "Is there any chance that little Lassen child wore black patent-leather Mary Janes?"

"How much do you know about her?" Tom queried.

"No more than Harry ever told me. It hit him extra hard, what happened to that child. He told me some of it." She took a gasping breath and shuddered. "Did you know what happened to Harry's little daughter?"

Yes, I know all about that, Martha. Harry and I were pretty close." Tom paused a moment then went on, "And another thing, I don't believe the resident of that house was brought in for questioning, either."

"He wasn't, Tom. Harry and I drove through there one night. We drove past the houses of those that had been questioned. He had a list. As we passed that house on Delgado Lane, we saw the pick-up with a camper on the back. It was seeing that truck that set me on edge. I was sure it was the same truck that followed me home from Hillside Hospital one night. It was after eleven p.m., and the driver stared right at me. Whoever lives at that address definitely wasn't on Harry's list of interviewees." She shifted in her chair. "I didn't see what he was driving tonight, though. I had to get out of there."

"And just in time, too." Tom had a slight smile playing across his lips.

Martha thought a moment. "If he isn't one of the known child predators living in that area, you won't have a DNA sample from this man, either then, will you?" She remembered something else. "Guess where the man works?

She saw his face pale and tighten.

"Where, Martha?"

"By the uniformed shirt hanging on a chair, he works at the nearby Longworth Elementary school."

"Goddamn!" Tom paced about. "Of course, if this man is a predator, he would find a job around young children, they often do."

Martha nodded. "There needs to be a reason for the police to enter that house and do a complete forensics study on the place. Of course, that would include taking that shoe as evidence. The family would be the one to identify it. If it belonged to the Lassen child, that would be one devil off the streets. If you think he could be the predator that raped and murdered that poor child, I can figure a way to get the police inside there." The Serena side of her came to the fore, and her heart began to race with eagerness. "You'd need an ambulance, too—no doubt."

"Isn't it past your bedtime, Martha?" Tom's pulse rate increased as he saw the light of Serena's eagerness glowing in Martha's greenish-amber eyes.

It froze him inside, but he noticed in some other ways, it excited the hell out of him. *Whew! This woman is something else!*

☙☙☙

Martha had slept fitfully, but the sun was out, and she shook herself awake. She showered and donned jeans and a green short-sleeved sweater.

In the kitchen, Tom sat at the table, a newspaper in his hand and a cup of coffee before him. The phone sounded, and Martha took it up. It was Lizzie. Alarmed, Martha wondered aloud what this call was about. "Lizzie never calls at this time of the morning. She always calls later in the day—sleeps late, I think." She answered, "Yes," and put the phone on speaker.

"Martha, I hired a guard because of what you warned me might happen. He has just reported seeing a man sneak out of our garage. I called the police, and they are checking things out." Lizzie lowered her voice. "My husband is going to be furious when he gets wind of this." She went on in a near whisper, "He is a lawyer, Martha, and doesn't like any kind of publicity, adverse or otherwise, you know."

For the first time in their years together, Martha detected a note of fear in Lizzie's voice, and she felt a load of guilt for bringing this kind of trouble into her friend's life. "Liz, I'm so sorry about this, but after that attack on Martin's car while he was at work—I had to warn you. I hope it will turn out to be nothing."

"I need to know more about this business than what I read in the papers, Martha, but I see another squad car pulling up outside. I hate the way they flash their lights around. Darn, now the whole neighborhood will know we have some kind of trouble here. They're a bunch of gossips and love to dish the dirt on anyone they can. I have an awful feeling—this is going to be bad news."

Martha waited long moments, heard a door open, male voices, and Lizzie gasping for breath. Then she heard Lizzie breathing rapidly into the phone. "Martha, they found an explosive device beneath my steering column! They're impounding my car. My God! What will Norman say?"

The near hysteria in Lizzie's voice nearly tore Martha to pieces.

But Martha also wondered why Lizzie all of a sudden seemed to be afraid of her husband. She'd never heard a hint of anything like that before today. Martha tried to calm her but found it nearly impossible to do so over the phone. What could you possibly say to someone who had faced a near death experience, and all because of her friendship with you?

She cautioned her friend. "Liz, get hold of yourself. This is exactly why I warned you about. Whoever this person is, he must be crazy! And I don't even know who it is or why he's doing these things." She listened for Lizzie's answer.

"I do appreciate it, Martha, in spite of being a little hysterical. This *is* what you warned me about when you cautioned me to be careful a few days ago."

Martha felt sick at hearing the cooler tones her best friend's voice had taken on. Was that rotten bastard going to ruin the best friendship any woman ever had? "Oh, God! Lizzie! I'm sorry, and I don't know what to do about any of it. It seems being close to me has become a dangerous thing for everyone who is related to me, or comes to visit, including you. I don't know what to do, Liz."

"Aw, Martha, I'm sorry if I sounded bitchy. I'm scared out of my wits right now, girl, and not all of it because of my husband. Whoever it is, nearly nailed me. If I hadn't hired that guard, I'd have been blown to kingdom come like that poor man who tried to drive your son-in-law's Buick."

Martha heaved a small sigh of relief at Lizzie's friendlier tone. "Liz, do you want me to come there?"

"No, Martha, you've got enough on your plate. I'll be all right. Norman will take some work, but little ol' Lizzie can handle that situation, don't you worry your head about that."

"All I can say is, I'm so glad you're okay. I couldn't handle it if harm came to you because of me—I just couldn't, Lizzie."

Her friend's voice had calmed when she said. "Martha, you know you've saved my life." She gasped and Martha heard her make a small squeal. "Oh, wow, there goes my car. They're hauling it off like some old wreck." Then she added, her voice tense again, "And here comes my husband home early from his office. I've got to hang up. I'll call you when I can."

Lizzie clicked off, and Martha reached for the nearest chair. "This cannot go on—something's got to be done to put a stop to this monster. Now this fiend has my friends and family living in fear for their lives." She sank into the chair as her anger turned slowly into a cold rage, one that set her on fire inside.

Yet, it also worked to clear her mind. She tried to imagine which of her so-called victims had the ability to make something like this happen. "Freddie boy? Never." Shaking her head in the negative, she easily ruled out the first destroying pervert she had clipped. She had never regretted what she'd done, nor could she bring herself to call him a victim, not after what he'd done to Will.

"Denny Garver—how could he—on death row?" But she couldn't dismiss him. In her heart, she knew he was a

man who had the smarts to pull something like this off—
if he could find a way. And so could that evil Pederson,
another one with a devious, evil heart. She realized the
list was rather long, and she'd never be able to do the
checking needed. And, she no longer had Harry to help
her with something like that.

She looked about for the ever present Tom Wells.
"Where is that man? He might be able to do some good
instead of lazing about the place, driving me crazy."
Looking out the kitchen window, she saw him tossing a
stick for the dogs. He must have left the house while she
talked with Lizzie. She went out to see him.

As she approached, he turned to look at her. His
black eyes bore into her with a questioning look.
"Ma'am?"

"Tom, I've been thinking."

"Yes?" He could see she had something on her mind,
and it was pretty big. She was strung out tight as hell.

Martha got right to the point. "The only person with
enough moxie to pull a vendetta like this against me
might be Denny Garver, or possibly Anson Pederson. Of
course, there's a slight chance it could be Ed Gilmore. I
didn't do anything physical to him, but he hates my guts
without a doubt. And of course, I don't think Pederson
ever knew who did him, but then again, word gets
around." Martha halted her words, at the look on Tom's
face.

"My God, woman, how many men have you fixed,
neutered, altered, or clipped, anyway?"

She could see he fought back a smile. "Well, there
were a couple of sick creeps I met on the internet. They
thought I was thirteen. But believe me, they were a whole
lot older than the nice fifteen-year old boy looking for a
bit of fun, like they'd said." Martha shrugged. "Both of
them would have devastated a young teenaged girl." She

held her head high, remembering those men. "I was quite sure I wasn't the first one either of them had ever lined up. Imagine how many poor little, lonely young girls those two men alone must have raped and ruined. Not for either one of them, or any of the others, do I have regrets."

She felt her temper rise at the memory of those predatory males." That last fellow would have killed, or severely injured for life, a young girl with what he had." Martha felt she'd gone too far with that statement, and her face grew hot. "Sorry, I shouldn't have said that."

Tom let out a good, long laugh. "Hell, yes, lady, you should have. Best thing I've heard in ages,"

She noticed how his eyes crinkled at the corners when he laughed. "Tom, is there any way you could find out if any of the men I've mentioned might have something to do with what's going on?" She faced him, seeking an answer in those black eyes. Right now, they were full of fire and mystery.

"I've already had a few conversations with an old friend of yours in Colorado Springs." At the look of surprise on Martha's face, he held up a hand. "Hold on, ma'am, he really is a friend of yours. He has the highest regard for you and applauds the work you did in that town. He has an ear out, down there, now that we've talked."

"You speak of Detective Ryan Mapus, then, I imagine."

"The very one," Tom said, a smile spreading across his lips. "He speaks fondly of your last meeting in that running park."

"Did he have any answers or help to offer?"

"Not immediately, but he planned to quietly ask around if you or your past activities have been mentioned by anyone, or if there was any new gossip."

Martha shrugged and went back into the house. She was restless, she wanted to get busy, or Serena did. She couldn't stop thinking about that little girl's shoe. Was the man who lived in that house another child predator, even the killer of that little girl? Could he be one of those inhuman creeps? And to think he worked around those little children. Why would a shoe like that be in his house? She hadn't seen any family pictures or any pictures at all outside of the picture of the little girl on the bedroom wall. Somehow Martha didn't believe that child was a relative. Not of this man—no way.

She needed to know—had to find out—and she could if Tom would kindly disappear from her life. She paced the floor in her frustration.

Chapter 16

Ray sat in his chair, fuming. "Nothing's working out the way I planned. That miserable bastard, Denny will be turnin' me in if I don't get something right pretty damn soon. That damned bomb didn't go off on the daughter's husband. After buying three of them, I don't know how I can get a hold of another one. That shifty dude is leery of me already." He groaned aloud. "Haven't heard of the daughter having a car wreck. It's not in the papers—not yet anyway. Maybe the one on the fancy dame with the Caddy will go off. The bastard who makes them was looking real funny at me, like he wondered about me—if I knew how to use them or something. Must read the papers to see what blew up. So he knew why I needed them. Why would anybody buy bombs, for God's sake? A man who buys shit like that ain't doing it for no Sunday school picnic. The bastard knows that and don't need to be lookin' funny at me. He's in business to make a few bucks, ain't he?"

He downed another beer and grabbed the empties to toss in the kitchen garbage can. "Damned thing's full up again." He grabbed up the bag and headed out the back door. Finding it unlocked, he raised his eyebrows. "Hell if I didn't forget to lock-up last night."

He made his way to the alley and walked to the big receptacle kept there. "Looks like fresh foot prints out here." His eyes followed them long enough to see they went out to the end of the alley, but he felt a shot of alarm race through his body when he noticed they went to and from his back gate, but nowhere else.

He felt a streak of ice crawl up his spine as he followed the tracks and verbalized his thoughts, as was his habit. "Shit-damn, these look like they're going both ways—in and out like. Not real big ones, now are they? Maybe some kids playin' around back here, and sneakin' into my yard." He hoped that was what they were, but a lick of fear began crawling through his veins like insects taking over his body, eating at him. It gave him a sick feeling. "Is there someone nosin' around my house? Those tracks could have been made by a woman."

He followed the tracks through his yard and around the house. "Hell's bells, if I didn't lock the damned back door last night, it could have been somebody coming in here and lookin' for something to rip off."

His fine china—his crystal? He uttered a disgusted laugh. He couldn't imagine what he had that anyone would want. That consideration sent his mind in a totally different direction. "Supposin' somebody's got a line on me, maybe getting curious for some reason?" He remembered seeing that older truck cruising past several weeks ago, and wondered about that at the time. "Maybe I got a guilty conscience or something to be feeling this way." He slumped back into his chair and snapped on the TV.

His head snapped up when the announcer blared out the news. "There was a car bombing attempt today in Colorado Springs. The bomb was planted on the car of a city official's wife. The attempt was thwarted by a very alert security guard. Authorities are on the case. We will bring you follow-up information on this story later as the details come in. This is the second attempt of this type in the past week. The last event occurred in Denver and caused the murder of garage attendant, John Lucas, age twenty eight, who leaves a wife and two young sons."

"Shit-damn, this rotten business is spreading all over the place, and Denny will sure enough be reading about it, too. I can't be going to that damned place to see him anymore, people will get wise." Ray got up and paced about. He had botched both jobs, failing to do the things Denny had demanded. "Hell, I got his money now. I'd give a hell of a lot to shove a damned knife between his ribs for what he's making me do." He grimaced. "It'd feel a damned site better than killin' off innocent folks."

But Ray hunched his shoulders. "They can't be watching every minute. I'll get that ritzy bitch yet. She must be real important to that damned Lavery bitch, or Chance, or whatever the hell name she's using these days. If that rich bitch spent a week out there with her, she's got to be somebody real damned important to that nut-clippin' bitch. After I do her in, I'm going for that boy. He's a little old for my taste, but he's been the start of all this trouble from what I hear."

Sick inside from his failures and his fear of Denny Garver, Ray took another two pills and sought his bed—dirty, tattered sheets and all. He needed the dark oblivion of sleep.

လ၁လ၁

"Mom, Jimmy Prentiss wants me to come over and study with him." Will looked up at his mother. On his toes, edgy, he waited for permission.

"I'll drive you over. You know full well it's not safe for you to walk the streets." Hands on hips, Jeannie questioned, "Where does this boy live?" No way did she plan to let Will out of her sight.

"Mom, how do you know that man hasn't put a bomb under your car? It's sitting right out in the open where he could get at it—maybe he fixed it up last night." Will wore a slightly smart-assed smirk on his face.

"Will! Don't you scare me with that." But Jeannie knew right then, she dared not get into her car until it had been checked out. This car was a loaner car until her own car had been fully repaired after her collision with the rock wall. "You can bet I'll keep it in the garage with the doors locked from now on." Muttering between clench teeth, she added, "After it's been checked out."

"See, Mom, you can't trust anything, anymore. None of us can. Not until they catch him." Will stood in front of her, his bottom lip stuck out a bit.

"Oh, Will, you are so right. I'm calling that nice officer that was here when Martin had that trouble at his office."

"You mean when Dad almost got blown up?" Will dodged a swat from his mother.

"Will, don't you say things like that!" Jeannie shook a finger at him as she reached for her cell and called the officer. After a short conversation, she told Will. "He'll be here in about an hour, Will. I guess he's very busy."

"It'll be too late to study by then. At Jimmy's house, they'll be having dinner at that time. He told me he has to get his studying done before dinner. It's only two blocks away, Mom, I can walk that far—I'm not afraid." He puffed out his chest. "I'm not afraid of that man or any other man. Not anymore, I ain't."

"Oh, big man now, are you?" She took another look at her son. His self-esteem had vastly improved, and she saw the beginnings of a man in the works. It struck her that her little boy was growing up. The thought of it nearly made her speechless, except to admonish him. "Haven't I told you not to say ain't?"

"Well, I'm not afraid, and I want to walk over there, Mom."

"Okay fine, but I'll be right beside you." She saw him begin a protest, but he held it. He knew the situation. They grabbed their coats and went out the door. "I need a breath of fresh air myself, son. The walk will do us both good."

She saw him to the friend's door and turned to leave, but cautioned him again. "Call when you're ready to come home. Dad will be home after a bit—he can come for you." She looked firmly at her son. "Understood?"

"In his brand new Enclave, Mom?"

"Yes, smarty!" Jeannie retorted then headed back the way she'd come. As she walked briskly along, a small dark tan car cruised slowly passed her. She didn't pay it much attention until it sped up and moved out of sight. A slight chill passing through her body. *That car...moving the way it did...Was that the guy?*

Jeannie knew it could have been. No one had described what the man might be driving, but it had been a tan car that nearly shoved her off the freeway. They believed he had gotten rid of the truck with the camper. After all the to-do about getting the license numbers, it hadn't been seen around lately. She could be in his sights as well as any other member of Martha's family. She'd been through that once already, with the severed brake line on her car. The police report had confirmed it.

She kept an eye out for that car, hoping to see it again, maybe get a license plate number. She'd gotten another glimpse of it as she turned the last corner heading for the house, but hadn't seen the plates. "If it was him, he knows where Will is right now." A tight case of nerves crept over her as she looked down the street hoping to see

Martin pull in any moment. She needed the comfort and strength of her husband right now.

She reached her home and hurried inside. Her heart beat rapidly, and her hands trembled. "If I call Mom, it'll just set her on edge." She got out what she had planned for dinner, but her mind was not on dinner preparation. She couldn't get anything started. Shaking inside, she made the call anyway.

"Mom, how's everything?" She couldn't keep the worry out of her voice.

Martha caught the panic in her voice. "What's going on, Jeannie?"

She explained about taking Will to his friend's home. "Mom, I don't know for sure, but I think that man might have driven past me as I walked home." She went on to explain the past hour then asked, "Have you noticed a smaller tan sedan cruising around lately?"

"Jeannie, I think I may have. I didn't pay much attention, but I certainly will after this." Martha went on warning and worrying. She couldn't keep the frustration from her voice.

"Mom, remember, the car that nearly side-swiped me? It was a smallish tan one, also. Do you suppose—"

"Oh God, Jeannie. It could have been, yes it could have!" Martha felt nauseous after hearing that new bit of information. Her daughter had come so close. She tried to find a few words of comfort for her if she could.

Jeannie listened for a short time then exclaimed, "Mom! I know what's really eating you alive. You want to do something. Harry had you settled down, but now—without him—I worry about you. You can't do those things any more, Mom—please!" After listening to Martha's story about entering that house, Jeannie gasped. "That shoe could mean something. What did that Tom say about it?"

Jeannie listened for another long moment. "The police can't go in there without just cause. So you want to go in there and do something. You want to make it so he has to call nine-one-one—fix him or something—is that it?" Knowing the forces within her mother, she cried out, "You must promise me you won't do anything so foolish." She couldn't help but add, "For sure, now, Mom?"

She heard the sound of the garage door rising. "Martin's home, now. Oh, thank God!" She felt her nerves settle almost instantly. "Mom. I'll call you later."

She clicked off and waited for the door to open. When Martin walked through the door, she threw herself into his arms and sobbed out the past hour to him.

ೞೞೞ

After Martha clicked off from her daughter, she felt a terrible fury rising within herself. She voiced her feelings aloud. "That monster has my entire family afraid to walk outside their homes, and Lizzie, too. They're afraid their every move will cause something hideous to happen." She wrung her hands and paced the floor, then firmed her jaw tight. "There's something about that man's place. I've got to go there again. I've just have to look around more closely. If he happens to be home, I'll attend to that, too." She wore a tight grin and her eyes narrowed.

She looked about for Detective Tom Wells. "I wonder if I could pull that vet business again. The man's no dummy, but then again, I'm not under arrest or anything. Basically, it's none of his damned business anyway." The sun had faded into dusk, and right now would be an opportune time right now to go check that house. She also wondered if Will had gotten home safely.

She called Jeannie back to find out. After a quick few words, she was satisfied all was well at the Moulton home. After another quick survey, she decided Tom was nowhere around. This puzzled her. To her, it seemed as though the man hounded her every step.

Feeling a touch of alarm, Martha stepped outside and began to search the grounds. Could that predatory devil have done something to Tom? She noticed the dogs were gone, too. "What's going on around here?" She voiced her apprehension into the soft blowing wind. His rugged old Bronco sat where he always parked it—he couldn't have gone far. Where on earth was that man?

She walked farther from the house, stopping to listen every few feet. After about a half hour of seeing no one, she turned back toward the house. It was then she heard the rattle of Skunk's collar chain and turned to see the faint shadow of a man and two dogs coming from the heavily wooded area down below the house.

She hurried back inside. She didn't want Tom to think she'd been worried about him. Maybe the dogs, but certainly not him. She slipped inside and decided to put the coffee on and fix something for dinner.

She heard him come clumping in and the familiar sounds of the dog's claws clicking on the tiled floor. He informed her, a half-smile across his lips. "I saw you out there looking for us."

"Excuse me, but I was hunting around for the dogs, that's all." Martha kept her back turned. She had opened a pack of hamburger to make some meat loaf. She got a cup to pour herself some of the fresh coffee. "Want a cup, then?"

"Why, I sure would. It smells real nice—fresh." He got a cup and came to stand next to her.

Martha poured the coffee and shoved it down the counter to him. She could smell the sweat on him from his hike with the dogs. That sharp male odor brought lingering memories of Harry flooding back to her. It filled her with such intense longing, she almost gasped aloud.

He moved away to sit at the kitchen table. Martha heaved a sigh of relief. "Have a nice walk with the dogs?"

"Were you worried about us, seeing as we were gone?" His voice was soft and low.

Martha didn't want to talk to him right now. She'd been on edge with worry and hadn't liked it. Caring about someone had never worked out for her, she knew that well enough. With family, it was different.

"I wondered where the dogs had gone, yes." She didn't like where this conversation was headed. "I'd begun to worry that nemesis of mine had shot them along with everyone else I have come to care about." She felt tears filling her eyes and kept her back turned.

"I have a very good idea what you are going through, ma'am. If you want to talk about it, I'd be glad to listen."

"If I did let you in on my feelings, you'd know I need to get back inside that ratty house in Longworth and look around. That's what's going through my mind right now. He could be the one who has driven past Will a few times, and now someone driving a tan car has been driving around my daughter's place, too." She felt a few tears drop onto the counter and grabbed a tissue to blot her eyes.

Tom leaped to his feet and came close. "Here now, ma'am, that's not all that's going on with you, now is it?" He took her by the shoulders and turned her to face him. "Tell me what's got you going like this."

Martha twisted away from his grasp. "You don't need to do that. I'm strong enough. It's just that I have to do something about this sorry predator business, and here you are, blocking my every move." She faced him, her tears unshed. "If Harry told you all about me, you'd know that."

"Yes, Martha, he told me as best he could. But there are some things no one can tell you. Some things you have to figure out for yourself." He uttered a half laugh. "You are one tough woman to get a line on, did he ever tell you that?"

"He never had to, we got along." She turned back to mixing the meatloaf, dismissing him and any help he had to offer. What she hadn't said was that she had been worried he might be one more casualty along with Harry.

Chapter 17

Tom rose from his chair. "Thanks for the coffee. I'll be in that room back there taking a shower. Martha heaved a sigh of relief as he left the kitchen. She wished he'd be some help to her. Why couldn't he go along and help her investigate that house? She decided to give it a try.

She whipped up a good sized batch of biscuits. If anything would soften a man's stubborn resolve, it might be those. With everything baking in the oven she set the table and made a salad. She decided when Detective Tom Wells made his appearance, she had something to say to him.

Tom appeared and took his usual seat at the kitchen table. He had rather settled in, appeared comfortable, and obviously enjoyed the fact of a woman cooking for him. Martha had spent plenty of time trying to figure out why this man was in her home. It had never made sense to her.

In no way would any responsible police department assign a full-fledged expensive detective as a personal body guard. If it was deemed necessary, she believed they usually assigned junior-grade officers, trained, but less expensive. And at no time did Martha believe it was necessary.

"Tom, I don't know why you're really here, and I don't want to hear any tall stories about it—or lies about your being assigned here. I never believed it in the first place. I know better than that." She set the meatloaf in the center of the table and turned to dish up the rest.

With the meal on the table, and over the stack of fluffy biscuits, he looked Martha in the eye. "You're no fool, lady, and that's the truth. But sorry, I am not at liberty to tell you everything as of now." He waited for her reply.

"That's ridiculous, and you know it!" Her temper flared and she felt her cheeks burning. "This whole scenario is beyond belief. To me, if not to you."

"I can't help how you see it, but I'm here for a while longer in any case."

Martha huffed about and let her disgust show on her face—she finally said, "If you're to be an anchor about my neck, you might at least make yourself useful."

"In any way I can."

She saw the mischievous twinkle in his eye, and it didn't set well with her. She found it disgusting.

"Really!" Martha decided to ask him what she wanted to know. "I need your help, if you'll condescend to give it." She took a deep breath. "I want to go back to that house, Tom. I know there's something there."

He had dished himself a generous plate. "I figured it was that. You'd lie to me and go anyway, wouldn't you? I'm glad you are letting me in on it."

"You wouldn't need to go in or do anything illegal for a man of the law, but it might be nice if someone heard my screams for help." Martha had a grin on her face that matched the lightness in her heart. This ornery law dog wouldn't stand in her way. It didn't sound right to her, but right now, she didn't plan to question him on it. She helped herself to the food, but her appetite had nearly disappeared in her excitement.

"I'd like to go tonight, Tom." She sipped her coffee.

"I'm ready. Seeing inside that house is on my list as well. But I'll play it your way."

Martha noticed nothing stopped the man from his food. He polished off several biscuits and all his meat loaf.

She left the table. "I'd best get ready then." She nearly ran to her bedroom and slipped into a pair of old, worn jeans, a big, sloppy sweatshirt, sneakers and then brushed her hair back under a baseball cap. The rest of her make-up was in the trunk of her car. She entered the kitchen and stood with her hands on her hips. "I'm all set, then.

Tom looked her over, nodded, and said, "You may be a grannie, ma'am, but to me, you look like a high school kid just now." He rose from the table and went to his room. "Be back in a minute."

Martha drove, and they were on their way. She carried a load of disbelief in her mind that he would come with her on a mission like this. "How can a man of the law get involved with a thing like this?"

"One day, I'll tell you everything, but Ebert thinks this way is best. His hands aren't too clean either if you want to know what I think." He hastened to add, "Not that he's in the wrong or doing anything illegal, but he is heavily influenced by what happened to Harry." He shook his head in the negative, giving thought to his partner's demise.

They entered the Longworth section of Denver. Martha drove past Rayburn McGill's home on Delgado Lane and on to another block. They did not see any vehicle in the driveway, and Martha heaved a sigh of relief. "Looks like he's not home again."

They parked, and Martha got out. "I need to get

something from the back, Tom." She opened the trunk then sat back in the car with a small bag, took out some dark make-up, and began applying it. "I don't know if this is needed, but I feel better with it on."

They left the vehicle and walked back to enter the alley behind Ray's house. She counted off the five houses and tried the gate. "It's locked this time."

"No problem." Tom whipped out a small leather case with a set of tools and quickly opened the gate. They entered the yard, encountered the same weeds and other objects left rotting on the ground.

"Messy dump," Martha said as she tripped over a half plastic bag of something lodged in the uncut grass. She led him to the back door. It too was locked.

Tom opened it with his little tool kit, and they entered. Martha whipped out her tiny light and cast the beam on the littered floor. They made their way carefully into the living room and on into the bedroom. Martha searched for the little patent leather shoe. She wanted Tom to see it.

She found it where she had left it and pointed at it with her light. "Looks like he doesn't know this shoe is here, Tom. Wouldn't that little item be deadly evidence against him?"

"It would if the parents identified it as Mindy's."

She pointed out the shirt. "It says Longworth Elementary School, right across the back, plain as day. That man works among little girls all day long."

Tom muttered something under his breath, but Martha didn't catch it.

"Wonder where this man goes at night? He wasn't home the last time I was in here, either." She remembered her fright as she'd barely made her escape that night. Somehow with Tom along, she didn't feel the same fear.

"Wonder what else we might find in here?" Tom moved into the living room and cast his own small light about. The place was messy. Paper wrappers of fast food lay about. He saw the edge of an envelope sticking out. "What do we have here?" He pulled the envelope out, and read the address. "Here's something. This letter was mailed from Florence, Colorado. That's up by Canon City. Big prison complexes up around there."

"Who sent it? Can you read it?"

"Nothing written on here, only Rayburn's address." He scanned the envelope again. "Wonder if it means anything?"

Martha felt a cold shiver run down her back. "There is someone up there on death row that I know." She wanted out of the place and fast. "Tom, a man I fixed is up there on death row. He had raped a little girl in Colorado Springs, and I heard him talking about it to another of the same sort. After that, I stalked him until I saw my chance. The police arrested him in his hospital bed. He had a bundle of hair ribbons from his little victims, some with hair and blood on them. He had murdered little girls all over the country. They got him on more than one sample of DNA from those ribbons, and, of course, the little girl he raped in Colorado Springs actually identified him."

"Sheese!" Tom interjected. "I say let's get the hell out of this place. He's bound to come home soon." As they retraced their steps, he locked the back door and the gate to the alley. They walked on to the car.

Tom settled in the car. "You know, that house has got to be checked and gone over by forensics. It's a veritable gold mine—it sure as hell is." He turned to look at Martha. "No wonder Ebert wants you handled with kid gloves. You, yourself, are a gold mine. In your own way, you manage to provide vital information and have certainly helped the authorities in the past."

"You mean by breaking and entering?" She said nothing about the kid gloves comment, but it didn't go unnoticed. "Ebert, huh?" she muttered.

Tom laughed, and she saw the way his throat looked as they passed a random street light. *He has a lot of strength, but he seems a gentle sort.* And once again she thought of Duke, an old navy SEAL friend of her and her late husband, Bob's. This man was much like Duke in his gentle strength.

"You must meet some friends of mine, Tom," Martha said. "They live in Denver, too."

"I guess it wouldn't hurt. You're letting me in a little bit—including me in some of your life, now—are you?"

"As long as you let me alone to do what I must. I'm not quite as young now, but I have the strength of two when I need it."

"I've heard about that, too."

She saw his teeth flash as he uttered a soft laugh. But her mind was on the place they'd just left.

"Why didn't we wait around and get the license plate of his current vehicle?" she said. "Wouldn't it help put his story together a little better?"

"I say we drive back and see if that's possible. If it's muddied over, I'll clean it off and get it. Actually, it ought to be the same plates, but not if he has a car now, when he had a truck before. They should have different plates."

"What if they don't?" Martha asked.

"I'd say he didn't give a damn about doing it right."

"Let's go back and take a look. We can stop for coffee if he's not home." She needed to know if he was the one driving around Jeannie's home, and maybe her home too. Aside from thoughts swirling about in her head that she wouldn't want Tom to even guess at, she wanted to know if this license plate matched the car driving around Jeannie's. That would be proof the man on Delgado Lane was the stalker out to destroy Martha's life.

"Suits me," Tom said, a slight smile on his lips that Martha could see by a passing street light.

She wheeled the car around a handy corner and turned back to re-enter the City of Denver. Nothing was said between them as she returned to the Longworth area. She turned to cruise down Delgado and saw a small tan car sitting in the driveway. A light shone from the grimy window.

"Let me out here on the corner and come around the block," he said. "I'll take down the license number and meet you out at that corner. Cruising slowly down Delgado might set him to worrying."

She saw his teeth gleam in the dimness of the street light as he departed her car.

When Tom re-entered her car, she asked, "Did you get it?"

"Sure thing. When we get back to the house, I'll check it out."

They headed back to Harry's house—that's what it was to Martha—with almost nothing being said.

Passing a small drive-in eatery, Tom said. "You want a coffee?"

She didn't want to get any closer to this man than she had to, but wanting to portray a cooperative persona, she replied, "I guess I could use a cup."

Doing anything with Tom set her off. She didn't know what he was about, why he was at her home, and where he'd come from. She didn't know any of those things, and he wasn't spilling. It was that very secrecy that made her suspicious of him and his every move—this one, too.

She parked and fixed her make-up to as near normal as she could under the circumstances. Tom ushered her in just like they were on a date. That pissed her off, too, but she hid it the best she could. They took a booth and a waitress handed them each a slightly tattered menu.

Tom studied his a while then looked at her. "Having anything besides coffee?"

"No, coffee's fine with me. I use cream," she told him.

Tom gave the order and included a hunk of cherry pie with his coffee.

"Hungry, are you? Didn't get enough meat loaf?" Martha had to smile with her question. She knew full well that a man his size would always be hungry.

They finished their coffees, Tom polished off his pie, paid the bill, and they left to continue on to the house.

He said, his voice soft and gentle, "I'll bet your cherry pie would lay that one in the shade, Martha."

"Or you'd think I was trying to poison you." She laughed heartily, and it felt good to her. She hadn't laughed about anything for a long time.

They entered the house, petted the dogs, and Martha said good night to him. She went to her and Harry's bedroom. The big wide bed was empty, and she wanted to weep once again for her loss but found the tears wouldn't come.

Chapter 18

Martha was desperate to get something done. She had the supply of Neutersol she'd kept hidden in her dresser, and her intended target was that man who lived on Delgado Lane. Feeling close to ninety-nine percent sure he was a child predator, she would use it. If this drug did anything at all to help prevent the kidnapping and rape of another child, she was ready to use it. And this was one venture she didn't plan to share with Tom Wells.

He'd willingly gone along with their invasion and investigation of the man's home. But Martha knew he'd want no part of this little venture. She also knew by instinct, and the things she'd seen in that home, that the man in that house was a prime suspect. If not for the rape and murder of Mindy Lassen, then how many others were there that were unknown to the authorities? If the police came to his home to investigate a crime against the man, they would find enough evidence laying about in that house to send him up for murder, she was sure of that.

Her immediate problem was to find a way to evade the ever present Detective Tom Wells. Wondering how to do the deed and get home unscathed without his knowing, took many hours racking her brain to find a way. The supplies were easy. She had plenty of access to syringes, so no problem there.

She had no sand bag, but that wouldn't be too big a problem. Martha had already decided to get one ready. She'd sew one up and fill it with small pebbles. It had worked well enough before. How well she remembered whacking the bag across the face of an older male. He'd been a predatory grown male, posing as a young teenager set upon a fun night with a silly girl his age. Martha felt increasingly strong and in charge, or maybe it was Serena.

The thought of what she had in mind had brought a flush to her cheeks, and her excitement did not go unnoticed by Tom Wells. He wisely said nothing, but Harry had put him wise to how Martha and her alter ego, Serena, worked. He knew that nothing short of handcuffs would stop her when she had a mission. Tom was very certain that Martha/Serena had something in mind. She would resort to any sneaky trick to throw him off her trail when she was ready.

He quietly left her alone unless he had meals with her or they went somewhere together, but he was fully on alert. And, in spite of it all, he knew he'd enjoy the whole scenario of her subterfuge and tricks. With a greatly increased sense of excitement of his own, he waited to see her in action.

When Martha felt ready, she waited until early evening. Dinner was past when Lizzie called Martha by their prior arrangement. When she got the call, Martha answered, "Yes, Dr. Gleason, I'll be right there." She looked at Tom. "I don't think I'll be long. He's trying to deliver some pups, and the bitch is in trouble. The family just brought her in." She grabbed her coat. "I think he's planning a C-section on her. She's an old dog, and he expects trouble." She nearly ran out the door with her purse flying through the air behind her.

Tom sat in the kitchen, a smile on his face. "Now, why don't I believe that woman?" He didn't. She'd been way too agitated, and the color in her cheeks too high. She was up to something. He waited about one half hour and went to his vehicle, saying, "Yes, Harry, I hear you way up there. I'm keeping an eye on her."

He often thought of his memories of a very fine man. Smiling at his remembrance of the lost detective, he knew Harry had been one of the best men he'd ever known, and he owed that man his life in the bargain.

He entered his Ford Bronco and headed into Denver. *Let's see what the little lady has up her sleeve.* He laughed in anticipation of the night ahead. He knew where she was headed and didn't hurry.

Tom didn't want her to catch sight of him, nor did he want to face her fury if she knew he was following her. He was in no hurry—what she had in mind took a bit of time. Would she wait until her target went to sleep? Could she do her business well enough if he was in his bed? Tom felt no pity for the miscreant in that house— none at all.

He stayed well away. She'd go in by the alley, he was sure of that. But if that gate was locked? He smiled to himself, wondering how she would handle that little problem. He neared Delgado Lane, parked a block away, and locked his Bronco.

He wore dark clothing, hoping to avoid her notice if he got too close. As he walked slowly past the little house, he noted the man was home tonight and also awake. A couple of lights gleamed through the fly-specked windows, and Tom figured the man either watched TV or read a book.

Had Martha already entered the place? He wondered as he moved carefully along the street. A sliver of moonlight, and some light from a few nearby street lights, gave Tom enough vision for his purpose tonight.

He continued down the street and turned the corner to the right, seeking the entrance to the alley. Once in the alley, he neared the gate of the fifth house. He heard a muffled thump near the gate and felt his pulse rise. "What the hell is going on?" He moved closer and saw the gate was closed. He tried it and found it locked. Looking through the slats, he saw a dark figure move close to the house and the back door, in particular. He knew what had made the thump he'd heard, and muttered softly to himself, "That dizzy dame has climbed over the gate and jumped down inside the yard!"

He heard a slight tinkling of glass and smiled. "God almighty, she's busted the window on that door. It must have been locked, too." He quickly picked the gate lock and entered the back yard in time to see her figure disappear through the back door. "Way to go, woman!" he whispered.

He crept close to the door. She had left it slightly ajar—he went in and moved along the narrow hall. Listening intently, he heard the TV playing softy, but nothing else. He moved closer to see what Martha was up to.

ⓔⓈⓔ

Martha felt her heart beating double time. It had been a while since she'd been active. She wondered, *Am I up to this*? But when she felt the flow of strength from her alter ego, she knew she could handle this stringy-looking dude any day of the week. After quietly setting her bag down, she slowly removed a long bag made of a burlap-like material. It was very heavy, but she'd handled it quite a bit in her bedroom before tonight. She wasn't one to leave anything to chance.

"Keep sitting in your chair, mister. I have something for you," she murmured to herself as she raised the bag high. But as she made ready to swing it, he moved his head to the side as he reached for his drink. She'd only grazed him—not enough to knock him out.

Martha raised it high again, but he leaped from the chair and turned to face her, surprise and shock across his face. She heard the surprise and fear in his voice as he cried out, "Who'n the hell are you?"

She swung that bag with all she had and hit him across his face. His hands were up, but they did little to stop the force of the bag of rocks. He dropped to the floor, knocking the table off its legs. It spilled his can of beer and upset the table lamp. The lamp kept on burning, however, and luckily, it cast a bright glow just where she needed it.

As she knelt over the man, she smelled the rich malty aroma of the brew that leaked from the overturned can. He seemed to be out, and she heaved a sigh of relief. "Good, you're out, let's get this done." She stretched his flaccid body out, so it lay straight, and knelt down, her bag handy. After unbuckling his belt, and unbuttoning his pants, she unzipped him. Then she quickly drew his work pants, and under shorts down to his ankles and turned him to his right side. Shoving his left leg high did a good job of revealing his testicles.

Martha reached into the bag and brought out two large syringes. Donning rubber gloves, she grasped one testicle and injected the full amount into the meaty interior of it. She then repeated the same procedure with the other one.

"I hope this works, or at least does something to put a halt to this devil's activities." She had to roll him about to pull his clothes up to cover his nakedness. She zipped up his trousers, but didn't bother to button the top button or fasten his belt. She kicked him in several places, including his testicles, and snarled at his inert form. "If this works as it is supposed to, you won't notice any extra soreness down below, you'll just hurt all over."

Ray started groaning and moving about. Martha quickly packed her equipment, stripped off her gloves, and shoved them into the pack. As she headed out the back door, she stepped in some glass and hoped the dazed man didn't hear it crunch beneath her heavy boots.

She reached the back gate and tossed her bag over it, found an old box, and used it to climb over the gate. "Wish I knew how to pick a lock like Tom does," she murmured as she jumped down. She landed hard and felt a sudden stab of pain down her left lower leg.

The pain in that leg nearly knocked her off her feet. She could barely walk as she moved down the alleyway, but fear of discovery kept her moving and dragging her left leg as she sought the sanctuary of her car. "Must have sprained something with that last jump," she murmured.

She couldn't stop a heavy groan. It hurt so badly she wanted to scream. The pain went all the way to her hip, and she limped even more. "Hurts like crazy, but I've got to make it to my car."

She kept going, limping painfully. "He must have awakened by now. I don't hear any sirens. He's probably afraid to call the cops," she said, relieved. "I would be, too, if I was him."

She finally dragged herself to her car and crawled in. The pain had become excruciating by now. "Could I have broken something?" she wondered aloud as she used her hands to grasp her painful leg and move it into position for driving. Martha was thankful she hadn't injured her right leg. She needed that leg for the drive home.

ᥫᩛᥫᩛ

Ray struggled awake enough to see the light from the TV and hear the words of an announcer giving the local weather report. He pushed himself to a sitting position. "What the hell happened? Who was in here?" He hurt all over, especially his face. He touched his nose and, when he held his hand out, saw the blood, he guessed it was from his nose. "It hurts like a son of a bitch there, too!"

He tried to get up and sit in his chair. "Shit-damn, I hurt all over. Somebody was in here. I saw him. Little bastard, it was. I oughta call the damned cops." He thought about it, but in checking himself over, everything moved, his arms, his legs, and he got his breath right enough. "Maybe I won't call those bastards—don't want no truck with the likes of them."

He struggled into his chair and sat for a little while, shaking his head. "Damn, I hurt all over—everywhere. Why'n hell would some son-of-a-bitch come in here and beat the shit out of me?" He felt confused. "Did he take anything?" He put his head back and shut his eyes for a few minutes. He tried to think but couldn't get his brain to work. Nothing made any sense right now. He needed time to get his head on straight. His small table was over-turned, and the lamp lay on the floor glowing away as if nothing had happened.

ᥫᩛᥫᩛ

Tom had remained behind. He stood quietly inside a closet in Ray's house, curious to see the effects of what Martha had done to this man. And more than that, he was curious about what, exactly, she had done. He hadn't seen any blood, and there ought to have been some if she'd castrated this man. Did she do the same to this man as she had done to several others? He was puzzled and very anxious to question her about it. He also wondered, *Why the syringes?* It didn't fit with anything he'd ever heard about her activities.

Finally, after sitting for nearly a half hour, Ray got up and staggered to his bathroom. "Need somethin' for pain and sure as hell for sleep." He knocked several bottles off the shelf of his wall cabinet before selecting a couple of pills. "Advil. Take two for severe pain. I got that all right." He downed the pills without water, staggered into the bedroom, and fell onto the bed.

Tom wanted to cover the poor dude but decided that he ought to just leave. He'd done what he planned for this evening and made his way quietly toward the back door. He ignored the broken glass and made his way to the gate. He opened it, went through, and locked it behind him, wondering if Martha had done her little jump-over on her way out, same as on her way in.

She'd miss seeing his vehicle when she drove into her driveway. "She'll wonder where I am, when she gets home, and I'm not there." It bothered him some but couldn't be helped. He'd have it out of her, everything out on the table before bedtime tonight in any case. He'd make damned sure of that.

Shaking his head at the kind of woman he was dealing with, he chuckled. "Harry didn't tell me half of what this babe is about."

❧❧❧

Martha pulled into her drive. She saw the dogs wiggling about and wagging their tails but no sign of Tom. Her leg hurt so badly by now, she didn't care where he was or what he thought. She struggled to drag herself out of the car and then limped heavily into the house. "I'll need to see a doctor about this, but I hurt too much to drive myself into Hillsdale tonight. I just want to sleep. She limped into the living room and lay on the couch.

After a brief struggle, she got her injured leg up higher on a cushion. The elevation relieved some of her pain, and she lay back, panting from the effort. Martha wondered again where Tom was at this time of night, but she hurt too much to really care. Nor did she care what Tom would have to say if he ever came home.

Suddenly, she heard his Bronco crunch on the graveled drive and tried to prepare herself for the onslaught of his inquisition. She knew there'd be one. Her heart rate increased as she waited to hear his footsteps. He was coming—

She shut her eyes as though asleep.

Tom wasn't fooled by her sham sleep. She heard him pull up a chair, right close beside where she lay. "Okay, Miss Martha, tell me all about it." He nudged her shoulder. "I know phony sleep when I see it." He looked down at the pathetic figure with the flattened hair, and that godawful make-up she'd used to blacken her face.

Martha opened her eyes and saw the concern on his face, along with a slight grin he tried to conceal. "What I do is no concern of yours, mister, and it never has been." She was so glad to see him, it nearly overwhelmed her, but she'd die before she'd let him know it. Her left lower left leg was pounding severely and throbbed to the point that she wanted to burst into tears.

"I beg to differ with you, ma'am. I've got a job to do, and you are making it tough as hell."

"What job? And what do you want to know?"

"I don't need to know a lot more than what I saw, but I do wonder what you did to that poor soul on Delgado Lane."

Martha rose up on her elbows. "You saw?" she gasped. "Are you saying you were there—in that house?"

"Of course. I know a lie when I hear it. I knew right away you weren't going to the vet's place. I made sure, of course. I knew where you were going and followed you."

He gave her a look that let her know she wasn't dealing with an idiot.

"I might have known." She sank back on the couch cushion she rested on. "You saw everything?"

He leaned over her, his eyebrows narrowing with his query. He wisely avoided a chuckle at the way she looked with her overdone make-up. It was a good idea of hers, not wanting to be recognizable. "I didn't see any blood, Martha, so what the hell did you do?"

"I learned about a new substance used on animals," she said. "Dr. Gleason doesn't use it, and he told me to destroy it—of course, I didn't." From then on, she explained about Neutersol and what she hoped to gain from its use. "If he loses his sexual urges, it might save some poor child. I did what I did tonight because I feel certain he was the one who murdered that poor Lassen child." She frowned. "But I admit, this is the first time I did this sort of thing without absolute proof. I am sure of his guilt, because of that little shoe, that he works at the school, and has followed me and scoped out Will at least twice. But that's not absolute proof is it? And yes, that lack bothers me plenty, it truly does."

"I see your point about that. And if I believed you were mistaken about the man, I would have stopped you, Martha." He grinned down at her as she lay before him. "That fact makes me as guilty as you, if we were wrong about him." He patted her shoulder to comfort her in her guilt before he added another little item. "You didn't button his pants or buckle his belt. He might remember that when he wakes up."

Martha frowned. "I did overlook that, but mostly I hope he hurts enough to overlook how his gonads feel. But since I put some Novocain in along with the Neutersol, it wouldn't be apparent right away." She'd worried about that little slip, but the man was waking up right then, and she had to get out of there. She looked at Tom. "I hurt my leg when I jumped down from the gate on my way out. I walked on it so it can't be broken, but I must have gotten a heck of a sprain." She indicated her left lower leg. "Maybe I should see a doctor about it."

He bent down to touch her leg. "I have some experience with these things. Mind if I take a look?"

Only slightly surprised at the extent of his knowledge, she agreed. "Turn away so I can remove a few things then." Tom obliged her, and Martha struggled enough to get her jeans pulled down but couldn't get them off. "I guess I'll need a bit of help with these, Tom."

She felt her face flame up, but there was no other option. Pulling a small snuggle blanket off the couch, she covered her hips with it.

Tom deftly pulled the jeans off, which action gave Martha the feeling he was awfully good at it. He bent down to have a look at her leg. Seeing the dark bruising on the lower left, he touched it gingerly. "This hurt?"

"It does."

He pressed about on several areas and moved her foot in several directions. "You have a heck of a sprain, but certainly not a broken bone. I can almost be sure of it by your pain level. A broken bone is excruciating, and your injury is painful, but not like that."

"I know about things like that myself, and I think you're right. A doctor could do no more than prescribe pain medication. If I could down a couple of Advil to get me through the night..." she said and trailed off. "I want to get into my bed, but I could barely walk before. I don't know how it'd be now."

"No problem." He scooped her up in his arms. "Where's your room?"

Martha felt like a silly school girl, but Tom was big and strong, and her weight meant nothing to a man of his strength. He carried her to her room and gently deposited her on the bed. She refused to mention her need to use the bathroom, and he didn't think of it.

"Thanks for the lift, Tom."

"No problem. Call me anytime if you need me—for anything." He raised his eyebrows a touch before he left the room and closed the door.

Martha sat on the edge of the bed for a long moment. "I've got to make it to the bathroom for several reasons."

She got to her feet and limped painfully into the bathroom, washed her face of all the make-up she could, and downed a couple of pain pills. Making it back to bed, she soon found oblivion.

Chapter 19

Ray roused himself enough to get up from his rumpled bed. "Damn! I hurt like a son-of-a-bitch! My face—oh God! My head!" He made it to the mirror. "I look like I've been in a street fight." He passed urine and noticed even that hurt a little. "What the hell was that guy in here for, anyway? I got nothing anybody'd want." He tried to remember more about his intruder—not a big man, the face was blackened, and a baseball cap covered most of the face. Was it even a man at all? "Had a hell of a swing, I know that for damn sure."

He made it to the kitchen and fixed a cup of coffee. It hurt to drink it, as it burned and stung his swollen and puffy lips. The ugly redness across his face had the beginnings of blue-shaded bruising. He examined his face in the mirror. "Don't think my nose is broken, but it looks like a damned light bulb. Ought to see a doc, but it ain't worth it. I'll call in sick for today." Ray had some pride in his looks, and he was reluctant to be seen looking this way, in spite of the scars and pits from his youthful acne.

He sat in his chair and turned on the TV. Nothing of interest came on, but he liked the background noise it gave. He made his call to the school, feeling disappointment at missing the excitement he always got from watching the little blonde first-grade girl. Ray always looked for her, spending more time sweeping the halls if he thought he'd catch sight of her, walking and chatting with her little friends. At times like that, he was transported into fantasies of how he'd take her and what he'd do to that soft little body.

He sat staring at the TV screen, his pain and misery overshadowing all other thought. He hurt all over, and it kept him from seeing or relating to anything on the TV. He kept going back to his intruder of last night. *Why did he choose this house—why me? What was the reason for the attack?* Ray held his head in his hands, and even that hurt like hell. No matter how hard he tried, he couldn't figure out what had happened to him, or why. "Shit-damn, my life is going down the toilet so damned fast, I can't keep track of anything. A man's got no chance. Nobody's safe anymore, not even in his own damned home."

℮∂℮∂

Martha awakened to the sun glaring against the drawn shades, creating the soft glow of early morning light. She struggled to the edge of the bed and looked down at her left leg. "It's swollen and blue. Wonder if it will bear my weight this morning." She wriggled off the bed and stood up. With most of her weight on the right leg, she hobbled to the bathroom. "It could be worse," she murmured as she washed and dressed. Pulling her jeans on took some work, but satisfied, she hobbled to the kitchen. The smell of coffee met her as she sat in a chair.

"Here's a cup for you." Tom placed a steaming cup before her. He'd even put the milk in it as she always did.

She looked up at him. "Thanks."

He had questions and looked at her for answers. "What now, Martha?"

"I don't know. Where will he strike next? Who does he have in his sights? Whoever is doing this must be stopped. I think we both believe he's a murderer, Tom."

She hurt so bad all of a sudden she wanted to cry out, and it wasn't because of her leg.

"Need some Advil again?"

"Yes, but I don't care if I hurt a little, I'm worried about my daughter, her husband, and Will."

"Has anything more happened?"

"No, maybe he's done with them. He'll be after me next. And I have to say, I'd much rather have it that way. I want to face him and have it out."

"Let's hope he waits until your leg improves."

She smiled at that comment as she asked, "Have you heard anything more from Colorado Springs?"

"I have, and I think we are on the right track." He took the chair opposite from her. "It seems our friend, Rayburn McGill, has paid two visits to your old friend, Denny Garver."

Martha felt a shock zip through her at what he'd said. "Oh, my God! Anything else on him? Is he a known child predator?" Remembering that little shoe, she felt her face tighten.

"I haven't heard anything more about him that way. He must go by different names in other communities, so it's harder to keep track. Even social security numbers can be phony or from people who died years ago. But I have little doubt this man has a nasty history." He held back a smile as he talked. "I keep wondering what your little treatment of him will do? How it will affect his sexual activities? You must wonder that, yourself."

"Of course, I do. The doctor told me he doesn't use the product because while it may stop the procreation of new animals, it doesn't seem to stop the aggressiveness of the male. He likes to be sure that any product he uses works all the way, or he won't use it."

"We need to find a way to get the police into that house." Tom scratched his head and looked at Martha. "Any ideas?"

"How about a fire?" She only said it for conversation, but it was an idea. "Or, shots fired in the air to frighten the neighbors enough to call the cops."

"Maybe, but we need something of a criminal nature and an impending arrest to have the house gone over by forensics." He poured another coffee and sat back down. "Can you imagine what's on that man's computer?"

Martha shivered. "I don't think I could ever look at things like that. Tom, I have seen a few of the children after they have been abused." The image of poor, battered, little Aliya Pederson, a lovely black-haired four-year-old had been etched into her memory forever, and this conversation brought it back in full force. She remembered the hideous things that child had suffered and felt herself grow cold.

"What's going through your mind, Martha? You look like you've seen a ghost." Tom's concern for her was on his face and in his voice.

"Just remembering a patient, Tom. One we lost."

"I'm sorry to hear it." He didn't ask for details as he couldn't bear to hear them, either. It was closer to home for him than Martha could ever guess.

"We'll never get rid of all of them, will we?" Martha said.

"No." He got up and looked out the window. "I wish you were up for a walk. It's wonderful out there." He looked back at her. "So, Harry left you this place, did he?"

"Yes. I'd much rather have him along with it, but it's a nice place with the Rockies looking so close, patches of snow still up there and all the trees down lower. He used to keep horses, he told me." She got up and hobbled a bit. "If you'll keep an eye on me, I'd like to walk outside a bit. Nothing is broken, and it feels better today." She limped to the door, and Tom followed.

They walked together out back of the burned out barn, and on into the wooded area beyond. Her leg hurt like crazy, but the freshness of the soft breeze seemed like a healing balm for her troubled soul. Out here, everything seemed unblemished and clean. The mountains soaring high above them were majestic today, with the highest peaks gleaming in the sunshine. A few snowy patches were still visible, even in the summer air.

She kept on as long as she could, but when they came to a handy stump, she sat down. "My leg is killing me, but it's wonderful out here, especially today, for some reason." She laughed. "Maybe I'm just glad to be alive after all that has happened—and all that I've lost."

Tom sat nearby and gathered a few pine cones. He said, looking at them in his hands, "I've always liked the way these things look. Each tree has a different sort of cone. Did you know the giant redwoods have a very small one, only about one inch long?"

"You're kidding me." She wondered about the man sitting so near—why he watched out for her, why he was there at all, and what Harry had to do with it. If Tom's being here to watch over her was Harry's wish, his idea, she couldn't figure why his department allowed Tom this much time away from his regular duties. Something didn't add up to Martha, but she couldn't ask. She believed he'd eventually tell her.

Martha sat on that stump, lost in dreaming. It felt like heaven having no worries, at least not at this moment. She wished it could go on for the rest of this lovely day, but nothing lasted forever. Martha shook herself and said,

"We'd best get back." She rose to her feet, but her leg had stiffened from the walk. When she took a step, she nearly fell, but Tom was right behind her and swept her up into his arms.

"Looks like I'll need to carry you back to the house. And it's uphill, too."

Her head lay against his chest. When he laughed, his big solid throat moved with it, and the deep rumbling sound came through to her. She was comforted by it and mesmerized as well. Feeling like an idiot, she fought those emotions. She felt the heat as her face flame up like fire, but her leg hurt so much, she said nothing and let him carry her back to the house.

છાજછા

Ray stayed off work a few more days before he returned to his janitorial work at the Longworth Elementary School. Looking in his mirror, he saw only a few scant remains of the bruising across his face, and his nose had nearly returned to normal. Everything seemed to be all right again. Yet, inside he carried the emotional scars of having had his home invaded. How could anyone feel safe after that? He was shaken and on edge by the attack on his person, too. But as he discovered, time had a way of easing even that.

Each day at work, as was his habit, he looked for the sight of the small blonde first-grade girl. Usually, when he saw her, he would become aroused to the point he had to stay behind his work cart for fear his bulging erection would show. But somehow, lately, she didn't seem to affect him in quite the same way. Maybe he was lucky, because a thing like that in a school full of young kids could get him fired. He'd heard of it happening at other schools he'd worked at.

Ray was puzzled by it. A thing like this had never happened to him before. He tried to ignore his lack of excitement and muttered aloud to himself, "I must be getting old or something. Something seems to be missing inside me. Could it be because of the way I was attacked right inside my own home, and for no good reason?"

Walking along the corridor, pushing his cleaning cart, he saw the little girl trip and fall down on her face. Her book and papers went spilling out to cascade across the floor. Ray rushed over to assist her to her feet. His hands were on her little arms. They felt warm and soft, smooth to his touch. He set her on her feet and looked into her wide, frightened eyes. "Are you all right, little one? Are you hurt anywhere?"

"Fank you, Mr. Man," she said, tears brimming in her lovely blue eyes.

A female teacher came to take her hand. She looked at Ray, a question on her face.

"She fell down, ma'am. I had to see if she was okay."

Nodding her head in thanks to Ray, the teacher gathered the strewn papers and led the little girl away, crooning soft, comforting words to sooth the upset child.

As Ray watched her walk away, he felt no rise of excitement, no increase of pulse rate, and no urge he had to work so hard to control. Puzzled, he felt fear rising inside himself and worried. *This is not the way it usually is with me, nothing is happening like it ought to be.* He moved away from the scene, deep in thoughts completely new to him as he tried to understand what had happened.

His immediate reaction to this unexpected encounter with a target of interest had been completely flat. He'd watched that child so often. She was the very one he'd had unhealthy and compelling designs on—that little soft body he'd had so many torrid sexual fantasies about. Today, he had actually touched the little girl and felt the softness of her skin. He'd had no reaction—nothing had happened—why?

Ray felt a terrible fear take hold. It surged to the point he forgot everything else, including the sight of the little blonde child. Restless, frustrated, and unsure of himself, he wrung his hands. *Something's not right— nothing's right with me anymore.* He went back to work, mumbling, "Am I getting old?"

Ray had worked at schools in other states, several of them, in fact. He'd never been caught by the authorities for anything he'd done to one of those nice little bodies when he'd gotten the chance. He'd usually moved to another state quickly after each kidnapping and sexual assault. But, sick of always moving, he'd decided to wait after this last event and see if the authorities would take notice of him.

They didn't.

His association with Denny Garver had happened several years ago in Illinois. They'd even shared one experience. Ray gave thought to some of those events, hoping for the same titillation he'd always had in thinking about it, but it wasn't there anymore. Something had gone missing inside him.

Finally, tired of trying to feel normal again, he gave up. Everything in his life seemed to have changed. Alarmed, he decided something must be wrong with him—he wasn't the same anymore.

Afraid he'd learn of some dreaded condition, he knew he had to find out and sought the services of a doctor.

❧❧❧

A few days later, Ray entered the offices of Dr. Erwin Cantor, urologist. His nerves, tense and stretched to the breaking point with anxiety and a lot of fear, made Ray's hands shake. He felt tight all over.

After a close examination, the doctor looked at him, a puzzled expression on his face. "Mr. McGill, I've never seen anything quite like this. For some reason, your testicles have shriveled up internally. They are barely palpable on examination. Your scrotal sac is limp and appears practically empty. I'm surprised you haven't noticed the emptiness."

"I guess I was too upset about how I felt inside to notice. What are you saying? Have my balls gone bad or something?"

"I don't know what to think. Have you had any sort of trauma to that area or any recent disease process that might have settled there?"

"Not that I know of, Doc." Ray felt his heart rate go double time as he tried to figure out what could have happened to him. He tried to think how he could have gotten hurt but couldn't. *The break-in couldn't be it— could it? I was all right down there afterward. A bit sore, but—*

"Someone broke into my house a while back," he told the doctor. "Knocked me out for a while, hurt my face, and kicked me in the slats, but no more than that."

"Did you call the police?"

"No, never thought of it. It's a sort of rough neighborhood where I live, but I haven't heard of anyone else having a home invasion like that."

The doctor shrugged. "Well, let's watch this for a while. Maybe it will reverse itself in time. I haven't seen this sort of thing before, so I can't be sure what will happen, without knowing the cause." He scribbled on his prescription pad, ripped the page off, and handed it to

Ray. "You can give this a try. It's testosterone. Can't hurt, might help. Just follow the directions on the bottle."

He ushered Ray out and told the girl to make him an appointment for one month from now. She asked Ray what day and time would work for him, scribbled his time and date on a card, and handed it to him. Shaken and fearful, Ray left the doctor's office.

Driving home, he puzzled over what he'd learned. "Could it have been something that happened while I was out like a damned light?" He wracked his brain over all the details he could remember. Finally, he drove into his yard. He hadn't gotten the medication and wondered what good it would do if he did. He felt sick all over, useless, and defeated. A light had gone out of his life. "I'm all washed up," he moaned.

Later that evening, as he undressed for bed, he remembered a small detail that had seemed unimportant at the time. "My damned pants were unbuttoned, and the belt was unbuckled. I was zipped up, but those things were left undone, now that I think of it. I hurt so damned much right then, I didn't give a damn."

He sank into his unmade bed, hoping those two pills he'd taken would do their job. "Who could have done something to me, and what exactly did they do?"

Chapter 20

Will came walking quietly into his home, apparently deep in thought. His mother had stood in the window watching him all the way down the street, up the steps, and into the house. He nodded to her and sat down with his books. Seeing his overly quiet demeanor, Jeannie feared something wasn't right with her son.

"How was school today, son?"

She received the usual non-committal reply. "Everything's fine, Mom."

"Oh, no, it's not, Will. I know that look on your face. Tell me what's going on. Things have been pretty quiet for a while. Are we getting careless?" She needed an answer and waited until she got one.

"It's just that we visited another school today. One of their janitors looked familiar—you know, with those same pit marks on his face as the guy who drove past me a couple of times. I stayed behind one of the kids—didn't want him to notice me. He didn't either, I'm pretty sure."

"You thought he was the same man?" Alarmed, she realized that if, indeed, this was the man, he worked among small children. "Which school was it, Will?"

"It was over in the cruddy part of town, you know,

Longworth, that school." She saw the look of distaste on his face and hoped her son was not becoming a snob because he went to a different, and no doubt better, school.

"Well, do your homework. I'll mention this to your daddy. You certainly have a good eye for things—details and such—don't you?"

Will nodded, pleased with the praise. Jeannie settled him with a snack and his books. In her bedroom, she called her mother. "Mom, Will may have seen the man who was giving him the once over from his car that first time. He saw him the second time, from a truck, you know, the one with the camper."

"Tell me about it," Martha replied,

After Jeannie mentioned Will's trip to the Longworth Elementary school, Martha felt an icy chill come over her. "Jeannie, I may know who you're talking about, and I happen to know he's a janitor at that school, too."

"And how do you know anything like that?" Jeannie demanded to know.

"Never mind how I know. This is important news, dear. More than you will ever know." Martha looked about for Tom. He had to contact the police or find some way for them to investigate that house. That man was already a known danger if that little patent leather shoe was any indication. She hurried to end her conversation with Jeannie and looked about for Tom.

She also 'wondered how those shots of Neutersol had affected that scrawny man who lived on Delgado Lane. Surely by now, he would have noticed some changes. Her curiosity ran rampant, but there was no way in this world she could ever find out something of that nature. Now that her leg had mostly healed, she stamped her foot in frustration.

Tom came sauntering through the door, his movements slow and leisurely, and an unhurried attitude which aggravated Martha in her impatience to see something done. The man Will had seen today was a potential danger to those children at Longworth Elementary school. Martha looked at him, her eyes narrowing. *What would cause enough violence against the man on Delgado Lane to attract the police and have them do an investigation of him and his dwelling?*

Tom understood the look on Martha's face as he surveyed the situation in the kitchen. *Now, what has the little lady got brewing in that mind of hers?* He was sure it dealt with ways and means of going after the man on Delgado. He said nothing, merely waited.

Martha wanted to snap at him but knew it would gain nothing. He was playing her, and she knew it. She had to do things his way, and it made her temper soar. He'd caught her in every lie and ploy she'd used in doing what that mischievous inner person had urged.

The situation was serious, of course, but he couldn't help egging her on when he had a chance. She had treated him like a damned non-person for way too long. She needed him—what he knew, and what he could do. But, he finally gave in and asked, "What's on your mind, Martha?"

"Something has to be done to get the police to investigate that house from top to bottom. Finding the little shoe alone will be enough to get him off the streets and out of that grade school."

"That's saying the parents identify it as little Mindy's."

"Well, yes, I suppose you're right on that," Martha conceded.

"I'm right on a lot of things, Martha."

Martha ignored that remark and went on to her point of interest. "So how can we bring this about? What can we do to get the police in there?" She grinned. "I could think of a few things, but I've done all I can do in that department."

"Don't you wish you knew how he's doing in that particular department?"

"All the time, every day, and I worry—is he still a danger to kids? What about the aggressiveness? The vet said that is not diminished." Martha threw up her hands. "How can anyone ever find these things out?"

"You can't, Martha. Just let it go, and stop wasting your energy on things like that." Tom sat at the kitchen table and cast a hungry look at the stove. "Isn't it about supper time?"

Martha sat across from him. "I'm hungry, too, but I can't think of cooking right now.'

"Let's go to a nice restaurant. You need a night off from things here. Why not just forget everything for once in your life?"

His look entreated her to accept, and the empty feeling nagging at her stomach made her decide in his favor. She shrugged. "Okay, let's do it." She jumped up and headed down the hall. "I'll be ready in a jiff."

Tom headed for his small room as Martha went to her and Harry's. She firmed up her jaw. "I hope he doesn't think of this as some kind of a date, because it isn't."

Shortly they met and looked at each other. Tom had a crisp white shirt on with dark gray pants that had a small black stripe in them. He wore a string tie, and, to Martha, he looked like a gambler—and a damned handsome one at that. He had a dark gray jacket slung over one shoulder.

Tom took a look at Martha, a widow, grandmother, and one hell of a handsome female. She wore a deep green, shimmery sweater over dark slim fitting pants, a pair of boots, and her hair was a rusty curling mass that

shone like liquid fire. Her eyes had shades of green Tom
had never seen on anyone. He easily understood the hold
she'd had on Harry Johns, and lately he'd begun to feel
the hold this handsome woman had taken on him as well.

"You're looking just fine, ma'am," he murmured, as
he escorted her to his Bronco and handed her in. She
didn't want him to, but he did it anyway.

Tom drove at a moderate speed. Martha relaxed and
gave herself over to the evening. At this moment, she
didn't know where he was headed nor did she care. It felt
good to forget all the troubles, mystery, and sickness of
the world about them for a few precious hours. She had
deliberately left her cell at the house so she wouldn't get
any calls during dinner. In addition to feeling relaxed for
once, she had the feeling Serena was enjoying this night
out as much, if not more than, she. Martha had begun to
suspect her Serena side had forgotten about Harry Johns,
and had eyes for Tom.

After a bit, Tom pulled into a rustic looking place
Martha had never seen before. Not that she gotten out a
lot since living with Harry. They'd been so content just
being together, that going out for dinner hadn't been important to either of them. She looked over at him. "What
is this place?"

"It's called The Big Horn Steak house. Ever hear of
it?"

"Not really. I have an idea you have, and likely you
know from experience that the steaks here are more than
great."

He smiled at her comment, parked, and came around
to help her out. But Martha tried to refuse his help. "I can
make it without your gallant help, Tom."

"Not tonight, Miss Independent."

She didn't argue as he took her elbow and ushered
her into the place. As soon as they passed through the

door, she caught the odor of steaks broiling over mesquite. She also heard the rattle of dishes and cutlery,
along with the low murmur of diners' conversations. To
the sounds of occasional outbursts of laughter, they were
led across the straw-littered floor. The usher seated them
in a high walled booth. The entire décor seemed to con-
sist of branding irons hung about the outside walls, and
paintings. Those were mounted on the walls depicting
longhorn cattle grazing in pastures, and cowboys on rear-
ing horses. Their table was made of polished planks. In
the background, the sound of country music softly echoed
through the entire facility. Martha relaxed and settled into
her seat. She was far more comfortable with Tom these
days.

"How's this, then?" Tom asked. He was seated
across from her and had opened his slick, western deco-
rated menu.

"It looks wonderful, Tom." She hesitated then said,
"I haven't been out much lately." She didn't want to add
any more to that declaration. It was good of him to take
her out for a nice meal, and this promised to be just that.

Being in a similar situation a while back reminded
her of another meal with an officer of the law. She remembered a date with Ed Gilmore. The evening had begun so wonderfully, but it had ended with Martha in fear
of her life from his drunkenness and erratic driving.

Martha decided Tom was not the same kind of man,
but the memory lingered enough to increase her wariness.
She took up her menu and asked him, "What are you having?"

"I'm looking at a nice sirloin." He smiled at her in a
narrow-eyed way she'd not seen before, and that look
sent a sliver of heat flashing through her midsection.

The waiter, a slim, dark-haired young man, approached, rattled off his offers, and absentmindedly

tapped on his order book as he waited for their selection.

Martha selected a six ounce sirloin, baked potato, and a small Caesar salad, along with a dry martini.

Tom ordered the sixteen ounce sirloin with all the trimmings, and he added a vodka gimlet. Martha wondered about the alcohol. How many would Tom have? She wondered and watched. Tom had no idea he was on trial because of a previous event in Martha's life.

The drinks came, and they toasted silently, each of them an individual desire. The glasses clinked together and they smiled at each other as they sipped their drinks. Tom said, "You may be a grandmother, Martha, but you have no idea how fine looking you are, do you?"

Taken aback, Martha was speechless. She had no idea Tom would ever make a comment like that. He didn't seem a man given to such things, and she was amazed. She saw him as a big, quiet bear of a man, certainly not some slick ladies' man. She knew that assessment was unfair, but he'd surprised the hell out of her just now. Her pulse rate rose like crazy, and she wondered how the rest of the evening would go. Was this big man getting amorous?

Martha didn't know how to answer that, so she remained silent.

The music they had heard before had been canned. Now she heard the sound of a fully outfitted western band. Tom rose from his seat and held out his hand to her. "The band has arrived. Care for a dance, ma'am?" The look in his eyes made her forget her weak protest. She got up and followed him onto the small, slick-looking dance floor. Tom wasn't taking no for an answer.

His arm encircled her waist. He took her hand and swept her across the floor in a graceful waltz. Martha found herself amazed at the gentle grace of the man. He smelled manly, his cologne was downright heady—and she floated away in his arms, forgetting everything but the feel of this man's arms around her.

He was skillful on the dance floor, and by the way she felt in his arms, she had no doubt at all, he was skillful in other things as well. She murmured in his ear. "You are some kind of man on this dance floor, mister."

His smile burned into her eyes as he murmured. "Well then, we make a fine pair, ma'am. You are sure as hell some kind of woman—anywhere." The dance ended at last, and he escorted her back to the table. Martha, flushed and, almost panting, took another sip of her drink. "Whew! That was wonderful, Tom,"

"Me or the drink?"

"You know what I meant. You're a big man, yet you dance like some slick panther out on that floor." She couldn't think of a better comparison at the moment and flushed as she said it.

"Thanks, Martha, you're mighty fine out there, yourself. The grace of a beautiful wildcat suits you pretty damned well, too." Just then, the steaks arrived, hissing and popping from the metal plates they rested on.

He indicated the smoking steaks. "Better get at these before they cool off."

It was obvious her comment on his dancing had pleased him. He had a soft shine in his eyes she hadn't seen there before. It made her a bit nervous, wondering how this evening might end. But, Martha knew she wasn't ready in any way for more than a friendly steak dinner.

They ate in near silence. Martha couldn't help seeing how Tom polished off his big steak, along with all the rest of what came with his meal. She wondered what his cholesterol level was, but remained silent on that subject.

The mood between them was suddenly more restrained than it had been. Martha wondered if it was the compliments that had passed between them. Somehow, it had added a new dimension to their tenuous relationship.

Considering she couldn't figure out why he was in her life at all, she truly believed that when all danger had passed, she would see no more of Tom Wells. That being the case, she would make very certain she did not allow herself to have feelings for him or give thought to his caring for her in any way.

He didn't ask her for another round on the dance floor, and she would have refused him if he had done so. They finished the meal. Both refused dessert and sat quietly watching the dancers for a while, saying nothing.

Tom let out an explosive breath and faced her, his elbows on the table. "What's going on in that head of yours, Martha?"

"What do you mean?"

"You've clammed up—it's like you're afraid something's going on between us."

"If you think something is, you've got another think coming, Tom." She straightened in her seat and looked him in the eye. "I don't think I'll ever let myself fall in love again. If I ever did, I truly believe it would mean certain death for anyone so unlucky as to get involved with me." She felt her pulse rate rise as she voiced thoughts she'd always kept to herself. "I've lost three good men in my life, and that's enough. It hurts too much. I can't think of facing all that again. I believe I'm a black widow." She fought back her tears. "It's too hard, Tom. I'll never get involved with a man again."

"Wow! I guess that sets me straight." He held back a grin and kept his face straight. "Well, if we aren't going to get involved, how about another turn on the dance floor. I could use the exercise." He got up and turned to her, his hand held out.

Martha realized she had gone off the deep end a bit,

and, with a flushed face, she got up and took his hand. "Just don't hold me too close."

Tom laughed aloud and led her out to a nice two-step. She quickly discovered he was more than proficient at this dance, too. He spun her about and dipped her until she was laughing and relaxed in his arms. She clung to him to steady herself, and they finished the dance. He led her back to the table and seated her. "Now, was that so bad?"

Martha shook her head. "You're a tough one to figure, Tom. I wonder if I can really trust you." She laughed, in spite of her comment. "You're a lot of fun. I'll have to say that." She leaned back in her seat and fanned her face. "Whew, what a dancer you are."

He said nothing, but glanced at his wrist watch. It was getting near midnight. "Had enough for one night?" He grinned. "Or want another spin round the dance floor?"

"It's been a very nice night, Tom. I needed something like this to get my head on straight again." She reached for his hand. "I miss Harry like you can't imagine, but he's gone." She frowned in her confusion. "I really don't know where I'm headed anymore with all we have hanging over us—I mean myself and my family. I really do appreciate how you have stayed and helped me get myself together." She grimaced. "I know I wasn't very happy about you being here at first, but I've been glad of it more than once since. The way you've been there for me, I have to say, I've appreciated it—plenty."

He rose from his side of the table. "All right, let's get you home. That bum leg of yours might need a bit of rest after all this activity."

Martha rose and found her leg did hurt a bit. She walked ahead of him and did her best not to limp. He helped her into his Bronco, and they drove away. Neither said anything as they drove, and Martha compared this night out with the disastrous one she'd had with Ed Gilmore a year or so ago. *Not the same at all, not with this big dude.*

When they reached the house, she got out on her own and headed inside, still feeling the glow of a nice evening out. She was afraid for Tom to get next to her right now, not after how close they'd gotten on the dance floor. She planned to hurry off to her room. But as soon as she hit the kitchen table where she'd left her cell, she saw the flashing light and heard it beeping as it lay there.

Her heart jumped in fear—more bad news, and right now, she didn't want to hear it, not after a wonderful night of forgetting it all. *Please, let me have a few moments of forgetting that sly devil who plots his evil against me.*

Chapter 21

She had to pick it up and see who'd called. It was Lizzie. She laughed in relief and held the phone out as she told Tom, "It's only Lizzie. No way is she going to tell me a horror story at this time of night." She played the message.

"Martha, someone just blew up our entire garage! I wasn't in my car, but my husband was! Martha—he's gone!"

The message ended, and Martha crumpled into her chair, gasping and sobbing helplessly. She felt Tom's arms go around her. He swept her up, carried her into the living room, laid her on the couch, and knelt beside her, his arms around her, uttering soothing words, trying to comfort her as best he could.

Martha couldn't listen to his soothing words. Her guilt rose before her like a specter of evil. "Tom, I've brought this death to my best friend in the world! It's because of me that her husband's dead. How am I supposed to live with something like that?"

"You didn't do this, Martha—you know that. It's not your fault that some sick son-of-a-bitch is trying to kill off everyone you ever knew. You've never done anything that didn't need doing." He shook her shoulders gently, trying to make her believe him. "It's not your fault!"

"I've got to call her. She'll know why this happened. It was caused by me—she knows the whole story, Tom." Martha rose off the couch and headed for her phone, nearly sobbing. "I'm about to lose the best friend I've ever had."

Martha grabbed her phone and pressed Lizzie's number. It rang for several rings, and the voice that answered was not Lizzie's. Martha heard the words, "I'm sorry, Mrs. Marin cannot come to the phone." After determining Martha was a long-time friend, the voice informed her, "Mrs. Marin has been heavily sedated. I'll tell her you called. I'm sure she'll want to speak with you. She'll need her friends around her now."

Martha clicked off. Her heart felt heavy, and she had a sick feeling inside. Everything seemed so hopeless.

She turned to Tom, tears in her eyes, a heavy load of guilt in her heart. "Tom, how can I go on like this? Will it never end? Why can't the police catch that man? We know who it could be, and after finding that little shoe, he might be more than that in the bargain."

Ever since she'd found it, Martha frequently thought about what that small shoe meant. With the rise of her temper, her tears began to dry. Something had to be done, and soon.

Tom stood before her, his hands clenched, wanting to help.

Martha sighed. "I'm sorry to be such a basket case, Tom. I must get some rest."

She began weaving on her feet as she rose to go to her bed. He caught her in his arms and swept her off her feet.

"Martha, let me hold you a while. I think you need it." Holding her closely, he walked over to Harry's big leather chair. He sat in the chair and reclined it with her across his lap. Pulling a small blanket off the back, he covered her with it. "Just relax awhile. We have plenty of time. You aren't going anywhere, and you can't call Lizzie until the morning. You need to rest."

Martha couldn't resist him. She felt totally helpless right now. The terrible feeling that this predatory fiend was winning his battle against her had taken hold of her mind. Feeling lost, she relaxed against Tom's solid warmth, took in the healthy male scent of his body, and sank into the heat and strength of him. She had no fight left inside her.

Feeling desolate that her activities had caused her dearest friend in the world to lose a beloved husband in such a terrible way was almost too much to bear. She let her tears flow, wetting his fancy dress shirt.

Snuggling close to Tom's solid warmth, she slowly took in the subtle woodsy odor of his shirt against her cheek and the masculine odor of his big body beneath it. She heard his big heart beating a steady rhythm, and the warmth and security he offered felt like a healing balm. She reached out for the comfort he had to offer, unable to worry about anything else right now. Martha needed this, and she needed him, too.

∽∾∽∾

Martha rose from her bed, knowing she hadn't gotten in there by herself. It had to have been Tom, and right now it didn't matter to her. "I've got to see Lizzie. I don't care what she wants or thinks—she needs me. And I need to see her."

She threw on a robe, ran a brush through her hair, and headed to the kitchen. The heady aroma of freshly made coffee was there, and she saw bacon sizzling in the pan. The delicious odors made her stomach rumble.

"I'm going to see my friend this morning—I have to, Tom." She was adamant and would brook no words against it.

"You won't get any argument from me, Martha." He also said, "I'll check out your car, or do you want to go in the Bronco?"

"Check out my car—what do you mean?"

"After what's going down around here, wouldn't you want to be sure your own car won't blow up when you step into it?" His eyes bored into her with the question.

Martha felt like an idiot for not thinking of her own danger. Certainly, she could be next.

"Of course, Tom." She avoided his eyes. "I should have realized he might come after me one of these days."

"No worries, ma'am. I've been checking both vehicles out from the beginning anyway. And I'm glad if you do feel safer with me around, under foot, and dogging your every step." He couldn't hold back his grin, as he repeated her own words back to her.

"I'm sorry I said those things, but at the time I didn't know I was going to be a target." She shrugged. "How could anyone even begin to imagine a thing like that?"

"Well, I could have, and did—haven't seen a thing so far. The burned barn is all we've had from your friend to date." His eyes narrowed. "Martha, he'll come for you one of these days, and right soon unless he's caught."

"You're trying to scare me, aren't you?" She looked him in the eye.

"Yeah, that's what I'm doing." He nodded at her and headed for the door. "I'll call when I'm ready. Which vehicle?"

"We'll take mine, and thanks for checking it out," she called after him.

ℰ✦ℰ✦ℰ

They drove without saying anything more than a comment or two about the passing scenery. Martha sat in the passenger seat, feeling glad Tom was with her and doing the driving as well. She finally spoke. "I hope you don't get into your own Bronco without checking it."

"Never do, Martha." He looked about as they entered Colorado Springs. "Nice little city. Do you have her address?"

"Of course, but you know, I've never actually been to Lizzie's home. We always spent time at mine."

Martha directed him, and they arrived to see a lovely brick and stucco home. But, sadly, on the west side of it, they saw a few trails of smoke drifting up from the pile of wreckage where the garage had been. Two terribly mangled vehicles sat there, smoldering, black, and crumpled among the bricks, plaster, and tangled wiring. She noted part of the house wall had been blasted apart as well.

Martha gasped when she saw the wreckage of the Marin home. "Oh, Tom, it looks so bad. Poor Lizzie!"

They knocked, and a nurse came to the door. Martha introduced herself. "I am a long-time friend of Lizzie's. I'd like to see her."

The nurse opened the door and ushered them in. "You must be the one who called late last night."

Martha nodded in reply.

Lizzie sat in the living area with a blanket snuggled up to her shoulders. She saw Martha, and her tears began to flow. She sobbed and reached out to her friend then remembered to nod to Tom.

Martha knelt by the chair and gathered Lizzie into her arms, smoothed the tangled mess of her hair, and stroked her back. "I'm so sorry, Liz, I know why this happened, but I could never have imagined he'd come back after you again, this way. I hardly know what to say."

Lizzie put her forefinger to Martha's lips and said to the nurse, "Dear, why don't you take a break? Help yourself to anything in the kitchen. I'll be fine here with my friend."

When the nurse left, Lizzie dried her tears, her voice nearly a whisper, "Martha, I'm so glad you came. I don't know what to do. What shall I say to the police? How much should I tell them? This is all so bizarre."

Her hands fluttered about, and she looked puzzled as well as totally distraught.

Martha looked at Tom. "Could you have a talk with the police and explain what's happening? You know more than most about what's going on."

"Is there anyone out there right now?" He directed his question to Lizzie.

"Sorry, I don't know, Tom. I just woke up a little while ago. I think they sedated me—I was such a basket case. I never expected something like this to happen." To her friend, she cried, "Oh my God, Martha. I never did." Her eyes filled with tears again.

Tom nodded. "I'll go outside and see what's what."

After Tom stepped outside, Lizzie stopped crying. "Men can't stand the sight of tears, can they?" She not only had the hint of a smile, but Martha saw something of her old deviltry coming to the fore, too.

Martha began to get the idea that losing her husband wasn't the worst thing in the world for Lizzie. She waited to hear what her friend would say next.

"Martha, my dear, I can tell you, but not another living soul in this world—things were not as hunky dory around this household as everyone thought. I found out a few months ago that my lovely husband was seeing another woman." She looked at Martha, no tears in her eyes now. "I never said anything about it to him. I could hardly face up to it myself.

"Oh, Lizzie, I never guessed. It does rather shed a different light on things."

"If you are wondering how well fixed he left me—no problem there. I made sure of that as soon as I found about Miss Floozy. I kept close track at all times. He never suspected I knew a thing. I made sure he had the most trusting, loving wife a man could have." Lizzie's eyes clouded over. "I never imagined anything like this would happen, though. Even though I knew about his plushy little love nest, I wasn't sure what steps to take—I hadn't figured it out yet." She blotted her eyes with a rather soggy tissue.

"You had some feelings for the man, I can see that," Martha said.

"The first few years of our time together were pure magic. But I suppose, in time, some men will look elsewhere. I have heard it said, and it makes sense to me, 'some men *will* cheat, and some men *won't*.' It's just as simple as that. There is no explanation necessarily, but it rings true, doesn't it?"

"I guess it does. I don't think I had that problem. I hate to admit it, but my men never lived long enough to look elsewhere."

"Martha!" Lizzie had to stifle her laughter. She didn't want anyone to see her as anything but a deeply sorrowful widow. "You're the best medicine any woman can have at this time, or any other time."

"Not better than you, Liz. How many times have you brought me back to some semblance of sanity? You've seen me through some tough times, girl."

Tom reentered the house. "I had a good chat with the officer out there."

"There's still one out there? I wish he'd have been

here when we needed him," Lizzie said, her voice heavy with grief.

Whether it was real or put on, Martha wasn't sure, and she silently applauded her friend's resilience in the face of a tragic disaster.

"I let him in on a few things." He looked at Martha. "They needed to know what's going on up in Denver. It's spilling over from Denver, clear down here to Colorado Springs."

"Are they going to do anything about it?" Lizzie asked. "Or are they just planning to sit on their asses and let more people get killed?"

She had straightened up in her chair, and Martha was happy to see some of her old fight returning.

A knock on the door startled all of them. Their eyes turned to the entry way as the nurse stepped out to answer it. She opened the heavy paneled door, and Martha caught a glimpse of an old friend from earlier days. Her heart rate went double time when the nurse ushered Detective Ryan Mapus into the great room where they sat.

Ryan spotted Martha and made a slight bow. "Martha Lavery, as I live and breathe." He took her hand for a moment and then sat down.

Martha was completely happy to see the man again. "Nice to see you again, Detective. My name's Chance these days, though."

Ryan nodded. "Tom here tells me you might have a good lead on this man for more than one reason."

Martha smiled. "Since I'm not in your jurisdiction, I will tell you everything I know and how I know it."

"Believe me, you're in no danger from me. We need all the help we can get. I'm all ears, Martha."

Martha quietly told him her suspicions, what she had done, and what she had seen. She finished with a worried frown. "That man works among small children, Detective

Mapus. It makes me ill to think of that, aside from that little patent leather shoe." She had impressed upon the detective the feelings she had about finding the shoe, when such a thing should not have been there.

"Whew! He needs checking out, and that house needs a good forensic examination." He beamed a smile at her. "Will he be as likely to single out one of those children—now?"

"Possibly, but maybe not. The vet seemed to believe the medicine, vaccine, or whatever it is, stopped the pro-creation urges, but not the aggressiveness." She shrugged, but her grin was wide. It was good to be able to tell someone about what she had done to Rayburn McGill. Mapus was an officer of the law, but that hadn't mattered at all.

"Maybe time will tell us more about that." Mapus smiled at her. That he admired and appreciated her was a given. Martha felt completely at ease with him. He had proven he was on her side.

Tom quietly sat, listening. Martha could almost see the wheels spinning inside his head. "I'm going to have another chat with my boss in Denver," he said. "This Rayburn McGill, if that is indeed his name, must have a history somewhere. We need to get a line on him. I'll see to it."

Martha smiled at him, grateful for his support. "We need to take another look inside that house. I think I can find a way." She hid her delight as well as possible, but both men knew her well enough to understand that Martha had inner help, an alter ego who had no moral stand-ards at all.

Chapter 22

Ray threw his newspaper across his living room. "Shit-damn, if I didn't get that damned ritzy bitch's husband, and not her!" He drank a slug of lukewarm beer and slammed the can down. "I wonder if Denny knows who that dame is anyways. Most likely, he's never heard of her. I need to get closer to home. I've got to make a good hit soon, or he'll have my ass in jail."

Ray felt the sweat running down his neck and back. It itched and stung its way down his shirt front, too. He mopped his brow. "Shit-damn, I need a shower." He frowned and firmed his jaw. "I've got to get to that damned kid. I don't need no bomb for that job." He laughed, but it sounded hollow, even to him.

Something was missing inside him these days. He no longer got excited or engorged when he saw the little blonde child playing with her friends. She often walked along lugging her books in a small backpack. It was small like her, with cartoon characters scattered about on it. But the sight of that small bottom wiggling along had lost its excitement for Ray. He couldn't believe it or understand it. It had happened to him every time he saw her, and its lack frightened him as nothing else ever had.

He was sure something had been done to him, but what? He remembered that night. His home had been entered—invaded. He'd gone over it time and again, trying to figure things out. When he'd come to, his pants were zipped. He'd gone to the toilet. He remembered unzipping, but he also remembered, the button had not been fastened, nor had his belt been buckled. Why? It had not been open before the incident. It was not his habit to go about with those things undone.

So why had he found his pants that way after the attack that night? He hadn't been cut or mutilated in any way. If he'd seen a bloody cut or something of that nature, he would have known something had been done to him. But he hadn't seen anything like that. Now the doc told him that his testicles had shriveled into mere nothings. And the doctor couldn't figure out any medical reason for it.

Ray shrugged in confusion and felt his heart racing. He moaned aloud, "What the hell, I'll be sittin' in there with that bastard Denny if I don't get the job done." He got up and headed for his bedroom, feeling lower than a snake. "Everythin's going down the damned toilet, and me along with it!"

∽∾∽

Will headed to his regular bus area. It was in front of his school, where he awaited a ride home. Sticking his chest out a bit, he walked wide-legged. He thought that looked the same way a Rambo-type guy might walk. He felt like he could lick the whole damned world these days with all the new things he'd learned at his training sessions with the Self Reliance Team, and the physical fitness classes. He strutted along, walking his special way—his arms swinging, sort of like Popeye did in old cartoons he'd seen. He felt stronger these days, too. His backpack felt like it was full of feathers instead of heavy books, and he hardly bent forward when he walked like so many kids did.

Will almost looked forward to needing those skills, even though, with a slight inner shiver, he realized it would probably involve a full-sized adult male. But if his back was against the wall—if he faced that sickening degradation once again, he'd know what to do. He wondered sometimes, would he—could he—do what he had to do to survive?

Will had never forgotten the sickening degradation he'd felt when that man, Fred Callahan, had molested him, doing those evil things to his body that evil day. He'd only been five years old. But now, he'd never handle being a weak little wimp like that again. He'd rather die. He'd vowed many times, he'd never be the helpless little victim again. Putting aside those evil memories, he knew if it ever happened again, he'd use the things he'd learned. His new knowledge gave him confidence.

He reached the waiting area and came face to face with Ricky, a boy he knew. He didn't like Ricky all that much, but mumbled, "Hi, Rick," and looked him in the eye.

Rick moved toward him, a sneer on his face. "Hi, yourself, snot-nose."

Will felt his temper rise and recognized it for what it was. He knew how to handle this too—he'd been trained. He remembered the words he'd been taught: *'Keep a cool head, son.'*

Will returned a stiff smile. "I'll let that pass, but you're playin' with fire, insulting me."

He kept his chest out and a dangerous glint in his eye. *Maybe if I look like this, using my Rambo face, it'll cool this fool kid down. I ain't supposed to deck him.*

He's the one makin' trouble, but if I paste him one, I'll be the one in trouble. He turned away to greet a couple of girls he knew.

Will had noticed that, with the rise in his own level of confidence, the girls seemed to look his way a lot more. He wasn't sure he liked it, but it did seem to tick off guys like Rick. That fact alone made it worth the effort to talk to them.

Will asked the two girls about a class they had together. Out of the corner of his eye, he saw Rick fuming and clenching his fists. Will silently complimented himself on his victory over the snotty-nosed Ricky.

Will felt a sharp blow to his head and saw a few stars. And then he felt the pain above his right ear and knew he'd been attacked. It shocked him. He knew instantly it had to have been Ricky, and a raging anger took hold of him. He turned back, ran at Ricky, slammed a shoulder into him, and sent him crashing into the ground.

Ricky started crying and moaning. "You bully, you hurt me!"

Will was worried his mom would stop his self-defense classes if she found out about this. But for all Ricky's sniveling, the only blood Will could see was a smear of blood on his elbow where it hit the ground.

One of the little girls yelled at Rick, "You threw a rock at Will. Shame on you—you're a dirty coward!"

They heard the brakes squeal as the bus pulled up and came to a stop. The door swung open, and the driver piled out to come and stand spread-legged in front of the boys. "All right, what's goin' on here? What's this about?"

"He knocked me down, mister." Ricky blubbered the words as he pointed at Will.

The driver faced Will. "Is that so, son?"

"Yes, sir, right after he hit me with a rock." Will remembered the girl's cry and knew the cause of his injury. He turned his head to show the blood on his right temple. The blood had begun to drip down the side of his head onto his shirt.

The driver examined the bleeding from Will's head, and the small amount of blood and scraped skin off Ricky's elbow. "Well, neither of you looks the worse for wear. You're only bleeding a little. I can report this or leave it up to you two to decide." He waited, his hands on his hips. "Boys, which do you want?"

Will, eager to escape attention relating to his anger, had pulled his shirt off and wrapped it around his head. "I just want to get home, sir." He.

Ricky nodded. "Me too, sir."

"Well, get on the bus, then, and we'll get going."

During the bus ride, Will glared at Ricky but said nothing. He left the bus, walked the short block to his home, and up the steps. He entered his house quietly, hoping his mother wouldn't see him come in. He tossed his back pack in a corner and headed for his room.

"'Hold on there, Will, what happened to you? My goodness, Will, you've got blood dripping down the side of your head, and from underneath that shirt you've wrapped around it!"

He feared his mother's voice was heading into a hysterical scream. He knew the sound. "Aw, Mom, it ain't nothin'." He turned his head, trying to see what blood his mom was talking about. He pulled the shirt off his head, and it shocked him to see so much blood—all of it his own. He instantly understood why his mother was so upset and scared. All of a sudden, he felt faint.

Jeannie grabbed his arm and sat him in a chair. "What happened to you, Will?" Her eyes were wide, and her face looked awful white to Will.

"I got into it with Ricky. He's always picking' on me, Mom. After he hit me with a rock, I gave what him for. I flattened him right to the ground and made his elbow bleed." His chest puffed out as he remembered Ricky laying on the ground, his face white as a sheet, worried about that little bit of blood.

"You were hit with a rock?" Jeannie peered closely at his bleeding wound. "Let's clean this up. I need to know if I have to take you to the ER." She led him into the bathroom, closed the toilet lid, and sat him down on it. After she tucked a towel around his neck, she tenderly cleaned and sponged the bloody mess until, at last, she saw the entry site. "It's only a tiny cut, little more than a nick. My, how it bleeds." She touched his shoulder. "Son, sit right here and wait. I'm calling Gramma. She'll know what to do."

Jeannie called her mother and explained about the cut to her. "What should I do?" She listened to the answer. "Okay Mom, we'll see you in a little while." She turned to Will. "She's worried those self-defense lessons are getting you in trouble, son." Her eyes narrowed suspiciously. "Are you sure it happened the way you said?"

"Yes, it did, Mom. He started it by saying rotten stuff, and I ignored him. I think it made him mad that the girls like me better, so he threw a rock at me."

❦❦❦

Martha parked and entered Jeannie's house. Her face felt tight. Her hidden worries seemed to be surfacing right before her eyes. What was happening to her grandson? With these deadly threats hanging over them, was this just the beginning for Will?

Her eyes sought the boy. When she spotted him sitting with a towel around his head, she went to him. "So,

Will, you got into a little fracas, did you? Let's take a look, son." She unwrapped the towel. The bleeding had stopped. "Small and clean. Might need a tetanus shot, but looks like it'll close without a stitch. It doesn't take much of a cut to make the scalp bleed like crazy. It always looks worse than it really is."

"He had a tetanus shot a while back, so he's good on that," Jeannie said.

"He's seems clear enough in the head—no blurred vision, is there, Will?" Martha asked.

"Naw, I can see okay." Will was getting sick of this whole thing. "Mom, can I just go do my homework?"

At her nod, he left them sitting together, talking, grabbed his bag, and went into another room. No matter what his mom said, he felt like a victor. He'd handled the situation, and it made him feel like he could handle almost anything.

If some dirty rotten man came at him again with his sick ideas, Will would show him a thing or two. You bet he would. He grabbed his book bag from where he'd tossed it and laid out his homework. He checked over his last assignments, his pulse racing, as he thought of situations that might come his way.

With his thoughts on his next conquest, he felt confident. He'd know what to do—how to act. He spread out his work book and tried to remember what his teacher had said about geography, or was it math?

Martha sat with her daughter. "He seems quite proud of himself, Jeannie. Is it this new training he's getting?" Her brow lifted a bit, as she wondered.

"I think so. He isn't quite the same anymore at all." Jeannie shrugged and smiled. "He's helpful, does his homework, and gets himself ready for school most mornings. These are wonderful changes in him." Then she frowned. "But I wonder what else the boy is learning, Mom."

"Well, he's been taking self-defense lessons, and I was more worried they had gotten out of hand than I was about the head wound. We all have to approve of the positive changes we've seen, however. If it's doing all this for him, I'd say it's all for the good." Martha chuckled. "Makes him more attractive to the girls, eh?" She rose from her chair. "Well, Jeannie, I've got to get back."

ৎৡৎৡ

Ray had followed the school bus at a safe distance. He'd been careful because his goal had to be that certain boy and not some other kid that looked nearly the same. He knew where the Moultons lived so he would be sure when he saw the boy enter that house.

The kid had noticed him looking his way a few times already, and Ray had seen his face go white and tense. That boy knew he was being observed and was alert and wary. Getting his hands on that one needed some very careful planning. Ray had had so many failures that he knew he had to destroy that kid to satisfy Denny. A deep seated-rage possessed him because he felt it was wrong.

If he didn't have that other purpose, the aching desire to satisfy his desperate inner needs, he couldn't see why he had to do it. He'd been guilty of killing his victims, but it often happened during those passionate, sexual needs of his. Ray had always justified those deaths. He believed it wasn't his fault if the kid died during a thing like that—he couldn't help what happened to any kid right then.

That part of his raging anger was directed toward Denny Garver, and it came from nowhere. It was something new.

When the bus stopped to discharge a child, Ray stopped a safe distance away and watched. Finally, he saw the boy get off. Parked a half block away, he sat in his car and watched the boy walk up his street. Nothing about the kid excited him—not anymore. Was it the kid's age? No, that wasn't it. He already knew his fever for small, soft bodies had changed forever. In place of it had come a terrible anger he didn't understand.

After a short time, he drove past the Moulton home while noting the trees and shrubs the boy would pass walking to his house. "There are' a few good hiding spots along here," he mused as he drove slowly up Will's street. "Damned nice homes—husband must pull down a nice bundle every month." He remembered the new vehicle smell of the Buick Enclave when he'd wired it with the explosive. "Got another one right off, must like that model." He snorted. "Didn't go so good, that time—got the wrong damned guy."

He hadn't had the kind of luck he needed. "The wife got off too easy, too. Shoulda got her damned neck broken with the brakes out that way." He wiped his forehead. "Missed the ritzy bitch, too—got the husband instead." He shook his head, dismayed at his misfortune. "Shit-damn, things ain't goin' right a'tall."

Ray knew he had to step up his efforts if he didn't want to hear from Denny again. These days, Ray dreaded going to get his mail from the ratty half-silver mailbox box at the edge of the yard. He feared finding another letter from that damned Denny Garver, asking him to come and visit. Ray was running out of excuses. Trying to explain away all his failures meant nothing to Denny. Ray was sick of the man's threats and scared as hell because of them, too.

Chapter 23

Martha reached home and found Tom waiting for her in the kitchen. "How's the boy?" His eyes held the query, and she had no doubt he was interested in her answer.

"It wasn't much, just a nick, really. Head wounds tend to bleed rather profusely, and it frightened Jeannie. Will's fine." She chuckled. "He got into a little scrap with one of the other students while they waited for the bus. The kid threw a rock at Will and struck him in the head. Will bested the kid, knocked him to the ground, and was very proud of himself."

"Well, good for Will. He must be getting enough macho training to be sure of himself. I say that's all to the good." Tom sighed. "Martha, you know, he's tried to take out everyone, except Will, and possibly me." He faced her, his eyes boring into her. "So, who's next, then? You know one day soon, he'll be coming for you, don't you?"

"Of course, I know it. I wish he would. It's me he's after anyway, so leave my family alone. Let's get this done. Tom, I'm fed up with this business. We never get any respite from it. We must constantly be on guard and worry all the time." She took a deep breath. "You can't get into your car without checking the wiring or the brake lines." Martha flopped down in a chair. "Wow, how I do go on." She laughed at herself. "Look what he's got me doing—blathering on like a nitwit."

Tom laughed with her. "Nothing wrong with enjoying a bit of gallows humor, Martha. I believe you need another nice night out at a great place. You're a hell of a great dancer." She knew he meant it, by the serious look on his face. He nodded at her. "I had a lot of fun that night we went for steaks."

Martha's eyes narrowed. She worried Tom was trying to get closer than she was comfortable with. She still wasn't sure why he was lounging about her home under foot. What had gone on between Tom and Harry? Was it after Harry was shot? Martha didn't know the story but had puzzled over it very often. For some unknown reason, she hadn't tried to get an answer out of him. Was she afraid to find out?

She had been glad for Tom's presence more than once and probably owed her life to him. Things were rapidly becoming a real muddle, and she didn't like the feeling. Maybe if Tom got a few drinks in him, he'd tell her about it, and if she had a few under the belt, she'd be able to handle the answers.

"If you'd like to go somewhere, I guess it might be all right. If you know where we'll be going, let me know, so I'll know what to wear."

"Any place you know, that you'd love to see again?" he asked.

Martha remembered the night out with the navy SEAL and a nurse friend of hers. Judith was a girl she had helped to escape an abusive husband. How well Martha remembered. She felt a soft glow remembering how Judith fell in love with the navy SEAL after he became her body guard. She raised her head. "How about a visit to The House of Joy?" She almost giggled. "Ever been there?"

"The House of Joy—with you? Sounds great, girl."

"Tom, I'm speaking of a restaurant—only," she reminded him, firming her lips. "It's very nice actually, but I didn't see any dancing there."

They spent some time discussing where to go, where to eat, including where there might be dancing—it all seemed so frivolous. But Martha felt a long-absent joy creeping into her mind. Feelings like that had been missing for the long weeks and months since she'd lost Harry.

It felt good to her, and she had Tom to thank for that, too. In spite of the threat hanging over her and her loved ones, he had been a steady force that had held things together for her. He was with her, no matter what she was up to, and had proven it to her more than once. He understood her and what drove her. It was a comfort to know she had no need to hide anything from him.

His voice broke into her thoughts. "If I can break into your wool-gathering, I'm ready anytime you are. What do we wear to a fancy place like the House of Joy?" he asked, egging her on into giving him an answer. "But I'd like to dance with you again, lady, I really would. You are really fine out on the dance floor."

She didn't miss the look he sent her way—it shook her to the depths. This man had become interested in her in a way she couldn't face. Martha never wanted to feel those things again—never. She'd been all through this, over and over. She had also tired of facing the huge gaping hole it left in her life each time she'd lost that closeness. She'd been through it three times, and that was more than enough for any woman. If she allowed herself to dwell on her losses, she felt like a miserable failure and a black widow in the bargain. Thus, most of the time, she sought to ignore what had happened to her previous marriages or alliances.

"Tom, I'll go anywhere you like. I enjoyed dancing with you, too." Martha, tired of fussing about it, left it to him. Looking at him, she wondered how old he was. There were hints of gray in the lower edges of his hair, so he was no longer a young man. Shaking her head, she headed for her bedroom. That, yet another man, had taken a fancy to her had become too much for her. Her cheeks burned, and she felt like a silly fool.

Tom watched her go and smiled to himself. *She's getting a little worried about me, I can see it clear as daylight.* He narrowed his eyes as he thought, *My lovely lady, my guess is that you aren't through with the game of life, not yet. You just don't know it.*

❧❧❧

Near sunset, Martha and Tom settled into Tom's Bronco. "I know a great place—just the thing for us," he said.

Martha thought she heard his emphasis on the word *us* and the togetherness of it sent shivers up her spine. *What does this dude have in mind? He has changed toward me lately in some crazy way, and I'm not so sure I like it. I'm not ready. I can't face getting involved in an intense relationship again—I just couldn't take another loss. I've had enough of loving and losing!*

Thinking further, she realized she had been extremely fortunate with each and every man in her life. Smiling to herself, she knew Serena had been satisfied with them, too.

How bizarre is my life—I am sharing myself with another being. I don't care what the doctors say, I must be a touch crazy—I've got to be!

Tom reached over and nudged her shoulder. "Hey, are you with me?"

He laughed in his joy, tossed his head, and she saw his white teeth flashing as they passed a street-light. *He's handsome enough for any woman alive, I'll give him that*, she decided.

Martha had dressed in a skirt and loose flowing blouse that reminded her of Serena's wild-hearted outings to that sleazy nightclub in Colorado Springs, the notorious Paradisio. She remembered how frenetically she had danced to that wild beat, and those flashing lights beneath the floor that made the dancers look like puppets jerking on a string. She felt her pulse rate rise as she recalled how it had been back then.

Tom wheeled off the road into a wide parking space next to a neon sign that showed a glass pouring a liquid downward, and bubbles rising magically to the top of the sign. It was a building that promised food and entertainment. "The Bird's Nest?" Martha queried, looking at Tom in suspicion.

"It's a small place a ways out of town, but it's a lot of fun, girl."

She saw his big strong throat working as he laughed aloud and winked at her. She felt that heated streak run right through her middle and downward. It made her feel edgy and angry that he could do this to her. It seemed so easy for him, but she wasn't ready for that, or anything else—not anymore. Besides, she told herself, she didn't really know the man—him, or his history.

Tom parked his Bronco and stepped to her door. Martha didn't want him to take her hand, but when he held it out to her, she placed her hand into his, like a child. He helped her out of the vehicle and took her elbow to escort her inside. She heard the blaring of dance music as they neared the door. Her face heated, and she felt the excitement of the night ahead.

They were escorted across a sawdust-littered floor that gave the place the clean odor of newly sawn wood. They were seated at a small booth with the dance floor right beside them. Martha was sure Tom had called for reservations when she saw that.

They perused their slick menus and gave their orders for drinks. This time, Martha ordered a Stinger, like she had in her racy Serena days at the Paradisio. She saw Tom's eyebrows rise, but he said nothing, and ordered his own drink, a dry martini,

"What are you hungry for?" he asked her.

She felt the intensity. His question was so loaded she could barely speak. "You do mean food, I hope." She couldn't stop herself from making that comment. She tried to hold back a stupid blush, but she felt it crawling up her neck. She heard his low-voiced chuckle, and it angered her. "I don't know why I said that." she murmured, but she had, and it had let him know where her thoughts were.

"I have no ideas in mind at all, dear girl," Tom said, his voice low and steady, his black eyes fastened onto hers.

Martha tried to avoid his look, but she was sure his every word was a lie. When her drink was placed before her, she couldn't stop herself taking a good-sized sip of it to calm her nerves. The liquid burned a bit as it slid down her throat, but she welcomed the warm feeling in her mid-section. She had to keep her guard up—she'd become increasingly unsure what would happen tonight after the dancing was over.

When the band started a smooth waltz, Tom got up and without speaking, reached out for her hand. Without a word of protest, Martha rose to join him. He held her in his arms, and she melted into his heated body as he swept his graceful way around the floor.

"You are one great dancer, mister," she declared as she relaxed close against him.

"Only with you in my arms, dear girl."

He crooned the words softly in her ear, as he swept her into a long, slow dip. He kept on until the song ended, and he escorted her back to their booth. Martha hurriedly took another healthy sip of her drink and, fanning her face, sat back against the cushions.

She hadn't eaten since lunch. Just now she felt a touch of dizziness creeping over her. Worse yet, she wanted to giggle and almost did. Fearing to look foolish, she straightened herself up and stopped her nonsense. What on earth was she thinking? But she couldn't stop remembering the way he'd moved on the dance floor—how she'd let herself go along with him and closed her eyes. She had to face the fact that here was a man who was good at everything. She felt that overheated Serena rising within her mind.

She face went tight—she knew what her alter had in mind. *I can't go along with you, Serena. He'd think I was some kind of slut. Harry hasn't been gone that long. Oh, God, I wish he was here right now!* She felt her face heating into another blush as she fought against Serena's heated wanting, and her own will in the bargain. *It must be the Stinger*, she decided, as she took another healthy sip and felt it hit her empty stomach like a time bomb.

"I'd give a hell of a lot to know what's going on inside that head of yours, Martha," Tom murmured as he tossed off his own drink.

Martha felt those familiar streaks of lightning passing through her midsection as she watched that drink slide down his muscular throat. She couldn't even remember what she'd ordered for dinner, not anymore.

"I wish that stuff we ordered would get here pretty soon," she said, fighting that tremor in her voice.

"Stuff—don't you remember what you ordered, dear?" Tom gently chided. He knew full well, she was feeling that drink on an empty stomach and heavily so. With a smile on his lips, he held out his hand as the band struck up a lively Schottische. "Feel up to this one, Martha?"

She rose, feeling slightly unsteady, to take his hand, wondering if she had ever done this dance before. He carefully led her into it until she was stepping it off right along with him. Martha felt the blood singing in her veins as she kept pace with this big man. But she had her suspicions. He worked her carefully, cunningly, while he slowly mesmerized her into someone she wasn't sure she knew.

In spite of her suspicions of Tom, she'd enjoyed the dancing. With the effort of dancing, the effects of the Stinger had worn off as they sat down again. "Wow, Tom, that was great!" Martha saw a fresh Stinger sitting in front of her, and her suspicions went soaring all over again.

She was about to say something, but just then, her meal came. She had ordered a plate of tiny shrimps, broiled and resting in a great seafood sauce. A small portion of coleslaw sat beside the plate, and she noticed fresh, heavenly bread setting in the middle of the table.

She thought she should order coffee, but after tasting the food, she forgot about it and sipped her drink along with her meal. Tom had ordered a large plate of seafood, with some type of cornbread things this place was famous for. He had told her about them as he ordered. She wondered how he knew so many places. He was no drunk like that other man, Ed. Martha put it down to the life of a single man. He had replenished his own drink as well.

They ate without much conversation, but Tom sent an appraising glance her way many times. He offered a smile as he asked, "How's your dinner?"

"It's very good, Tom. How did you happen to know about this place?" She had wondered about his life before she knew him. He hadn't said a thing about his life before and nothing since she'd met him, either. To her, it seemed he had appeared out of thin air.

"I've been in this area for a while, Martha. Harry and I go way back, but we'd only started working together lately." He smiled slightly and took a bite of his sea bass, fried to a golden crusty delight. She heard it crunch between his teeth. She knew a bit more about him, but not much. She kept to her own meal and was relieved that her dizziness had evaporated with the intake of food.

They danced a few more times, had another round of drinks, and decided it was time to leave. Tom ushered her out to his Bronco, but before she got in, he caught her to his chest and gazed into her startled eyes. "I've wanted to do this for an awfully long time, my dear," he murmured softly as he kissed her on the lips, soundly but gently.

His kiss sent electric thrills coursing all through her, and all of them affected her legs, making them weak. Her heart pounded in her ears, and she felt faint.

She didn't resist him at first, but as he kept on, probing her lips with his tongue, seeking an entrance, she tried to draw away. He affected her far more deeply than anything she'd ever imagined. But Martha had decided she would not go this way again. She dared not allow this to happen to her—falling in love was out for her. Startled by the way her body responded to his, she began to struggle.

"This can't be happening," she cried, "Not again!"

"But it is, Martha, and you know it." He held her away from him. Her huge eyes were glowing, and her pale features were shadowed softly in the moonlight. "You feel it—you know it—don't you, girl?"

She struggled in his arms. "But I don't want this. I refuse to ever go this way again. I'm deadly to any man who mixes with me. I've told you that!"

"Martha, you can't hide from life. You have to live it out to the end, no matter what happens." He didn't let her go. "Are you afraid of me?"

"I'm not afraid of you or any other man. You ought to know that by now." She wanted to kick his shins but held fast on her temper. "I think you're a fine man, but if you got tangled up with me, I wonder how long you'd last." She felt her anger fade and the hopeless tears begin. "Can't you hear me? Don't you understand what I'm saying?"

"I know all that has happened to you, girl. I don't give a damn about any of it. If I die from being with you, darling girl, I have the idea I'll go out with a smile on my lips." He tossed his head back and laughed. "Do you hear me? I'm not afraid to take a chance with you—not in any way."

Martha gave up and slumped against his chest. "Let's get home, Tom. I can't fight with you anymore."

He helped her into the truck, and soon they were headed back to that little home on the outskirts of Denver. Martha knew what he had in mind, and she wasn't going to go along with it. They'd have it out when they got there. Her mind was made up. She refused to get romantically involved with Tom Wells or any other man. She didn't dare. Her conscience wouldn't allow it.

Chapter 24

They entered the driveway, got out, and went into the house. Everything seemed normal, but Martha had a strange sensation that something was not right. It was too quiet—eerily so. "Tom, something's wrong here."

"What makes you say that?" He looked at her. "Your face is white as a sheet, girl. What is it?"

"Well, for one thing, where are the dogs, Tom?" she pointed out. "They are always excited when we drive in. I don't see them at all."

"You're right, Martha. I guess my thoughts were elsewhere." She saw a frown slip across his face.

"Yes, I know just where they were." But she couldn't think about it, she was filled with fear for their two nearly-grown pups.

"Let's look around, girl. They've got to be here."

He grabbed his big flashlight, and they walked outside around the house, softly calling for Skunk and Max. Martha remembered another time, when their namesakes had been killed by another of her enemies. She prayed that wouldn't happen again.

Tom almost fell as his feet hit a soft pile in the grass alongside the house. He directed the flashlight down to see Max trussed up with rope and black electrical tape around his muzzle. "My God—Max! Who did this to you?" he cried as he quickly unwound the tape from the dog's cramped muzzle.

Max licked his hands as Tom untied the white cords around his feet.

The dog easily got to his feet, and, after a good exam, Tom said, "I can't find any sign of injury to him, Martha."

"What's going on, Tom?" Martha followed him as they walked on around the home, looking for Skunk.

When Max bounded away and let out a sharp bark, they went to him and found their other dog bound the same way.

Tom undid the dog's bonds, and they took the animals with them as they went into the house.

"Martha, I believe your nemesis has just left us a calling card," Tom said. "Thank God he isn't into killing dogs—it's just us, he's after." Tom paused, thinking. "I'm going to check around for anything else he may have left us."

Martha fought her anger. She paced the kitchen floor, clenched her fists, and tears fell across her cheeks, until Tom came back inside.

"He's got to be stopped. Tom. It's a wonder he hasn't gone after Will. He's tried to kill everyone else—well, except us." She realized that Tom, because he guarded her, had become a target for their predator right along with her.

Tom took her into his arms and held her against his body. "We'll get him, but not tonight. You need something I can give you, and I don't want any more nonsense about dying because of it. Let the dogs stay in, tonight. Come on, girl, I need you so much I can barely wait, and neither can you."

Martha didn't know why she allowed Tom to pick her up and carry her into her bedroom, but she found she had no argument against it. She murmured a faint, "I'm sorry, Harry," as Tom closed the bedroom door.

He held her so close she could scarcely breathe. He began to kiss her, and she could put up no struggle against him. The male essence of him went so deeply into her mind, she thought her bones would melt. She let him do as he wanted. Burning with heat and hopelessness, it wasn't long before she found herself his willing partner. From then on, she hardly knew who she was or where she was, as the night slowly wore into dawn.

୧⁓ଈ⁓ଈ

Ray sat in his musty old chair with a smile on his face. "Didn't want to hurt the dogs. It was so easy. They gulped down that delicious spiced-up meal I had for them. I didn't have to do any killing. I would have if I thought it would let that bitch know she's next. She sure as hell ought to know I'm coming for her by that nice little message I sent her tonight, though." He was pleased with himself. It was about time he got around to the main reason Denny had hired him—the woman called Martha.

He hadn't heard any more from Denny. "Maybe if I knock off that bitch, Martha, and that law-dog asshole she's got livin' out there with her, he'd see it in the paper and leave me the hell alone."

Ray worried constantly. *Shit-damn, something has been done to me. I know something was, but what? There ain't no fun in life for me—not anymore.* Still puzzled over the change in his sexual leanings, he was positive somebody had done something to him. He'd become even more sure of it after he'd happened to walk past the little blonde girl playing hop scotch on her sidewalk.

She'd been playing with a friend, and he'd spoken to her. But the usual, heated sensations he'd always had were missing. Nothing worked for him anymore. He didn't feel that familiar rise inside himself when he looked at her soft little body. Thoughts of what he'd lost had made his anger skyrocket, and that puzzled him too. On the other hand, he decided, it might be a plus. If he had no more desire to do those things to his little victims, it would keep him from running from the cops, now that he didn't feel the need to stalk and rape little girls.

As long as he had suffered these changes, he could live out the rest of his life quietly without the police breathing down his neck. But first, he had to get shut of that threat from Denny Garver. That meant he had to get the nurse, and as a bonus, her grandson, too. That would surely satisfy ol' Denny. Then Ray could move away somewhere and freely spend some more of the money he'd gotten from Denny. It was enough to get him a nice little house and spend a bit without anyone nosing around about it.

So far, he'd done all he could to please that devil on death row. But Ray wasn't done. He had to find a way to get that bitch, in spite of that big Rambo-type cop she kept out there. Ray spent hours figuring out how to do it. Wiring her vehicle had no chance, not with that bastard checking everything, every day. The boy, no problem. Ray could easily snatch the kid as he walked home from the bus. There was enough brush along that street to hide behind. One quick blow to the head was all he needed. He could manage that—he knew it.

Maybe in the night I could set fire to the house and burn the nurse and her live-in stud—send 'em both straight to hell. If I set the fires all around the place, they'd be trapped inside. They wouldn't see it until it was too late. He smiled to himself. *Well now, wouldn't that be too bad?*

From then on, Ray puzzled whether to get the kid, and then Martha, or Martha and then the kid. If he got the damned kid first, it would be one more sorrow for the bitch nurse and please that damned Denny Garver all to hell. And Ray believed the kid would be easier, being he was still a little boy.

He'd like to do those things to that small body like he used to do, but he knew he no longer could. Not anymore. But if the kid was dead, that ought to satisfy old Denny. Upset and angry, Ray took a few more of his pills and hit the bed. The sheets were so filthy, any normal man would have hated to touch them, but Ray didn't care about that anymore. He showered before he went to work, but that wasn't any fun anymore either.

ↀↀↀ

Martha awoke slowly. She pressed her hand down on her abdomen, reaching for the slight discomfort she felt. It alarmed her. She shouldn't have those feelings. But she did, and she knew just how she'd gotten them. How well she remembered that soft aching—so familiar after a big night with Harry. She came alert and leapt out of her bed to see her clothes laying about in tangled piles across her bedroom floor. She clamped her hand over her mouth to stifle a gasp and murmured, "What have I done, now?"

She already knew what she had done. She'd spent the night with that hulking brute who spent all his time dogging her footsteps and haunting her life. But a soft glow took hold of her mind when she remembered the tenderness with which he had treated her. With incredible skill, he had torn her reserves down to nothingness during their long night together. Big man he might be, but he was gentle where it mattered, and flushing hotly, Martha recalled it all in vivid detail.

Against her better judgment, she felt a smile cross her lips as she went back over the night in his arms. Then she remembered her vow never to get entangled with a man again. "What he must think of me! A slut at the very least." She felt her face burning as she slipped into the shower and stood under the heated flow, hoping it would wash away her disgust with herself. "What a gutless wonder I am! I have no will power at all," she chastised herself as she moisturized her skin and pulled on her clothes. She hurriedly picked up what she had tossed about across the floor. All the items were hers, none of them were Tom's. She made herself ready to leave the sanctuary of her bedroom and face him, but she wasn't ready to do that.

Martha imagined him waiting for her in the kitchen with a "cat that ate the canary" look on his face. The thought of it made her angry and that gave her the courage she needed to go out and face him.

She stuck her chin in the air. She would hold herself together and damn him or anyone else. She fussed with her hair until it shone like liquid fire, and even put on a bit of make-up. "What are you doing, you fool?" she said to the image in the mirror. "Why are you trying to look your very best?"

She wore snug-fitting jeans and a dark green sweater that fit all too well—and she knew it.

She entered the kitchen and found it empty. A pot of barely warm coffee told her he'd been up a while. She looked out the window. He wasn't there, and a small niggling feeling of fear grew on her until she began believing something had happened. She didn't hear the dogs fussing about outside, either. It was possible he was out somewhere with the dogs. That had happened before.

Now she wasn't so sure she could face Tom after spending the night in a passionate tangle with him. Those heated memories were fresh in her mind, and she found it difficult to face him now in the light of day. What he must think of her—she couldn't begin to imagine. Thinking about it, she felt the heat of another deep blush burning across her face and neck.

Her head snapped up at the sound of crunching gravel. She ran to the window again to see Lizzie's Caddy coming in the driveway. Her heart leaped with joy at seeing her best friend drive into the yard. She headed for the door as the wheels stopped turning.

Martha helped Lizzie out of the car and embraced her. "Hey, girl, I'm so damned glad to see you. Are you doing okay?" She searched Lizzie's face with anxious eyes. How was she dealing with her husband's death?

Lizzie grabbed onto Martha and returned the embrace. "I had to get out of there. I am sick to death of all the phony condolences." She laughed, her tone derisive. "I think one of my dearest comforters just might have been the lovely little shack-up my husband had. I don't know for sure, but her perfume had me wondering. I had caught the same scent on my husband a time or two."

"Oh, Liz. What gall!"

"It *was* brassy, wasn't it? Maybe she came to see what her conquest had at home. Who knows, Martha? I don't."

Martha hurriedly put the coffee pot on. "Have you had anything to eat?" She looked at the clock. "My God, Liz, it's nearly noon."

Liz looked into Martha's face, her eyes narrowed. "What's going on around here? Are you saying you just woke up, Martha?"

"Yes, that's what I'm saying." Martha's tone was clipped.

"Where's the big guy? What's happening round here?"

"I don't know. He was gone when I got up, the dogs, too. I'm not worried. Tom likes to go walking down in the thickest part of the trees, and takes the boys with him."

"Something's going on." Lizzie laughed. "I see the color of your face, my dear. Are you are getting it on with that big dude? Don't you lie to me. I know what I see."

Martha felt her face heat up and glow like a blast furnace as she admitted, "I don't know how it happened, Liz, but it did, and I feel like a damned slut."

It felt so good to have someone in her corner who it was safe to tell about such personal things. Liz had always been there for her, and here she was, ready to help her iron out this new twist of fate in her life.

Liz leaned forward and took her hand. "You have a lot of living to do yet, girl. Are you thinking what Harry would say about it?"

"Of course, I am." Martha tasted dust and ashes in her mouth as she thought about Harry. She'd been unfaithful to his memory, and it hurt.

Liz sighed. "He was taken from you, Martha. And in a very cruel way. Isn't that what you said was being done to you—a part of that hidden enemy business you have, just like Harry figured?"

"I think it is, but how are we to know for sure?" Martha hated the weak, indecisiveness she heard in her own voice, and it made her temper rise. She squared her shoulders and took another tack, pouring Liz another coffee. "Liz, I might know a part of this. A man followed me home from work quite a while back. He had this certain truck. Harry and I saw it parked at a house in a crummy housing area." She went on to tell Liz about her two forays inside that house. "I have a strong feeling that same man is a part of all this, somehow. He has even driven past young Will while he waits for the school bus—twice."

"You think you may have hindered his sexual ability a little?" Liz had a one track mind when it came to Martha's hidden inner person and her inclinations toward sexual predators.

"Liz, you get right to the heart of the matter, don't you?" Martha found her tensions had relaxed, and she laughed with Liz as they discussed her nighttime activities. "It's like my old days, isn't it?" She let out another giggle as she let it all out with her dearest friend—one she could be completely honest with.

"How are you going to find out for sure about this strange man?" Liz asked. "And he works with little kids—at a grade school?"

"I saw the shirt, Liz. He must be a janitor. Imagine a guy like that working around all those little girls—boys, too."

Just then, Martha recognized the jingle of Skunk's collar and felt her heart begin to race. Tom had been out with the dogs, and he was back. Now she had to face him after last night—and in front of Lizzie!

Tom boomed into the kitchen along with the two scrambling dogs. Their entrance created a mad stir in the kitchen with their whining, licking, and claws clicking on the floor. He welcomed Lizzie, walked over to Martha, and grabbed her in a big hug. "Good morning," he boomed out to both of them.

Martha found herself speechless, and Tom stood looking at her.

Lizzie jumped into the sudden quiet breach. "I just had to get out of town, Tom. It's always good to see my friend here and find out what she's been up to." She stifled a giggle. "And it looks like she's been up to plenty."

"We've had a lot of things going on, Liz," he replied, a smile as wide as the Mississippi across his face.

Martha felt the heat of anger rising within her at Tom's cavalier attitude. It didn't help her feelings of shame and disgust she dealt with after she'd spent a night of heated passion in the man's arms. She'd been unfaithful to the memory of Harry Johns, and it hurt her deep inside.

She lashed out at Tom. "How can you stand there and act like nothing happened?" She stamped her feet and felt like a fool for doing such a childish thing. "I can't begin to describe how hurt Harry would be if he knew of it." She felt hot tears streaking down her cheeks.

Tom reached out and took her in his arms. Lizzie's presence made no difference to him as he held her struggling body against his own. "Martha, dear girl, I knew Harry way better than you. Believe me, he would be happy for both of us—he would."

Martha pulled away from him to look into his face. "How can you say such a thing?"

"Harry and I go way back, almost to boyhood. I guess I'd better level with you about Harry and me. He was married to my sister, Anna. I was there when he lost his little Della, my niece, and later on Anna, too. I went through all of that hell with the man. We worked together, too, until he moved to Denver. He said he had to get away from where those things had happened."

Martha put a hand on Tom's arm. "By the time I met him, he'd found out—you can never get away from your memories, Tom. They were strong inside him and tormented him day and night. But it did help him to know that one man is on death row, possibly the one who was responsible for his daughter's death."

"And you're the one who put him there, aren't you?"

"Yes, I did. He could surely be the one who brought that sorrow upon Harry and his little family." Martha was able to smile a bit as she remembered putting Denny Garver where he was today.

"Your friend, Ryan Mapus in Colorado Springs, said our grubby little suspect on Delgado Lane has been to see Denny twice," Tom reminded her.

"Yes, he told us that when I went to see Lizzie, remember?" Martha broke away from Tom and paced the kitchen floor. "Oh, God, Tom, it has to be that man. It has to!"

Lizzie smiled in her certain, knowing way. "I guess you got all that business off her mind for a while last night, Tom."

At that comment, Tom, Martha, and Lizzie all broke into a good laugh. No problems were solved, but a lot of tensions were eased.

Chapter 25

Ray drove into his littered yard and sat in his car a while. He had things to plan—things to set straight. "That ritzy bitch is out there visiting the Lavery woman again, or whatever name she goes by for now. Wonder if they're sharing that big stud of a cop while she's there. That bastard's got the two of them to take care of every damned night now. What a chance for me! If I'm careful and wait until the wee small hours of the night, I just might rid myself of all three of them in one great swoop, if I do it right. Shit-damn, things have been goin' wrong on me most of the time." He shook his head. "So far my record is nothin' to write home about." He hated the threat of Denny Garver more every day.

He sat in his small Toyota pick-up, a newer, nicer model, too. He'd had the sense to change vehicles again and wanted something a lot better this time. He'd leave the area when he had finished this job for Denny, and that truck would hold all his stuff real nice.

Pleased with how it felt to drive a better mode of transportation, he sat there, letting his mind go wild with the planning and just how he might accomplish what he had in mind. What a chance—all three at once! And then, he'd be shut of the whole damned thing after he took care of the kid.

That would have to wait. "Hell, too bad I can't wipe out the lot of them all at once." He'd have plenty of time after the bitch was dead. But he felt bad she wouldn't be around to cry over that damned kid—she'd be dead. "She won't get to suffer over the loss of the kid, but burning to death won't be such a damned picnic, either." He snorted at his own losses. "Too bad about doing what I'd like to with that boy. But I'll see the kid dead, anyway."

He knew that someone fixed his sex drive. He had gone over it many times, trying to figure out how it had been done to him. He was sure it happened that night his home was invaded. Someone had cut him right down to zero—to nothingness. But, in any case, after what he planned for tonight—and the kid—he'd be free of that sick bastard sitting on death row in Florence, Colorado. Ray pictured himself driving on a lonely freeway with his stuff in the truck and some money in his pocket.

❧❧❧

Will had learned a new maneuver this past lesson. He had decided he'd keep this new skill a deep, dark secret. His mother would scream if she knew about it. He practiced it over and over in the privacy of his own room. "If someone tries to grab me from behind, or even face to face, I can fix him real good with this move. I know I can. I'm strong enough to do most everything we've learned so far, the instructor told me so." Then he frowned as he remembered. "But he had also said you can be a weak little woman, and, if you do it right, it will work for you." He felt his chest swell with pride, in spite of the comparison with a weak, little woman.

He had done a lot of thinking about telling his mother what he was learning and what he was thinking but had decided not to tell her anything. *She's such a 'fraidy cat over everything, thinks I'm going to get hurt again.* He felt good, smiled, and thought of that day, wondering when it would come. He believed he would have an encounter with that man with the pitted face. And when it happened, Will would be ready.

Inside himself, he had decided he would never be a victim again. He had his memories—they had dimmed a bit, but like a slow burning nightmare, they clung in his mind and made him feel dirty inside. He knew he was not guilty of anything. It hadn't been his fault, but those invasive, evil things had been done to him. He'd been helpless to defend himself, and that would always be a part of his memories, too. Will had faced that.

He'd seen that small tan car around his immediate neighborhood, too, but not the last few days. He believed it was that pock-marked man, but he had decided not to tell his parents about that, either. They always got so upset about everything. Will had constantly kept an eye out for anything suspicious. He'd even taken to checking out the thickest bushes along his short half block walk home after the bus let him off.

Each lesson he'd had helped him believe he was ready. He felt a nervous excitement about it, tinged with a bit of fear. Any new thing, untried, but well practiced, had its unknowns. "Come on, Mr. Molester. I'm ready for you, any day—I'll be waiting!" Deep inside his mind, he'd always felt a need to avenge what had been done to him.

I've been taught not to misuse what I've been learning, but...

e∽ɔℰℲ

Martha, Tom, and Lizzie spent the rest of the day laughing, talking, and walking about outside in the soft spring air. The sun was out, and a few fleecy clouds clung in the azure sky. It should have been a totally relaxing day, but Lizzie caught the undertones between Tom and Martha. Yes, they had spent a night together—she'd got that much, but she had learned little else.

Martha meant the world to Lizzie, and she always looked for signs of emotional peril. She remembered fondly how she'd always been there for Martha. Had seen her through her psych days, vigilante days, a night at the sleazy Paradisio, and the rest of her crazy adventures as well. In addition, Lizzie knew she was the only soul in the world Martha could feel truly feel free to tell her deep secrets—her darkest secrets—everything.

Lizzie watched those two with a worried kind of curiosity that nearly drove her mad. She easily understood that neither Martha nor Tom realized the depth of her concern. They were far too lost in their own thoughts.

Martha felt her heart swell with joy. Her friend was here, the weather this relaxing day couldn't have been better—until she looked at Tom. The sight of his big body brought a flood of disturbing thoughts and memories to mind. She couldn't stop picturing what had taken place in the dark of night. Things she hadn't had the time to sort out.

In a total dither of confusion, and embarrassment, she couldn't speak to him about it. How could she—what could she say? She felt so guilty, thinking of Harry. What would he think of her?

What were Tom's thoughts? She couldn't bring it up—he'd be ready for another night of it. Thank God, Lizzie was here. Out of pure embarrassment, Martha just couldn't permit Tom in her bedroom tonight. But what about when Lizzie left and went home?

Worrying over it dampened Martha's joy of the weather and her friend's visit.

It came as a relief when Liz sidled up to her and in a lowered voice, questioned, "What the devil is going on with you? Why are you are in such a damned dither, Martha, my friend?" She uttered a short laugh and grabbed Martha by her shoulders. "Get that Tom out of here. Send him to the store for something. I want to know what's going on in that head of yours."

Martha's face burned with a furious blush. "Lizzie, he'll be after me again. I don't know how to stop this!" She faced Liz, panting. "It isn't right. I know it isn't."

"You'd better send that man off somewhere so we can get this out on the table, Martha." Looking about, Lizzie giggled. "Or on a stump."

Tom, intuitive sort that he was, saw that the women needed some time alone. He whistled for the dogs, and waving to the ladies, turned away, heading down into the thick stand of trees below. The dogs happily followed him, tails wagging and tongues hanging out.

"Those dogs have really taken to Tom." Martha sighed. "In too many ways, it's almost as if Tom has stepped into Harry's shoes, even to his handling the dogs."

"And apparently you, too." Lizzie suppressed another giggle. "What's really on your mind, Martha, dear?" She wasn't letting this chance get away from her. "Come on, spill."

"How can I spill anything to you, when I don't know what's happening, myself?"

"Is it because Harry's only been gone a couple months or so?"

"Some of it, yes. I feel disloyal to him, Liz."

"Martha, I knew Harry, too. That man would be the first one to tell you to grab what happiness you can." Liz took a deep breath. "We aren't on this earth long enough to spend it mourning over what we've lost. Granted, Harry was one of the best, but isn't he the very one who placed this big dude right here, under foot, as you always say?"

Martha tried to hold back a laugh and failed. "Liz, my dear, you do make a lot of sense." She sat on another handy stump and wiped her brow. "I am so tired of trying to sort things out, worried over that idiot who is out to kill everyone I know or care about, that I'm just not ready to get into another relationship."

"I can't help you there. But in any case, if you do take that big dude on, I think he'll be good for you. Nothing fazes the man, and he seems to be a take-care-of kind of guy." Lizzie stopped and thought a moment. "Funny how those two got together, but of course Tom was a brother-in-law to Harry, wasn't he?"

Martha puzzled over that herself. "Liz, that's a mystery to me, too. Why did I never hear of Tom before this? Harry wasn't one to keep secrets, but he never spoke much about that time of his life. Losing his little one, and then his wife was tough on him."

"I don't think men are much on speaking of sad things. They just hide it inside and go on." Liz laid a hand on Martha's shoulder. "Thanks for talking about this business with Tom. I hope you feel better getting it off your chest."

They saw Tom heading their way and got off their rustic seats to meet him. He came striding up, the dogs at his side, and he looked like he belonged right where he was—right now. Martha decided she would not fight against this man. Maybe Liz was right. He was meant to be right where he was, even if he did hold her back at times.

Tom stood in front of the two women. He figured

they had done their talking. He didn't really understand what they'd gotten into a lather about, but just being in their company was mighty nice, so he didn't bother about it.

Instead of talking about things, he had other thoughts. "Say, you ladies fancy a nice steak dinner somewhere tonight?"

Martha flushed. "Like at that place we went the other night?"

He gave her a slant-eyed look that set her pulses racing. "Which one?"

She gave a slight kick to a pine cone and didn't look up at him. "How about that steak place, remember, the first one we went to?"

Lizzie enjoyed this intimate little interplay. She approved and believed each of them deserved all the happiness they could find as she watched two good people trying to find their way to each other.

"Sounds great. The Big Horn Steak House, it is." He watched Martha intently, wondering how she was handling their torrid encounter of last night. He didn't think she'd allow it again tonight. Not with Lizzie present. But the friend would soon leave...

He wanted this woman more than he'd ever believed possible. He'd thought all that business was past for him. He'd had a few of his own personal sorrows—and they were deeply hidden. But he knew, and she knew it too, he'd have it on with her again, and plenty.

It was early yet, and the day was beautiful, cool, and breezy, but Tom's emotions ran high. Thinking of how his life was headed for change, he felt the sweat pouring off him as if he'd just climbed the Matterhorn. *Damn me, I must be crazy!*

"Catch you two, later," he called. He headed away from the ladies and took the dogs toward the house.

ℯↄℯↄ

They rode in Lizzie's brand new Caddie to the steak house. Tom drove, and Lizzie sat in the back. Little was said until Tom ushered them into the place. They were led along by the hostess through corridors of straw-covered wooden floors; seated at a highly polished, thick plank table, just like the last time they were here; and handed menus.

Lizzie looked about, staring momentarily at the straw-covered floor. "My, how rustic." The soft strains of western-themed music filled the air. Along with the hint of Mesquite tinged bar-b-que smoke, they heard the murmur of voices, and the clatter of dishes and cutlery. Lizzie smiled at Martha and Tom. "You've been here before?"

Martha was quick to reply as she fought the flush that crept up her neck. "Yes, it was a while back, and we needed a night out."

"The dance band isn't tuned up yet, but they're pretty good," Tom put in. "Especially for dancing." He cast an eye at Martha, his eyebrows raised. "This lady is magic on the dance floor."

"It's a far cry from the Paradisio, Martha, isn't it?" Lizzie said.

"Any place is a far cry from that sleazy hell-hole."

The waiter came and took their order for drinks. Tom had a dry Martini; Martha, a Stinger again; and Lizzie ordered a white wine, saying, "I've got to watch it. Since my husband is gone, I can't seem to take much in the way of alcohol."

Martha looked puzzled, but now was not the time to ask about that. In spite of Lizzie's husband's infidelity, she still had to learn to live her life as a single woman. Martha knew from experience that it wasn't easy.

As they sipped their drinks, the waiter took their food orders. Tom ordered the full-pounder again, and Martha the six-ounce sirloin. Lizzie took a broiled shrimp platter. The waiter set a plate of small bread rolls and butter in front of them. Lizzie murmured, "Oh, don't those little fatteners smell divine!"

They settled into their booth, munching on rolls slathered with butter. When they heard the strains of the western band tuning up, Tom slid out of the booth and held out his hand. "Martha, I'd like this first dance with you." Looking at Liz, he nodded. "You're next, my dear."

At the strains of a softly played waltz, Martha followed Tom out onto the small dance floor. He held her close, and looked into her eyes. "I know we have a lot to work out, but we will. Don't you worry about a thing. You'll be fine, Martha—and Harry would approve."

"How could you possibly know that?"

"We were close, as I said. We go back, nearly to childhood, Martha. He loved you completely and spoke of it more than once. He was a generous man in everything—this too."

"This too?" Martha queried.

"You know what I'm talking about."

He gently swung her about and into a graceful dip. She had to cling to him. Despite her worries over things, he felt so good to her, she was giving in to the wanton side of herself. It had to be Serena, and that angered Martha. She merely smiled at him and never let on how much she continued to despise herself for her wayward thoughts.

He returned her to her seat and took Lizzie out on the floor. Martha watched him handling her friend. He swept her along, swung her about, and Martha saw Lizzie laugh with joy. "He certainly has a way with women. Oh, yes, he certainly does," she murmured softly to herself.

Tom wanted to ask Lizzie about Martha, but it wasn't something he felt he could do. He'd wait and sort it out with Martha. They finished the dance as the waiter brought their dinners, which were sizzling on metal platters and fine enough for the most-particular palate.

Lizzie was impressed by everything. "This is very different from what I'm used to, but I have to say, it's wonderful. Thanks for bringing us, Tom."

"Not the usual country club fare?"

"Nothing is usual about this place, Tom," Lizzie said as she dug into her shrimp.

Martha cut into her tender sirloin, and they both watched Tom devour his meal, one befitting a man of his size.

They finished the meal, danced a bit more, and decided to head for home. Tom held his worry inside, but he had the feeling Martha might be next on the predator's menu. His anxiety had risen during their joyous, relaxing time out, and he wanted to get back and check out everything, inside and out.

Chapter 26

After the ladies were settled in the living room, Tom went outside with the dogs. He carefully checked around the perimeter of house and, seeing nothing to arouse his suspicions, headed back inside. All seemed fine. Both dogs were quiet, sniffing and wiggling about in normal fashion. Finally, satisfied, Tom entered the house and sat with the ladies in the large living area—or great room as Martha always called it.

"Tea, or coffee, anyone?" Martha offered. "I have ice cream, too."

Seeing no takers, she sat back and tried to relax, but she felt on edge. Did Tom have designs on her for tonight? She wouldn't consider anything of the sort with Liz in the house but wondered what she would do if Lizzie was not here. She couldn't stop feeling she had dishonored Harry's memory.

She had willingly let Tom take over. He had taken all of her as if she had no will at all. Even now, thinking of him, Martha felt those heated streaks running rampant through her body. No wonder she felt like a damned slut. A label she had fastened on to Serena.

But she was Serena. What did that say about her character? Could she face the truth? Even now, a feeling

of disgust came over her, and a slight feeling of disappointment—Tom was the perfect gentleman and made no
move toward her.

Nearing midnight, Martha said, "Liz, why don't you
sleep in with me? The bed is king size, and there's plenty
of room." She saw Tom squint his eyes a bit, and twitch
his lip, perhaps to let her know how he felt. But that's all
she saw. If he'd had any other plans, it wouldn't be for
tonight.

"Sure, Martha, I'd like that. We could talk all night
long, then." Liz got up and headed for the small room
where she'd put her bag.

Martha got out of her chair, and Tom caught her in
his embrace. "Nice going, girl." He smiled his narrow-
eyed smile at her, and she knew that he was on to her.

"Tom, we have a guest. We can sort this out much
later." Martha pulled herself out of his arms and headed
down the hall, saying, "Good night, Tom." She wanted to
smile at him and giggle like a damned fool but held it in.

Both she and Lizzie got ready for bed and slipped
between the sheets. "I miss having someone in here with
me, Liz. I had gotten so used to Harry. I believe I will
mourn him forever. He was such a great guy."

"I know how it is myself, in spite of knowing my beloved was screwing around. For sure, they leave an empty spot when they're gone—good or bad."

"How are you doing, getting used to widowhood?"
Martha wanted to know, but she didn't want to bring on
an emotional storm. Lizzie had plenty of things to get off
her chest.

"I have had the repairs done to the garage and house.
I bought a new car as you have seen. And all the estate
matters are done with, too." Lizzie choked back a sob.
"As you know, Martha, I have plenty of reason to actually celebrate this loss, but it's still a major change." She

shrugged, and her hands splayed out in the semi-darkness of the room. "But now there are no more fancy dinners with his coworkers or dances at the country club, either. Being single is tough when you've been married forever."

"We have a lot in common, don't we?" Martha wanted to comfort Lizzie and didn't really know how. "You'll get things straightened out and begin a new life, Liz." She knew that time was the best healer, and it took a lot of that to adjust your habits and feelings to a big change in your daily life, happy or sad.

"I wish I was a guy magnet like you, girl." Lizzie giggled. "You seem to have wonderful guys pouring out of your ears."

"It wasn't my idea to have that big lout hanging about the place!" Martha replied, a silly smile on her face.

"Big lout? Oh, how you do suffer, my dear." Lizzie laughed and turned to her side.

Both women slowly succumbed to fatigue and drifted off. Martha heard the soft sounds of Lizzie's slumber, and soon she drifted off herself.

ↄↄↄ

It must have been after three a.m. when, outside the property and down the road a bit, a car pulled up and parked. A figure crept close to the yard, moving quietly. Ray stayed down wind to avoid alerting the dogs. When he came close enough, he hurled chunks of meat into the yard. The chunks were laced with heavy doses of sedative. He waited and watched.

He saw the dogs raise their heads as they sniffed the air. The bigger dog caught the scent of the meat. At first, he only sniffed. Then, whining softly, and growling low, the dog headed for the tantalizing smell of a tasty treat. Also catching the scent, the smaller spotted dog was right behind him. Their tails were wagging, but their fur ridged up along their backs in suspicion as they approached.

Ray started worrying the dogs would get in a snarling match over the meat, and his plans would fall apart. But he could only watch. If he approached closer, they would catch his scent and set up a storm of barking, and that big bastard cop would be outside in a flash, looking for an intruder. Ray didn't want to chance having that happen.

Excited, he murmured under his breath, "Oh, God! They've got it. It won't be long until both those furry critters will be out like a light."

He had bags of rags and cloth back in his car, ready to soak in alcohol. He'd found it cheaper than fuel, and going to several stores, he'd gotten quite a lot of it. In fact, he had several gallons of the stuff, enough to set fires on all sides of this house. His plan was to completely entrap the occupants. Here was his chance to take out three of them—and all at once, too.

He also decided it was lucky this old-style ranch house had that nice wood siding all around. He was relieved it wasn't asbestos—that shit was fireproof. Ray knew this old, sun-dried material was bone dry—just waiting for a match to set it off. Luckily, it hadn't rained for more than a week. The siding was dried out real good and would burn like paper.

The thought of it made his heart race. That damned nut-clipping bitch was quietly sleeping or getting it on inside there with her current stud. This woman was the cause of all his trouble. If it hadn't been for her, none of this would have ever been started in the first place. She was the one who put Denny where he was. Everything was her fault, and tonight she would pay the price.

Tonight would be the end of all his troubles. He hadn't taken care of the kid, yet, but he couldn't pass up this opportunity to rid himself of Denny's main goal. Maybe this would be enough to satisfy Denny and get that sick bastard off his neck. And tonight this chance was too good to miss. He muffled a giggle, "And I'll get the fancy dame with the caddy while I'm at it."

As all the lights were out and he heard no sounds anywhere, Ray decided the house held only sleeping occupants. He was ready to go to work. The dogs were laying spread out asleep, and he freely moved about setting his fire trap.

He carried the rags, already stuffed in small bags and soaked with good old rubbing alcohol. It was heavy in his own nostrils and nearly had his head spinning by the time he had them all re-soaked and placed every three feet around the outside of the ranch house. He'd left all the tops open and torn a small hole in each bottom so they'd burn real hot. Then he snapped his cigarette lighter into action and quickly moved around the outside of the house, setting them ablaze.

The dogs were laying out on the driveway and wouldn't get hurt. That satisfied Ray for some reason. His heart leaped with excitement as he watched the blaze erupting in each spot, all around the outside of the house. The dry cedar siding quickly caught fire as he had hoped it would.

As the blazing erupted into a roar, Ray moved away. He wanted to watch this fire take hold and end of all his misery. He'd like to stand right here and watch the bitch and her friends burn to death. But he knew he had to get away from the scene. He didn't want to be caught standing around watching the building burn to the ground as some arsonists were known to do. He headed for his nice Toyota pick-up and drove reluctantly away.

രൗരൗ

Tom came alert in a sudden jerk—did he smell smoke? His pulses raced as he leaped from his bed and pulled on his clothes. When he saw the glow of flames from his window, he knew the house was on fire. After he'd raced to a few other rooms and saw the same thing, he cursed, "Holy shit! He's set fires all the way around this damned house." He snarled in disgust at such a cowardly act. "That bastardly son-of-a-bitch is trying to burn us out!"

He raced to Martha's bedroom as smoke rapidly filled the house, thick and choking. Every window had a glow of fire outside of it, and he wondered how they could escape. The smoke had gotten so thick and heavy inside the house, he could barely breathe unless he went down to the floor. "We're trapped in here!"

He didn't plan to die by the hand of some miserable lowlife. He found Martha's room—the smoke had become heavy in there, too. He reached the bed and thumped her on her back. He pulled her awake. "Martha, the house is on fire!" He shook Lizzie awake. "Get a move on, ladies! We're on fire, all around the house. We've got to get out!" He pulled Lizzie to the edge of the bed, and she sat there in a daze.

Martha snapped into action. Still a bit confused from her deep sleep, she leaped out of bed and saw Lizzie sitting up, looking confused. "Get some clothes on, Liz. The house is burning—we have to get out!"

Tom stood in front of them. "Get clothes on, get in the shower, and get wet. We have to get out, but I haven't found a way, yet. Soak a lot of towels and breathe through them. You have to, the smoke is too heavy. Be ready." He left them.

Lizzie was fully awake now, pulling on her jeans, a top, and shoes. Martha was already in the bathroom, running the shower, and grabbing towels from the cupboard.

Tom appeared. "I've found a way out, but it'll be fire all the way."

He grabbed the wet towels, except one for each to hold over their mouths and noses. He told the women to follow him. In the great room, he approached the larger, main window pane. Flames were visible outside, on all sides and he believed it had reached the roof as well. He saw the edges of the roof bursting into flames. But glass didn't burn, and he found there was less fire by the big window that was their only way out, their only chance.

He faced them. "We have to go out through here. I'll smash the glass and pad the bottom edge. The inrush of air will make the fire hotter, but we have to get out. Our air is about gone in here. Get down on the floor to get a breath of air until I'm ready." He coughed. The smoke was so thick that he choked on his words.

He rolled a towel around his arm and smashed the glass in several places.

I'm glad these aren't duel-paned windows. Martha thought. *Harry never got around to having them changed.*

Tom laid towels across the broken glass and grabbed Lizzie off the floor. "Out you go, girl." He picked her up and gave her a good solid shove past the smoldering shrubs, hoping she landed clear of the glass and flames. Then he did the same with Martha.

Martha landed hard, but Lizzie had gotten to her feet and helped Martha get up. They looked back at the gaping hole that had been the window. There was no sign of Tom, and Martha felt a terrible fear for his life.

"Tom, where are you?" she screamed.

She heard no answer and choked again on the swirling smoke as she tried to see him. Off in the distance, she heard the scream of sirens as she struggled through the smoldering shrubs to the window's edge. She looked inside, trying to see Tom. The shrubs had burned almost completely, but she felt the remaining heat of them searing her thighs and legs as she tried to find him.

Looking over the jagged edge of broken glass, Martha saw him laying inside the window. He appeared to have passed out before he could get himself outside the big window. "Lizzie! He is laying just inside. But, he's so big, I can't get him!"

"Martha, the fire truck is here!" Lizzie turned and ran for the truck.

Martha backed away from the encroaching flames. Her eyes burned from smoke, and she gasped for a breath of air. As she gulped in the fresher air away from the fire, she saw the firemen coming to help. They followed Lizzie.

"Please, there's a big man right inside this window. He's passed out on the floor. Please get him out!" Martha pointed to the gaping window and saw the flames burning inside the house moving ever closer to Tom. In fact, taking a quick glance, she saw that the entire house was now a hopeless mass of fire. The roof was nearing collapse.

The firemen had her step away. One of them took her to a place of safety. She watched them go through that window. They wore smoke masks, and shortly they lifted and tugged to pull Tom's inert figure out the window into the fresh air.

"God, this'n here's one big dude—you got him?"

She heard the grunting comment as she saw them haul Tom to safety. Another man brought a stretcher, and they placed Tom onto it. Was he alive? Sick at heart, she didn't see how he could be—that choking, poisonous smoke had been so thick. She tried to go to him, but the fireman gently moved her away, saying, "We'll attend him, ma'am."

She felt Lizzie's arm around her. "He'll be all right, girl. Those paramedics are very good." She tightened her hold on Martha. "That man set this fire, didn't he?"

"I'm sure it was him—had to be. Oh, Liz, he tried to get all three of us this time." She suddenly remembered the dogs. "I wonder if he killed the dogs." She looked around. "If they were alive, wouldn't they be right here under foot, barking their heads off?"

Martha moved back and took a moment to look at the burning home where she and Harry had been so happy. It was a total loss, now nothing but a pathetic pile of burning embers. She couldn't feel anything right now, but she knew who had done this evil thing. She clenched her fists as her anger rose inside her. She would attend to him herself. And without further thought, her mind settled on that scrawny little man on Delgado Lane.

It had all become too much. After they'd put Tom on a stretcher with an oxygen mask over his face, she knew he lived. She breathed a sigh of relief and let the tears flow. She wanted to see if he could speak to her. That big man had saved her life again.

Martha approached the ambulance and the EMT caring for Tom. "Please, let me see him. He saved our lives tonight." And this time, she did not plan to take no for an answer.

At the man's nod, she approached the stretcher. Lizzie was right beside her. Tom had his eyes closed, and she thought him unconscious. But he must have sensed her closeness. He slowly opened those bloodshot black eyes and looked at her. "Martha, are you all right?"

"Yes, thanks to you. The question is—are you all right, Tom?" She had cried enough already, but seeing that big lout as she had always called him looking so pale and weak, nearly tore her heart out.

"I must have passed out somewhere. Who got me out?"

"The firemen. You were inside, Tom—we couldn't do it—we couldn't get you out. Thank God, they came just in time." She tried to smile. "They had a tough time dragging you out, but they managed it. One of them called you a big dude, Tom."

"House is a goner?"

Martha could only nod. She smoothed his sooty forehead with her hand. "Sorry you're lying on this stretcher, Tom. You saved both Lizzie and me tonight—you know you did. Thanks are not enough for something like that."

"I won't be on this stretcher for long, Martha. You will be dealing with me for a long time to come." He looked into her eyes with his bloodshot black orbs, and then his eyes closed, his head rolled to the side, and he appeared to be unconscious.

Martha wanted to scream, but instead, she got the EMT. "He's passed out, sir."

"Yeah, happens a lot in these cases." He nodded at Tom. "He's a strong dude, ma'am. For sure, he has smoke inhalation, and maybe some searing of his lungs, but the doc will know best about that. He'll be right as rain in a few days." He checked the oxygen flow and told her, "Looks like he'll be the only case I'm taking in. I'll be taking him to Riverside Emergency, ma'am." He got into the vehicle. Another man got in with Tom, and they sped away.

Lizzie said, "Sounds like Tom has you in his plans for the future, doesn't it, Martha."

"What future?" Martha replied. "Look around you. The house is gone."

"Come on, Martha, you're in shock right now. You'll rebuild—won't you? You must have insurance on the place."

"Harry had a fireproof safe. I suppose it's in the rubble somewhere with all our important papers," Martha muttered, her head in her hands, blathering about things, and not making sense.

Hearing her friend babbling senselessly, Lizzie became worried. "Martha, I think you should have been in that ambulance right along with Tom."

"Oh, that's ridiculous!" Martha exclaimed as she sank down on the grassy area near where the ambulance had been.

Lizzie called another of the firemen over. "Look at her, will you? She's not right in the head at the moment."

The fireman knelt beside Martha and touched her shoulder. "Ma'am, can you talk to me a moment?"

"Who, me?"

"Yes, ma'am, can you answer a few questions for me?" He knelt down on the grass beside her.

"I can't think about things like insurance or valuables, right now. That man almost killed us. It just isn't important after almost being burned to death." Martha shivered at her thoughts, and the EMT took notice.

Chapter 27

The EMT turned to Lizzie. "What is she talking about? What man? Are you saying she knows who may have set this fire?"

"Someone has set out to kill Martha. But from what little we know or believe, he is trying to destroy all her family and friends first. Tonight, he tried to get the three of us. But before this, he has tried to kill me with a bomb in my car. Martha had warned me, and I hired a guard. When he saw the man run out of our garage, we called the police. He failed that time, but later on, he did kill my husband, by mistake, I think. Before that, he had tried to kill Martha's daughter, her husband, and now he has finally gone after Martha. No wonder she's a bit off, right now. That's a big load for anyone to carry."

"My God, woman, is anything being done?"

"I think they're trying. But so far, nothing has been solved or any one arrested, to my knowledge. Martha is my dearest friend in the world. I need her and so do a lot of other people. This shouldn't be happening!" Her tone had accusations in it, but Lizzie didn't care. No one was safe with that monster running amok the way he was.

"Good Lord, no wonder she's in a dither right now, if not in shock. I wish that ambulance was here. I'd send her in right now." He bent down to Martha, prepared to take her blood pressure and pulses. "She may be suffering from smoke inhalation in the bargain."

"Why can't I take her to the hospital?" Lizzie looked about. Her car sat where she had left it. But was it safe to drive? She wouldn't touch it now until it had been cleared. But then she remembered something else. "I'm from Colorado Springs—I don't know where the hospital is."

Martha spoke up. "Look, I know I'm shook up, and plenty. Who wouldn't be? But I do not need the hospital. I want to go to my daughter's home, and I know the way there, Liz. I need to go see how Tom is. He looked so bad, Lizzie."

"Okay, Martha, we can do that, and if you get sick or something, your daughter can take you in to the ER." Then Lizzie remembered, and hands on her hips, she faced the EMT. "Would you look at my car? I'm afraid to get in it unless it has been checked for a bomb. That man has tried to kill me three times so far, and these days, I can't drive anything without it being checked out for a bomb first." She pointed. "It's over there—the Caddy,"

"I'll get right on it, ma'am." He walked away, shaking his head.

Martha got up from her grassy spot. "I can't call Jeannie, my phone was in there." She pointed at the smoldering ruins of what had been a very happy home. "Look at that, Liz. It's all gone." She allowed more tears to flow. They felt good and cleaned the smoke and ashes from her eyes.

"It was such a nice place, Martha. What a damned shame."

Martha narrowed her eyes. "If it's that runty soul on Delgado Place, I hope I fixed him good."

They were interrupted by the returning EMT. "Your

car checks out, ma'am. I had to use a slim-jim to open the door—to get in. How about the keys, do you have them?"

Lizzie flung out her hands. "Keys weren't on our minds when Tom got us up and shoved us out that window, sir. Have you got a cell we can use?"

He handed his cell over, and Martha put in a call to Jeannie. It was daylight by now, and she'd be awake. Martha hated putting this latest news on her daughter's shoulders, but there was no other choice. She waited for her daughter to answer.

Jeannie said hello, and Martha had to tell her all that happened during the dark of night. It took a while. Jeannie's near hysteria had to be quieted, and she had to be reassured her mother was all right. "Hey, I'm talking to you, right?" Martha demanded.

Finally, Jeannie said, "Mom, I'm calling Martin. He'll come out there and bring you in to our house, and of course, Lizzie also. We can attend to any other details, after that." She rattled on, but Martha knew she had settled down and was making sense. "Mom, if you barely got out with the clothes on your back, you must need everything. Imagine it! You'll have everything new— clothes, make-up, hair brushes—you name it. Dishes, glassware, oh, Mom, it's endless! And certainly, we'll go visit Tom." She sounded excited about having a chance to help her mother, and Martha was glad to hear that in her voice.

She informed Lizzie, and it was settled. The firemen were still spraying water on the ruins of her home, and the dogs slowly dragged themselves about. They were barely on their feet. Martha realized the dogs had been very heavily drugged and worried if they were going to be all right. But when she saw them wag their tails, weakly and slowly, she believed they would be fine. Worn out and overwhelmed as she was, that was enough for her. It was a positive sign.

The chief fireman came to Martha. "What can you tell me about this?"

Martha replied, "Please, let's sit down here in the grass. I'm sort of shaken by what has happened."

He agreed and sat across from her—all ears, and a recorder in his hand.

Martha did her best to explain about her nemesis, all he had done, and even who she had in mind. The man had a strange look on his face, but he seemed to have a lot of sympathy. Martha was sure it sounded rather insane but went on to explain that he ought to speak with Tom if he needed more information about the person who had started the fire. Being encouraged to speak to a detective about all this seemed to satisfy the man.

"What are your plans now, ma'am?" he asked, looking about at the devastation.

"I'm not sure of anything, sir. There is a safe somewhere in those ashes. I'd like to have it, if your men can locate it. All our papers were in it. It's supposed to be fireproof, Harry said." She sighed. "Harry Johns was the previous owner. He told me about the safe."

By the time Martin drove up with his Buick, the firemen had recovered the safe. The dogs had mostly regained their strength and were busily sniffing about the ashes and smoldering shrubs. Their barking sounded decidedly weak as Martin drove into the yard.

"My God, Martha!" He whistled and walked all around the still smoking rubble. "That bastard sure made a good try on your lives. Jeannie told me Tom tossed both of you out that big window in front, is that right?"

Martha hugged her son-in-law. "Martin, you're right. Whoever he is, he made a heck of a try to burn us to death. Tom saved our lives, without a doubt." She shook her head as she looked over the pile of rubble that had held a lot of good memories. "It's all gone, isn't it?"

Martin nodded. "Well, if the firemen are through with you, let's get you back to our house." He looked at the filthy, rubble-encrusted safe. "What about that?"

"We have to take it along, Martin. I have never been in it, and I don't know how to open it, but we can't leave it here, either."

"I have an old blanket in the back. I'll wrap it in that." He walked around it. "I wonder if I can lift it."

℘ℭ℘

Later, Martin had squared everything with the fire chief, loaded the safe with the help of the firemen, and they were headed for his home. Martha sat in front with Martin. She dreaded going over the whole thing again with Jeannie but knew she couldn't escape it. She felt so tired, she could barely hold her head up and dozed off on the way into Denver.

Lizzie sat in one of the back seats. There were two rows of seats behind the driver, and she let herself relax, though she wondered how she would ever get her car going. It had another set of keys at home, but the set she had driven here with had been in her purse, and that no longer existed. She knew there'd be a way, and feeling completely wrung out and tired, she dozed off on the way into Denver, herself.

℘ℭ℘

It was mid-morning by the time they arrived at the Moulton home. Martha came awake to see her daughter fling open the front door and come rushing out to her. She dreaded going over it all again, but she knew that would happen many times in the near future. Right now, she felt defeated. Serena was quiet, and she had no Harry to bring her around—nor did she have Tom. She wanted to curl up somewhere and sleep for a day.

Jennie took one look at her and said, "Mom, come in the house. You need a shower and some sleep." Looking at Lizzie, she added, "You too, dear."

Martha remembered feeling proud of her daughter's take-charge attitude as both women were escorted inside, given a small light breakfast, and allowed the time they needed to clean up and put on some fresh clothes that Jeannie had found somewhere.

She told her mother, "Mom, get some rest, I'll find out all I need to know from Martin."

Martha had Will's small room. She had no idea where Lizzie was, but they were both clean, clothed, and given time to rest. She and her friend needed it. Martha snuggled into bedding that had the faint scent of a young boy, her grandson Will, and let go.

Martin told Jeannie all he knew about the fire. "It's a total loss, but she can rebuild if she wants to." He had twisted his hands together without thinking, as he worried aloud to his wife. "Jeannie, it could be Will he'll go after next. There is no one left he hasn't gone after—it has to be."

Jeannie nearly screamed at his words, but she clapped her hand over her mouth as Martin held her close. He muttered, "Jeannie, hold on. Whatever this is, it's almost over. It's coming to a head, like a damned filthy boil. I have a feeling the end is near.

As Martin comforted his wife, he wondered what Martha would find in the safe. She had never actually seen it—only knew there was one. He hoped the insurance papers were in there. Martha would need some money to rebuild.

He had no idea how to open it, so he decided to call one of his coworkers. "Hey, Jim. I have a little problem." He laughed and thought it sounded a bit nervous, even to his own ears.

He carefully explained the problem and was immediately given a clue. "Two paper clips and a pair of needle nosed pliers?" Martin uttered a contemptuous laugh. "You're kidding me. I thought these things were safe from burglars." He listened a bit longer. "Okay. I've got an idea how to do it. I can look on the internet if I get lost. Good Lord! They have everything on there, don't they?"

Martin rang off and got busy. It took a good two hours, but he finally felt the handle give way. The door creaked open. Inside he saw slightly singed papers, several silver bars, a stack of gold pieces, and a photo album. He looked inside the album and saw a family shot of Harry with a lovely young woman at his side and a tiny blonde girl on his arm. Martin felt his throat tighten, remembering all Harry had lost.

From then on, he scanned the insurance papers, the title to the home, and the one to Harry's old truck. It had sat useless since his death, but Martha had kept it. She had not gotten rid of anything of Harry's that Martin knew of. There were a few other things, but he was satisfied Martha had insurance coverage on her house. He decided she could deal with the album and the rest of the contents. He closed the door part way, afraid it might lock again.

Martha came out after three in the afternoon, wearing clothes that were not hers, and her hair knotted and mussed. Lizzie stumbled out behind her, rubbing her eyes like a child.

"Martin, I must go see Tom. He saved our lives last night." She went on, "I'll be ready in a while. I have no makeup, no comb, no—my God, Martin, everything is gone!"

Lizzie sat in a chair, her head in her hands. "Martha, your life is *not* gone, and that's what *really* matters. As we know all too well, death is the one thing you can't come back from. All the rest are just 'things.' It's sad to lose special items, certainly, but everything else can all be replaced, and it will be. What's important right now is that no one was lost in the fire."

Martin took Martha in his arms. "That filthy bastard planned to kill all three of you. He set those fires all around the house, so you'd have no way out. He has failed again, kiddo. What a klutz! If it's in the papers, he must feel like the world's biggest failure right now." He uttered a small chuckle, but Martha wasn't laughing. Lizzie wasn't either.

"I know it's that sleazy little man on Delgado Place. I feel it in my bones. He followed me home from the hospital I work at. He was seen checking out Will, too. We know that much. I've been inside that house, Martin. I saw a little patent leather shoe in his bedroom. If it belongs to that Lassen child, that proves that Rayburn McGill is the soul of evil, a child molester, and a killer too!"

"Martha, what are you saying? Has Serena been active again?" He grasped her by the shoulders. "You know his name?"

Yes, Tom checked the license numbers from what Will had taken down, and from what Harry and I had taken when we were driving past that house." She smiled, her lips tight. "He has ways to find out things like that." She shrugged. "Martin, Tom followed me the second time I went there—he watched everything I did."

"Everything you did?"

"Yes, I knocked McGill out and injected a certain product that I hope has made his gonads dry up into tiny little nothings." She saw a certain smirk cross Lizzie's face. She already knew this story.

"I'm speechless, but with your history I shouldn't be surprised." Martin sat down and wiped his brow. "How will you ever know if what you did was effective?" he added, "What did you use, Martha?"

"It's a preparation used to neuter puppies. I had to use a lot, maybe enough for a St. Bernard, a real big one." She couldn't stop the giggle that escaped at Martin's expression. "There is no way to know. I can only hope. What I don't get is why nothing is done about him. Tom said they cannot arrest him without cause, or do forensics on his home, either." Martha flung out her hands. "What I *can* do is go visit Tom. I owe him everything." She turned to her friend. "Lizzie, would you want to go see our rescuer?"

"Thanks, Martha, but look at me, I am not presentable enough to visit the city dump, right now." She headed back to bed.

Martin informed Martha that the safe had been opened and her insurance was in effect. "There were pictures and other thing in there, but I didn't bother with it. That will be up to you."

"Thanks for everything, Martin, but I must see Tom as soon as I can." As he grabbed up his keys, he noticed her head was held high, and she seemed brighter—like she'd gotten over the initial shock of the fire and was ready to face what had happened and go forward. Martin smiled at this amazing woman who was his mother-in-law.

Chapter 28

Martin ushered Martha into Riverside Hospital. At the front desk, she faced the elderly clerk. "May we see Detective Tom Wells, please?"

Receiving the room number, they took the elevators and went to the second floor. This was a medical floor—one Martha had worked many times.

She felt her nerves rise to match her racing pulse. She was almost afraid to see how Tom fared after she'd seen him passed out on that stretcher. He'd survived that smoke-filled holocaust, but had he been seriously injured? Neither she nor Lizzie had possessed the strength to get him out—to save his life—when he'd just saved theirs. Tight as a wound spring, and forgetting Martin was with her, Martha stepped inside.

Worried as she was over for Tom's condition, she also faced the realization she cared a great deal for this big man. He'd become so meaningful and important in her life that her feelings for him had come about almost against her will, or better judgment.

He lay asleep, propped up with several pillows, with oxygen via nasal cannula. Seeing that, Martha feared his lungs had indeed taken a severe hit—by smoke if not actual fire.

At the sound of their footsteps, his eyes opened and

fixed on Martha. "Hey, now, how are you, lady?" he said to her and nodded at Martin, who stayed back.

"I'm just fine, Tom, thanks to you."

"Think nothing of it. Just doing my job." He choked out a harsh, non-productive, rasping cough.

Martha noticed he brought up nothing and believed his lungs were severely injured. Was his cough nothing more than a natural response to local irritation? She choked up, and tears filled her eyes at the sacrifice this man had made for her.

"What does the doc say about your lungs, Tom? And don't lie to me about it. I can get the truth, and you know it."

"He told me I had a lot of smoke inhalation, but not so much real tissue damage. That's what he said. I'll be right as rain, my dear, and he said I could leave here in another day or so." He frowned. "The problem is, I'm not sure where we'll go. I still have my obligations."

"We? What obligations, Tom?" Martha had always wondered why Tom guarded her. She never believed it was because of his boss and waited for his explanation.

Tom coughed again and, in his newly hoarse voice, started his story. "Right after Harry was shot, I found him and called for help. Right then, Martha, he made me swear to keep you safe. He believed you were the real goal from this predator, right off. He didn't know how it came about, but he was onto the game from the beginning." He coughed that harsh, rasping cough again. "That's why I've been the big lout under your feet all this time, dear girl. It was Harry's last command to me."

"Oh, Tom, that sounds so like him." Martha took his hand. "And he knew I wouldn't like it."

"He said you wouldn't." He chuckled softly. "But he was very afraid for you—your family, too."

"Oh, Tom, he must have been in such pain, right

then. How could he think about me at a time like that?"

"He always thought of you, Martha. And now that I know you so much better, I can understand it." He let the rest of what he meant by that flash in his narrowed black eyes.

Martin broke into the conversation. "Tom, you'll come to our home until we decide what to do about...everything."

"Where did you live before you came to my house?" Martha asked.

"I gave that place up, Martha. It wasn't big enough for two, anyway."

"What do you mean?" But Martha knew exactly what he meant.

"Never mind, you two." Martin laughed and took her arm. "We need to go, Martha. I'll leave you here for a moment or two, while I bring the Buick around front. But I have a locksmith going out to Harry's place to fit some keys in that Caddie so Lizzie can drive her car, and I need to get out there and see to it. She wants to head for home." He looked at Tom. "I think he'd best make some new keys for the other cars while he's out there, hadn't he? I'll have him do that."

"Hey, Martin, thanks."

Tom had another fit of dry coughing, but Martha detected some moisture and the beginning sound of normality in it as well. She felt that familiar streak of heat zip along her spine. *He'll get better quick enough, and what will happen between us then?*

After Martin left, Tom addressed her, sounding almost formal in tone, "Martha, I will not leave you alone until this man is caught—I cannot." He grinned at her with a twinkle in his eye. "It was very good between us, my dear, and you cannot deny it—no way can you. We'll get this straightened out between us, and you know I can be persistent as hell."

"I don't know what to say right now, Tom." Martha felt flustered. Her heart hammered relentlessly, and the feeling of being trapped, slowly crept over her as she mumbled, "I've got to go right now, we'll take this up later—you must be crazy!"

She left the room and stumbled to the elevators on her way to meet Martin with the car. "What am I to do with that man?"

⌯⌯⌯

Ray went out and picked up his paper, but he'd already heard the news. He'd felt the ice creeping into his bones as soon as the TV blared it out. He knew he had another failure to add to his sorry account. "Shit-damn, Denny will be after my ass now, for sure. This is all I need—another botched up mess!" He cursed, using words he'd never used before as the fear of failure settled in. "How in the hell did that damned stud Martha's got living there figure out how to escape that burning house?" He again felt that new kind of anger festering inside his useless soul.

He was ready to kill and main. And that would be all he could do these days. Something had been done to him. He was a sexless eunuch, a creature he'd read about in books and had pitied. He flopped aimlessly down in his worn-out chair. "I've got to leave this area, this state, and maybe this country. Damned that devil, Denny Garver. How could a man on death row ruin a man's life from a prison cell? How in the hell could that happen?"

But it had happened. Now, all that was left to him was to get rid of the damned kid. Ray knew it was all he had left. He cursed aloud. "That damned nut-clipping woman, Martha Lavery, Chance, or whatever to hell her name is these days, is still alive—and free as a bird. Her house has burned to hell and back, and her lover is in the hospital. Even her snooty society-bitch friend has gotten off without a scratch. It's enough to make a man go crazy! I've got to get a different car again, too. This nice Toyota pick-up has been seen way too often."

Ray was tired. In his excitement over the fire, and the hoped-for result, he hadn't slept a wink since he'd gotten home. His big arson attempt had gone up in flames, along with that damned house. He got up and paced the floor, kicking an empty beer can in the process. "Maybe I'll try a different car lot. That last salesman looked sort of funny at me. Maybe he wonders why I need so many different cars."

He couldn't rest. He got out of his chair, went to his money stash, and headed out, the unregistered title to the nice Toyota pickup in hand.

ᶜᵛᵒᵉᵛᵒ

Lizzie was ready to head for home. Martin had brought her car to her with a new key in the ignition. She turned to Martha. "Girl, you can call me anytime. If I come to visit again—can we keep things down to a dull roar?" She hugged Martha. "Life with you has never been a dull anything, my dear friend, but you've outdone yourself, this time. A nice dinner out, dancing, and on top of that, a nice toasty night at home."

"You wretch!" Martha returned, squeezing Lizzie half to death before ushering her into her Caddy.

"I'll be back to see you all, dears," Lizzie cried to Martha, Martin, and Jeannie as she drove away.

By the time Lizzie left, it was near time for Will to get off the bus and come walking up the sidewalk to his home. Martha, more fearful for him than ever, said, "Why don't I go down and meet his bus?"

Jeannie shook her head. "No, Mom, it might embarrass the kid. He's getting to that age."

Martha nodded her acceptance of her daughter's advice, but nothing she said soothed her apprehension. He only had to walk one short block, and she was anxious to see him safely home, but she said nothing to upset her daughter.

She hadn't told her daughter that Tom, along with Martin and herself, believed Will was next on that devil's hit list. But those words were ever in her thoughts. *He'll try to get Will but how—and when?*

She told her daughter, "I feel sort of cooped up. I'm going out for some fresh air. I need a good long walk."

Jeannie watched her set out, so Martha walked up the street, away from the direction Will would leave the school bus. Undeterred, she quickly went around the block and headed back to where she could see the bus stop.

It was time for Will to come home. Shortly, Martha saw the bus pull up and heard the breaks squeal as it came to a halt. Will was the only one to get off. He waited for the bus to leave then slung his bag of books over his shoulder and trudged up the hill to his house.

Martha barely noticed a small maroon sedan sliding slowly by but that it slowed just a tiny bit caught her attention. Her heart rate sped up at the thought of who could be driving that car.

She hadn't seen it before, which tended to allay her suspicions, but the man changed vehicles so often it could be him. She didn't get the license number or see the driver enough to be sure, but her alarm system was on full alert.

Will was safe for this day, but later on—what then?

eɔeɔ

Two days later, they brought Tom home to the Moulton household. They insisted he stay there. Neither he nor Martha had a home to go to. It would have to do for now. When to build another home for Martha, or what kind of house, remained to be decided. The police had finished their investigation and labeled it a murder attempt, as well as an arson case.

But as far as Martha could determine, nothing had been done to find the culprit. Not one thing! To her, the time had come to get the authorities to do forensics on that home on Delgado Lane. Yet, she hesitated. She puzzled over how to get that done and stay out of jail herself. Her disguise and make-up were in her car, and Martin hadn't brought it in to her. It needed a set of keys as well. And she had no purse to put keys into.

She wanted to discuss these things with Tom. Was he well enough? He was resting in Will's small room at present. She tapped on the door and heard his voice beckon her inside.

He looked much improved, and his coughing was productive now as his body slowly repaired itself. Clinically, Martha knew he coughed out what had been damaged as the lungs grew new tissue to replace the old. "Tom, can we talk a bit?"

"You bet, dear." He was fully dressed in some rather snug-fitting clothing of Martin's. He was sitting up, his bare feet on the floor. He looked expectantly at her— waiting.

"I think our man has a different car again, a small maroon Toyota sedan. He drove past Will yesterday as the boy was getting off the bus. I saw him—I was out for a walk."

"A walk, huh?" He cocked an eyebrow. "It isn't

over, Martha, not yet. I'm not all the way back but getting there." He motioned for her to sit beside him, and she did. "It feels good to have you close against me like this, my dear."

"Tom, you can't keep on with this business."

"And what business are you speaking of?"

"You know very well what I mean. We haven't settled a thing between us. After one night like that—" She felt the heat burn up her neck and flood her cheeks. "Good Lord, I'm too old to be blushing like a young girl!"

"Hey, girl, I see by that rosy face, your memories are as good as mine. We aren't done yet, Martha, we never will be. We're just getting started. Our business with that predatory bastard is coming to a close. I feel it, and strong."

Martha trembled and pressed against him. "I know it is, I feel that, too."

He encircled her body with his long arm. "I just don't quite see how this will end. But it will, and it won't be pretty."

"We have to keep Will safe from this man, Tom. If he is actually the one we suspect, he is most likely a child abuser and murderer. Will has suffered terribly from things like that—and he's doing so well these days." Martha shook her head. "If he has to go through an encounter like that again—I think it would destroy him."

Chapter 29

Will sat in his seat alone by the window. As the bus lumbered along, he barely noticed the passing trees, flowers, and people out walking. He rode the same bus home each day but always with an eye out for any sign of a lurking stranger. When he thought of meeting someone like that, it sent his spirits soaring. But he was a child, compared to a full grown man, and the thoughts of a confrontation like that filled him with fear and anxiety, too. He was untried—a term he'd learned in his self-defense class.

While the excitement of it was always there, he wondered how it would happen. But he knew it *would* happen—and soon. He'd overheard Tom and Martha talking about it and knew he was the next target. They thought he didn't know and were worried about how to protect him.

Each week, he'd waited eagerly to attend his self-defense lessons. They had gotten more strenuous, but at the same time, a lot more exciting. He felt his small boyish chest expand as he remembered the latest moves he'd learned.

His muscles were sore sometimes. But he had noticed they had grown bigger as he faithfully practiced all he'd learned. He'd kept it all in the privacy of his room.

Was he ready? He didn't know a thing like that for sure, but he had gained assurance by the week. He believed he could handle himself and do a lot of damage if he had to. He might not win, but he wouldn't lose either.

The bus pulled to a halt, and Will jumped off from the second to the last step and hit the ground. His book bag banged heavily on his back, but these days it felt light as a feather. The bus drove away, and he looked carefully around as had become his habit.

Don't see anything or anybody. He felt a touch of disappointment, along with a touch of relief—it wouldn't happen today. He crossed the street and headed to his house. This time, he had a lot of homework, and maybe his mom would take him over to Jimmy Prentice's house again. Jimmy's mom put out great snacks, and he was a good kid to study with, especially with science stuff.

Will's mind was heavily into what the science teacher had said and how muddled up it was in his head. Jimmie was the kid Will needed this afternoon. His mom could walk him over there again. He smiled to himself and, with his head down, trudged his way up the slow rise to his home.

Will felt a shock streak through his body when he felt a strong male hand seize his shoulder. Instant fear shoved an icicle all the way through him. He felt himself being jerked backward toward the thick shrubbery along the sidewalk. At first, the harsh, strong male strength, and the male odor of his attacker made him paralyzed. He did nothing at first.

But then the man jerked his arm up behind his back and clamped a salty tasting hand over his mouth. That act brought back dreadful memories. For a moment, Will was five years old again, and the terror of that past encounter took hold of his mind and body.

Will felt frozen inside as he saw the thickness of the bushes he was pulled through. He felt the burning scratches of them across his face and the painful twisting of his arm. Then the helpless feeling of being dragged to a hidden lair where terrible things would be done to his body began to send signals into Will's newly trained mind.

He had learned about things like this, and now— unless he wanted to suffer those sickening, degrading things that had been done to him before—he had to make use of his new skills. *First of all: Stop being afraid. Plan you're attack and your escape.*

Suddenly, Will let himself go lax in the man's grasp. His limp body weight immediately slowed the man's progress. Just this little bit of change in the man's move- ment proved to Will that his training was right. He felt the sense of elation within his mind. He knew how to take care of himself.

Will wondered where he was right now. In another yard? He caught a glimpse of a mowed lawn somewhere close. Just then, Will felt the man's hand leave his mouth, followed by a heavy whack against his head. He knew now his very life was in danger. Was this the man—the one his folks worried about all the time?

Twisting his head, he spotted the pockmarks and scars on the man's face. Seeing that, he knew for sure this *was* the man who had driven past him more than once. Was he a stalker, a child predator? If so, Will's life, his pride in himself, was in danger. He strengthened his re- solve. He was on his own. There was no one to help him. Weren't those the kind of situations he'd learned how to handle?

He lay limp, watching through the narrow slits of his eyes as he did his frightened best to remember the moves he'd been taught. He heard the man panting with his exertion and muttering through his clenched teeth.

"I gottcha, you little bastard." He squeezed Will's neck with both hands. "I can't do what I'd like to do—oh God! I can't—I need it—want it so bad!"

Will heard the man actually wailing in anguish and found it hard to believe. What did the man need? Will didn't know but saw the man's anguish as an advantage. Will needed to get to his feet and struggled to get up.

"What do you want with me, mister?" He rasped out the words. His throat hurt real bad after the man had choked him so hard. Yes, he was frightened, but he was trained now—not some scared little kid. He waited, delaying until he had the right moment. Maybe this time the man wouldn't get away, and everyone could quit worrying about him. Will had a plan.

The man raised him to his feet and turned Will to face him. "What do I want with you? If you only knew— but forget all that. It's over for me, anyways," he scoffed. "What does it matter to you? I can tell you anything I want because you won't have the chance to spread it around all over the damned place." He held his pock-marked face close to Will's. "What I'm going to do to you, kid, will be a message to that bitch granny of yours. She'll get the message loud and clear when they find what's left of you, sonny boy." He gave Will's neck another long, hard twist.

Then the man said, his foul breath blasting in Will's face, "Come on, we're goin' back to my place. I need a lot more time for this job."

Will saw a crazy kind of anger and a sick grin come over the man's face. Will wanted to vomit from the evil that he saw on that man's face and heard in his voice. Will didn't have much time left to live, and he knew it.

One more twist of his neck might be the last. For a skinny kind of guy, the man's hands were real strong.

Suddenly, Will twisted in the man's grasp and tuned his back to him. Holding both feet in the air, he forced the man to hold him tight. Seeing the stance of the man, Will knew how to strike. With both his feet, he kicked backward as hard as he could. He threw his whole body into it—the way he'd been taught. He felt his shoes smash straight into the man's right knee. He heard the crack of bone and felt the man's grip loosen on him.

Will fell to the grass. Twisting around, he saw his attacker rolling about on the ground. His hands clasped at his right knee, from which his lower leg kind of dangled in a funny looking way. To Will, the whole leg looked kinda useless, and it must have been really painful the way the man was howling and crying. Will knew then that what he'd learned worked just like his instructor had said.

He heard the man's words, screaming in vicious hatred at Will. "Oh God, you little son-of-a-bitch!" The man rolled to his side and tried to get up, but, instead, he fell back and clutched at his knee. "You've ruined my leg!"

The man screeched out the worst cuss words Will had ever heard—a long, unbelievable stream of them. Then the man collapsed and lay motionless, his face a pale mask of misery and pain. Tears streamed down his face.

Looking about, Will realized his attacker's screams had drawn the entire neighborhood, including his grandmother, Tom, and his mom, too. They pushed through the same bushes the man had dragged Will through. They rushed to his side. His mother let out a scream, as she saw the man lying on the grass with his leg at an odd angle.

"Mom, he tried to take me," was all Will could manage at the moment. He manfully fought his tears as the scream of police sirens filled the air.

Martha murmured to Tom, "I guess I won't need to do a thing to have forensics done on this dude's house, now will I?"

"No, my dearest girl, you won't." Tom seized the moment to get in a bit of sweet talk to Martha. He wasn't one to let a chance like that, pass. He heaved a sigh of relief. "It's all over, Martha. I believe this is our man."

"He's definitely the one from Delgado Lane, Tom. I'd know him anywhere." Martha went to Will and knelt down on the grass where he sat a good ways from his assailant.

His face was pale, but his eyes were shining.

Jeannie sat beside Will, her arm around him, but only as tightly as he'd allow. Martha heard him tell his mother, "I'm not a baby anymore, Mom."

Martha asked him, "Will, is that the man who has driven past you so many times?" She only had time for one question as she saw the police approaching, but she wanted to hear him verify this was the same man.

"Yep, he's the one, Grammy. Got those same pockmarks and everything."

From then on, Tom dealt with the police. He informed them, up to a point, with what he knew. He put in a call to his boss, Marcus Ebert, to let him know what had gone down.

Jeannie called her husband and told him what had happened. Then she told Will, "Your daddy will be along soon, son. I think he'll be very proud of what you have done today. Those lessons, no doubt, have saved your life." She couldn't stop her tears, and Will patted her on the shoulder.

There were many details to deal with. Martha and Jeannie sat together, letting Tom and the police do their jobs. They watched the nosy onlookers being warned away and heard the police saying, "This a crime scene."

They had strung that crime scene yellow tape around the area, too. Martha thought of the many NCIS programs she'd watched. It had looked quite real on TV—but, this time, it was totally real.

After a short examination, the paramedics placed Will on a stretcher, Jeannie stayed close, her questioning eyes on the officer. "Does he have to go to the hospital, sir?"

"He was handled rather roughly, ma'am—has bruising all around his neck and throat. His arm hurts. He said the man jerked him around quite a bit. We'd best check him over—good evidence in court when that time comes, too."

"I'd like to ride in there with him then." With that settled, the ambulance sped away with Jeannie sitting beside her son, and an attendant along with them. Martha noticed the brave little guy didn't mind having his mother along for that ride, not at all.

Another ambulance was called for Rayburn McGill. The paramedics had his leg splinted and wrapped. But by the man's moaning cries, Martha decided they hadn't given him a shot of morphine, which would definitely be called for with a painful injury like a dislocated knee.

His identity had been established by the police and his residence discovered. Martha knew it would be all downhill for that man from here on out. She wondered what the little patent leather shoe would mean for McGill. Was it the shoe of little Mindy Lassen?

Martin drove up, hastily parked his Enclave, and came rushing to the scene. Martha and Tom filled him in on everything that had happened. After the initial shock of what had happened had passed, Martha saw the relief in Martin's eyes. Their siege of a having someone trying to kill them was over. He sped off to Riverside Hospital to be with his little son, and had anyone looked, they'd have seen the shine of a very proud father in his eyes as he drove away.

Chapter 30

Tom escorted Martha back to the house. The crime scene had emptied of onlookers, but the yellow tape remained. Two remaining forensic men poked about for further clues or information.

"I'd give all I have to be with them when they go through that man's house." Tom looked at her. "The danger to you is past, Martha—I can return to my duties as a detective, but—" He paced about the great room where they sat. Beads of sweat formed on his brow. "The thing is—what about us? It's been something special getting to know you. I'm not planning on giving you up, girl. I can't do that."

Martha sighed. "Tom, we can discuss this later when you have a cooler head. Today has been too much for all of us. I'm all messed up myself. I must go to the hospital and see Will. He's all I can think of right now."

"All right—later then. We'll have a good long talk, girl." Tom fidgeted and paced about, unable to hide how much he wanted to go along with the police when they did forensics on Rayburn McGill's home. She smiled and waved him on his way.

❧❧❧

Martha felt a deeper kind of relaxation spread throughout her body as she drove the familiar streets to the hospital. Was it really over? Did she no longer have to watch for a tail or check under her car's hood for a bomb? At Riverside, she entered Will's room in Pediatrics. This was one ward Martha had carefully avoided since the time she had the care of a very unfortunate child.

The memory of that little black-eyed girl haunted her to the point she couldn't face seeing another child in that terrible condition.

Will sat up in bed, a popsicle in his hand. When he saw her, his eyes brightened. He said, in a soft, croaking sound, "Hi, Grammy. This Popsicle is icy cold—it makes my mouth and throat feel lots better."

Martha grinned at him, looked at Jeannie, and asked, "How is he, really?"

"He'll be fine, Mom." Jeannie held her emotions in check. "He has some severe bruising about his neck and throat. His right arm and shoulder hurt when he moves them, but thank God, nothing's broken." She pulled Martha out of the room, fighting tears as she murmured, "Mom, he was so brave!"

Martha hugged her daughter. "Jeannie, it's over now, and believe it or not, we have Will to thank for it." She thought a moment. "You know, this whole thing began with Will, and now, look what's just happened—it's ending with him, too." She laughed joyously. "He's a little hero, Jeannie. It's amazing what that self-defense course did for him. He's a different child in so many ways."

"Oh, Mom, it *is* ended now, isn't it?" Jeannie giggled a bit and quickly turned to another subject. "What are you going to do about that Tom? He's loony tunes over you. He is—anyone with eyes can see what's going on there."

"We're going to sort that out when we can. But, right now, he was so hot to get in with that forensic team when they go through that house on Delgado lane, he couldn't see straight." Martha hesitated a bit then, with a sly grin, admitted, "That Ray is in the hospital now, and I can't wait to find out what his physical exam reveals. That's what's on my agenda."

"Why is that? Mom—what have you done?"

"I visited that man's house a while back, Jeannie. The first time I went, I stumbled over a little patent leather girl's shoe. This was shortly after the Lassen girl's murder." Martha took a breath and continued, "At that time, I also saw a work shirt with the lettering—Longworth Elementary School right across the front of it. A handy job like that put the filthy devil working among those little kids every day!"

"Oh, my God, Mom!" Jeannie cried then asked, "Did you say the first time—are you saying you went back in there again?"

Martha noticed her eyes had brightened—a sense of mischief had replaced her shocked expression.

"Yes, but I had a different mission that time." Martha went on to tell her how she had used Neutersol, and how she had injured her leg jumping his gate that night. "What I don't know is what, if anything, it did to the man. I don't even know how it works on dogs, since my vet friend won't use it on puppies."

"Mom, that was Serena, wasn't it?"

"And me, too. I wonder if we aren't one and the same these days—and now Serena has some heavy feelings for Tom." Martha felt the heated flush come over her face and could not stop it. "I didn't want to get involved with a man again, Jeannie, especially not so soon after losing Harry." She got up and paced the floor. "If a man falls in love with me, Jeannie, they always die. I can't take that chance anymore—I just can't! It's too much!"

"Mom, I don't think Tom cares two hoots about that. You shouldn't either. You're not dead, in spite of how hard that horrible man tried. Why on earth would you want to live alone, like you are?"

"You're no help, my daughter. It's not only too soon for me, it's that I'm afraid for Tom."

"You can't tell me Serena is the only one who has feelings for him—no way, Mom." Jeannie giggled at Martha's red, telltale face. "How far have you gone with that man? By the flush on your face, I'd say quite a ways."

"Oh, Jeannie! Let's forget about that. Let's go back and see Will."

"Not before I tell you something else, Mom." Jeannie's voice was low and insistent. "I have some happier news. Something that has come as a complete surprise. Martin is floored by it."

"What?" Martha knew it couldn't be bad news by the shine in Jeannie's eyes. Her eyes narrowed, as her suspicions rose. "Speak up, girl. What is it?"

"Mom, Martin and I are pregnant! I will have another child in about six months. And here I thought it was over for us." She giggled. "Martin thinks it's the water here in Denver that has caused this."

"It wasn't the water here that caused you to become pregnant, and you know it. Oh, Jeannie, I am so happy for you both. You know what? This is a sign that good things are ahead for all of us.

After she gave Jeannie a good hug, they reentered Will's room. He was sound asleep at the moment. Martha asked, "Does Will know?"

"Not yet, Mom, but we'll tell him very soon." Jeannie smiled. "I think he will be a great big brother, don't you?"

"Yes, I do." Martha nodded. "I plan to find a nurse I know and see if I can find out more about this Ray person." She looked at Jeannie. "That's on my mind right now, too, daughter."

She left Jeannie sitting at Will's bedside. Martha didn't want to discuss Tom anymore with Jeannie. But the shine in her daughter's eyes told Martha, she approved of Tom and wanted for the best for her mother. Or was that shine the glow of impending motherhood?

Chapter 31

Tom caught up with the forensics team just as they entered Rayburn McGill's home. "I'd like to come along with you boys. I have a personal as well as professional interest in what you'll find in here." He flashed his badge since these men did not know him or that he was one of them.

They easily picked the lock on the front door and went in. The smell of garbage and stale beer assaulted their noses. "Phew! Get a load of this place."

"Well, let's get at it," Sergeant Jack Bender said.

Tom stood back, not touching anything, merely watching as the two men went about their business. His major concern was to make sure they discovered the little shoe.

Sergeant Hal Markham went to the computer and turned it on. Within minutes, he cried, "Son-of-gun, Jack! This dude is heavy into kiddie porn." He bagged it and took it out to the patrol car.

Sergeant Bender found the little patent leather shoe after a quick look through the bedroom. He placed it in a plastic evidence bag. He held it out for the other two men to see. "Now what do you suppose this means?" He had a sick look on his face as he carried the lettered work shirt in another bag and held it out for inspection. "Guess where the bastard worked?"

Tom stood out of the way, watching those men cover that musty little house from end to end. One officer found the letter from Denny Garver among a few other letters and bills. Tom had seen the empty envelope, but not its contents. It was taken for evidence, as well. Tom was sure that the evidence they found there, along with Ray's attack on Will, would send the man up for years. If the little shoe had belonged to Mindy Lassen, Ray would end up on death row right next to his old acquaintance and letter writer, Denny Garver. Tom shivered, trying to imagine how Will had faced that nasty situation. Without his new training, a thing like that would have paralyzed most kids with fear. Tom waited for the chance to have a good long chat with that boy.

❧❧❧

Commander Marcus Ebert sat holding a computer printout, staring at it in disbelief. He called to another detective. "Hey, Ron, take a look at this." He waved the paper at Detective Ronald Helm. "This Rayburn McGill, the guy that kid took down, had multiple aliases. He was also Delbert Black, David Wilkins, and several others." He shook the paper. "All of them wanted for child abduction, molestation, and some of them murders. My God, this man was a monster!" he exclaimed with disgust and shock. "And now we find he was a janitor at the local Longview Elementary School—dammit all to hell!" Marcus heard his own voice getting higher and louder. "Hell's bells! What a way to zero in on your victims— little girls, all around him, every damned day of the school week!" He paced about the office. "We got a lot of the stuff off this sheet from his DNA. I guess they weren't so fussy about who they hired at that Longworth School. Those poor damned fools who run these schools—don't they check on who they hire? I've got kids, too." He went on a bit more before he asked, "Have we got a call out to the Lassen's? I'd like to be there when they see that shoe."

e/ce/o

Martha called a nurse friend who worked at Riverside. "Judith, I need a favor." She went on to explain her need for information to a nurse she had helped out in the past. "Jude, I don't care a thing about his knee, just find out the rest of it, and you know me well enough to know what I mean. Appreciate it, girl." She laughed as she rang off.

Maybe now, I will know if those nice big shots did their job. And luckily, Judith was on duty today. Martha wondered if she would get the information she sought any time soon. Will was still asleep when she returned to his room.

She decided to see if she could get a peek into McGill's room. With him being under arrest, she didn't know where he would be held. She called Judith again for that answer.

Later on, with Judith beside her, they approached a secluded room kept for severely disturbed mental cases. Judith wore her uniform, which they thought might be helpful. They knocked softly, and a guard came to the door.

"Yes? This patient is a no info. State your business." His tone was friendly, but firm.

Judith told him, "This lady is the grandmother of the boy he attacked. We are merely asking his condition, sir."

"He's sleeping right now, full of drugs, I believe." Peeking past the guard, Martha saw Rayburn McGill manacled to the bedrails. He had a large plaster cast on his right leg, above and below the knee. They both knew they'd get no further information from this no-nonsense guard.

Judith nodded. "I'll see who has him this evening. Come on." She led the way to the nurse's station and checked the board. "It's Dan." She looked about to see the nurse, Dan Mendez, going into a room down the hall. Judith pulled Martha along as she hurried after him. They met him coming out of the utility room. Judith took his arm. "Hi, Dan." She spoke quietly to the man, a questioning, yet conspiratorial look on her face. Martha saw him smile, nod his head, and, with a sly little grin, murmur a few words to Judith.

Judith took Martha's arm as they walked to the elevators. "Martha, you really did it, didn't you? Dan helped with him earlier, and he is one nurse who reads the patient chart thoroughly. He tells me that Ray is flat as a pancake, girl!" She giggled and squeezed Martha's arm in her excitement. "Apparently, there's nothing worth mentioning left in those little doo-dads he's got between his hairy legs."

"Thanks for finding out that little tidbit for me. I have wondered for so long." Martha knew that the desire to injure a child might remain with a predator, but that one part would be missing. That gave her a distinct feeling of satisfaction.

Judith gave her a hug. "I'd better get back to my floor. Thanks for a great dinner hour, Martha. It was wonderful to see you, very informative, and I wasn't hungry anyway." With that, Judith sauntered away to return to her duties.

Martha returned to Will's room to find Tom sitting by the window. She knew he waited for her. He was dressed in new clothing, and she surmised he'd done a bit of shopping for himself. She had the need for everything, herself, but being with Will came first.

Tom nearly leaped to his feet when she entered the room. "Hey, girl, where you been?"

"You won't believe it when I tell you about it." She smiled at him and, sitting down next to him, confided what she'd learned from Judith.

"So it must have worked." He nudged her. "How about dinner out somewhere tonight, just us two?"

"I'll have to do a bit of shopping first, but, yes, Tom, I'd like that very much." She went on to ask, "How did the forensics go at Ray's house?"

"They found the little shoe, and the officer's face was white as a sheet when he held it out." Tom shrugged and nudged Martha. "You had that dude pegged, didn't you?"

"Sadly, I did." Martha looked at him intently. "At dinner, I want to know all about you—okay?"

☙☙☙

This time, they did choose the House of Joy. It was a small part of Martha's past, and Tom was eager to visit it. They pulled in, and Tom handed the keys to Valet Parking. "Here we go, Martha, into the House of Joy. Here's to a fine night out with a beautiful woman."

Outside, they saw the gartered leg of a by-gone-days prostitute, sticking out of a window, and old style lamps burning behind red lacy curtains. The décor worked to create the look of a fancy bawdy house from the 1870s.

They found the inside lush with lace, fine dark wood, and paintings of the rugged saloon days of old time Denver. They were ushered to a soft, secluded nook, which appeared to have been created for the quiet assignation between a woman of the night and her overheated consort.

"Wow, lady, this is some place. I have an idea the food is great, too." Tom enjoyed the idea of being out with Martha on a real date. He asked her, his voice soft as feathers again, "What would you like to know about me, Martha?"

"Tom, all the time I knew Harry, he had never mentioned your name." She cast her eyes on him, puzzled. She really needed to know. "Where have you been, and what were you doing?"

Tom looked into her eyes. "I will tell you what I can. But there are things I can never discuss with anyone." He leaned forward on his elbows and began. "I've been out of the country, until shortly before I started working with Harry. I had just moved to Denver." He laughed—he anticipated her next question. "I had planned an evening with you and Harry, but it didn't happen. He was shot that very afternoon, Martha."

"What sort of training do you have that you can walk in to the Denver Police Station and become a detective, just like that?"

"I was a ranger and did undercover work in many places—many countries. None of which I will speak of. There's no better training anywhere than what you can get in special forces. It's no sweat to get a job anywhere, and Harry put in an additional good word for me. So after my discharge, I came here."

"Were you ever married?"

"Once, a long time ago. Being in the military and undercover makes it tough for some women to hang in there. My wife couldn't." He shrugged and reached over to take her hand. "I've never run into a woman like you in any country in the world, Martha. Harry felt the same way."

"What about your job, while you were watching me?"

"I took a leave of absence. I hadn't been there long enough to warrant that, but they knew I would have quit if they didn't grant it to me. Anything for Harry, that's what I told Marcus."

"No wonder you were so tough and bossy." Martha felt her mouth curve into a smile. "You were there for me. If Harry's looking down, I hope he is happy for us both."

"Speaking of us, my dear Martha. Tell me where I stand with you." He leaned toward her. "I warn you, I want to hold you, sleep beside you, and make as much love to you as possible for as long as our time on earth time allows. That's what I offer. Well, I have a few bucks set aside, too." He grinned as he waited for her reply. "I hope you know me well enough to know I mean what I say, and I do mean everything."

His words had set her insides on fire. Her face felt the fire of the heated glow he'd set inside her. She remembered very well how he could be. "Is this a marriage proposal, Tom Wells?" she murmured softly.

"Yes, it is. I don't want to spend another day without you, Martha. You've made me come alive—I can't lose that again." He reached out and took her hand. "And, I want us to be man and wife. I don't hold with your nonsense about being a black widow."

"It's so soon after losing Harry, but if you think he'd approve, I'll say yes, Tom." She met his kiss across the table and, taking his hands in hers, she asked, "Where would we live?"

"We'll live right out there at Harry's place. But it will be the Wells' place, wouldn't it?" he added. "After all, we have the two dogs, and it's their place too.

"You've been warned, Tom. I still say you are taking a very big chance if you get mixed up with me."

"One I'll happily take."

"How are you at being a new grandfather?"

As they laughed together, completely delighted about Jeannie's news, as a waiter came to take their order.

The End

About the Author

Ramona Forrest is a retired RN. She keeps busy writing novels—and traveling whenever possible. Forrest has resided in the back country of Arizona, assisted in round-ups, worked in Saudi Arabia, and has had the pleasure of traveling extensively. She now resides in Phoenix and spends much time in gardening, writing, entertaining friends, and family.